WAYWARD SPIRITS

WITCHES OF PALMETTO POINT BOOK 2

WENDY WANG

Copyright © 2018 by Wendy Wang

All rights reserved.

No part of this book may be reproduced in any form or by any electronic or mechanical means, including information storage and retrieval systems, without written permission from the author, except for the use of brief quotations in a book review.

v8.4.20

CHAPTER 1

Jason Tate parked his black Dodge Charger and surveyed the scene. The call had been for a possible suicide. Usually the worst kind of call, and not exactly the way he wanted to start his Wednesday.

The two-story tan house with dark red shutters was more like a mini-mansion, and must have been at least 5,000 square feet, by Jason's estimation. The forensics people were already milling around, as well as the coroner and his people.

A knock on the window startled Jason. His partner Marshall Beck stood outside the car door holding two cups of coffee and wearing a what-are-you-waiting-for expression on his face. He and Beck had worked together for the last couple of years. Beck wore a sour look on his long, thin face, but at least he came bearing coffee. Jason got out of the car. He pulled off his mirrored sunglasses and tucked them into his front pocket.

"How's it look?" Jason accepted the paper cup and took a sip.

"Like a bloody shit-show." Beck smirked. "I don't know what the hell she was doing out on the roof. There was a storm last night."

"I thought this was a suicide." Jason glanced at the body suspended halfway in the air, impaled on the wrought-iron fence surrounding the house. The coroner and several of his techs were working on the best way to move it.

There was something mismatched about the house and fence to Jason. The oversized low-country styled house beckoned for white pickets. Something simple. Not this Gothic monstrosity that surrounded it.

"Maybe. Maybe not. The coroner won't even give a preliminary because the woman landed on her back."

"Maybe she changed her mind halfway down? Tried to flip herself?"

"Hard to say." Beck shook his head. "No note that we can find so far."

Jason grunted. "So?"

"Lieutenants?" A forensic tech stepped out onto

the porch and signaled Jason and Beck with his hand. "I think you're going to want to see this."

Jason and Beck gave each other a knowing look. They stopped at the front door and donned a pair of gloves and booties.

"And so it begins," Jason said.

* * *

"What the hell?" Beck tilted his head and narrowed his muddy brown eyes.

Jason leaned over the bathroom vanity to get a better look at the mirror. The long piece of reflective glass was mounted to the wall just above a pair of double green glass sinks. On the left end, halfway between the top and the bottom, was a single palm print.

"When I went to dust it—I couldn't find any oils for the powder to adhere to. Then I realized that the handprint is not on the mirror," the tech said. He folded his arms across his chest and his thick bushy eyebrows tugged together, forming a deep line between them.

"Where the hell is it, then?" Beck said.

Jason touched the edge of the mirror to see if it was loose. He pulled a small penlight from the front pocket of his uniform shirt and put his forehead against the wall. The penlight illuminated the tiny crack between the wall and the long sheet of glass. He could see the bead of adhesive running the width, holding the glass firmly in place. The mirror's silvering seemed intact.

"How did that happen?" Beck asked.

The tech shrugged. "I don't know. It's weird. I can take the mirror off the wall if you'd like, but it's so big, it might break."

"No, that's not necessary," Jason said. "Can you scan it so we can run it against the database? We can always come back later and get the mirror if we need it."

The tech nodded and left to get the tools he needed.

"Okay," Beck said. "That's weird. Probably doesn't mean anything though. It's probably her print."

"Well, that's easy enough to prove. We'll just have the coroner take a palm print and compare them." Jason turned off the penlight and returned it to his pocket.

He walked into the bedroom and looked around. The furniture looked expensive and antique. The bed was rumpled, obviously slept in. He glanced at the open window to the left of the bed. What had made her crawl out there and jump? There were much easier ways to die. Most of the suicides he'd seen with women involved pills and alcohol. Impaling yourself on a wrought-iron fence? Yeah, that would hurt. He made a mental note to check for drugs and any firearms. He heard a whistle and followed the sound to find Marshall inside the large walk-in closet.

"Well, one thing's for sure—she liked shoes," Marshall said. He stood near the back wall, which had floor to ceiling shelves and at least a hundred pairs of shoes lining it. There were more shoe boxes on top of the shelves of the clothing racks. Lots and lots of suits hung pressed and ready to wear. Most were gray or black or navy. The fabric looked expensive.

"All right, well, I'm gonna let you document her clothes and shoe fetish. I'm going to head back downstairs and start talking to neighbors."

"Sure," Beck said. "I'll finish up in here; we'll compare notes later."

"Okay. Just a heads up. I need to take a ride out to Givens' this afternoon."

Beck shifted his gaze from the woman's closet and fixed his stare on Jason. "You're giving them false hope. That little girl is dead."

"Maybe she is… but they're the ones who asked."

Beck's lips twisted with disapproval. "And you just happen to know a hot psychic." He shook his head. "Good luck with that."

Jason felt heat creep up his neck. "She's helped us with a lot of cases."

"Three. She's helped us with three."

"Three cold cases. And don't forget the kidnap-murder case."

"Fine. Four cases, then."

Jason scowled. "You know I ought to just make her read you."

Beck scoffed and rolled his eyes. "Right. 'Cause that'd make me a believer. Just admit it. You wanna get in her pants."

"Fuck you." Jason turned and left the room before Beck could get in the last word.

His relationship with Charlie Payne was strictly business. He'd been a doubter, too, once, but the scales had fallen from his eyes and he could see her for what she was—an asset. She helped close cases, and if she was nice to look at, that just made it all the easier to work with her.

* * *

DUST MOTES SWIRLED AND SPUN, DRIFTING IN THE BEAM of sun streaming through the partially closed curtains of the girl's room. As the dust settled, it added to the thick layer coating the furniture. No one came here anymore, and nothing had been moved in the two years since the girl went missing. Not a doll. Not a book. Not the purple backpack still sitting on the white desk chair. Enormous pink and green letters spelled out Macey and hung above the bed. Each was skewed and affixed to the wall for an artsy effect.

Charlie Payne picked up the teddy bear from the zoo of stuffed animals piled in front of the ruffled pillow of the twin bed. She hugged it close to her chest, breathed in the stale air and waited for some sign. Usually the dead didn't hesitate to show her something. She waited. Nothing. Maybe there was hope. Maybe the girl was alive after all.

Lieutenant Jason Tate sidled up next to her. He shifted the sheer ruffled curtain to the side. The Givens' lush green backyard was large with only one tree, a large oak. A swing hanging from the thickest branch moved back and forth in the late afternoon breeze. Trees lined the back of the property, extending for quite a way from what she could tell.

"Anything?" His voice was soft, but tense with anticipation. He had been the one to suggest her to the parents. He was the one sticking his neck on the line, and nothing was clearer than his desire for her to see something. It was almost as palpable as the girl's parents had been when she met them earlier. They *wanted* to believe. But it didn't always work that way, which was the hardest thing for Charlie to explain, and, of course, made people doubt her when she couldn't give them what they wanted.

She shifted her gaze, glancing over her shoulder and smiling at the parents. Jimmy and Marla Givens stood in the doorway. She spoke in a whisper, and looked at him directly, "Maybe if I was alone?"

The skin around his hazel eyes crinkled as he narrowed them. One corner of his mouth twitched into a half-smile, and he gave her a quick nod. Before he turned to face them, she saw him put on his game face. He called up an easy-going, reassuring smile, but it was a lie. Jason Tate was anything but easy-going.

"Folks, why don't we give Ms. Payne a few moments alone to concentrate?"

Jason ushered the couple out and glanced over his shoulder before closing the door. "Call me if you need me."

She gave him a nod. "I will. Thanks."

The door clicked and Charlie walked around the room, still holding the bear in one hand while letting the other hand drift across the surfaces of the dresser, the desk, the bed frame. There should have been some piece of the girl emanating from her things, residual energy that could be read, but there was nothing. It was almost as if the girl had never slept here or played here or done her homework here. If the child was dead—she must have moved on. If she was still hanging around—well, she wasn't calling for help—at least not to Charlie.

Charlie stopped in front of the window. Her gaze settled on the thick line of pine and hardwood trees. A well-worn path disappeared into the gloom of the trees. This neighborhood was full of sizeable houses on one-acre lots, and most backed up to more undeveloped acreage. Some areas still hadn't fully recovered from the recession a few years back, so no builder had snapped up the land to turn it into more houses.

A glimmer of sunlight bounced off something in the yard and blinded her for a second. She blinked and when the brightness was gone, she noticed a girl by the path. She must have been about eleven—redheaded and so pale. Translucent. Cold dread coiled around Charlie's heart and gave it a squeeze. The child was dead. Like most spirits, she must have sensed Charlie's presence and sought her out. Was she a neighbor girl? Did she know Macey Givens? Charlie sighed and put the bear back on the bed. There was only one way to find out.

Once downstairs, she passed the living room where Jason and the Givens' sat forcing conversation and sipping iced tea. She gave him a brief wave and her most serious expression but didn't speak. He hopped to his feet and followed her through the house.

"Charlie? Is everything okay?" Jason's voice echoed behind her as she made her way out the back door. She heard him stop at the bottom of the steps and felt his stare on the back of her neck. Watching her. Waiting for her. He knew better than to get too close when she was like this. They'd only been working together a few months, but there was a comfortable trust between them. She would call if she needed him, and he would be there, which was all she could ask and all she knew he expected.

Charlie made her way across the yard, her eyes fixed on the apparition. The closer Charlie came, the farther into the dim forest the girl moved. Once Charlie was walking along the path, the child disappeared. The girl could have been any of a million shadows. Charlie stopped and glanced over her shoulder. Through the trees, she could see Jason. He had moved halfway between the house and the woods, and concern etched lines into his angular face. She could go back. Tell him she found nothing, but something inside her wouldn't let her. That child had come for a reason. Charlie could feel it in her bones. She took a deep breath and continued walking into the murky light of the thick trees.

The path wound its way through tall pines. Up high in the canopy, Spanish moss clung to the branches of the oaks and other hardwood trees. The silvery-gray beards of moss swayed in the late afternoon breeze. The woods were alive with squirrels and birds. They made the trees move and filled the space between them with their sounds. It would have been downright peaceful if she weren't looking for a dead girl to have a conversation with.

"I know you're here." She gazed around, inspecting each shadow. "I know you saw me. I know you want to talk to me." She stopped and turned in a circle. "It's probably been a long time since anyone has noticed you, but I'm here. Noticing you. Please come talk to me." Charlie waited, listening. Somewhere above her head, a mourning dove cooed in response. "I'm gonna leave if you don't come out." The sound of tree branches cracking made her look up. A squirrel launched itself from one tree to another, sending a spray of pine needles flying.

An icy finger traced its way down her back, sending a shiver through her. When she turned toward it, the girl was standing there.

"You can see me." There was no astonishment in her tone. No real emotion.

"I can." Charlie called up a reassuring smile.

"They said you could, but I had to see for myself."

"So, you're a show-me kind of girl, huh?"

The girl's nose wrinkled with confusion and her soft gaze met Charlie's.

"I'm Charlie. What's your name?"

"Trini."

"That's a pretty name. Is it short for something?"

"No. It's just Trini." The lack of affect in the girl's voice made the skin on Charlie's shoulder's crawl.

"Have you been here a long time, Trini?"

Trini shrugged one of her slender shoulders. The stylized rainbow and smiling sun on her soft white T-shirt reminded Charlie of T-shirts her mother wore as a teenager in faded pictures from the seventies.

"How about others? Are there others like you here in the woods?"

Her blue eyes must have been dazzling in life, but in the thick gloom of the canopy, they were bleached and dull. "Sometimes. There are others in the house, but I don't really talk to them much. They cry a lot."

"Why do they cry?"

Trini's throat undulated, as if she were swallowing hard. A habit from when she was alive. She did not need to swallow now. Charlie had seen this type of thing before—spirits using physical gestures they used in life. "Sad, I guess. They want to go home. But they can't."

"Do you remember meeting another girl, sort of close to your age?"

Trini scrunched her lips into a frown. There were still freckles on her pallid skin. "They're all close to my age. Some older. Some younger. But not by much."

A pang squeezed Charlie's heart. "Have you ever met a girl named Macey? Her parents are very worried and sad. They'd like to know what happened to her."

The wind kicked up, swirling leaves and pine needles along the path. Trini's eyes darkened. "She's dead. We're all dead. That's all anybody needs to know."

Charlie's arms broke into goose bumps, and she took a step backward. She wasn't sure if the child had learned how to harness energy. Some spirits learned early. Others never did. The last thing she needed was an angry spirit with the mind of a child throwing rocks or downing trees on top of her.

"Trini—"

"Shhh. Did you hear that?" The girl startled as if she'd heard a clap of thunder, and her eyes widened.

Charlie glanced at the canopy of trees, looking for the source of the girl's worries. A gray squirrel skittering across a branch stopped and stared down at her. His black eyes locked on her and he chattered as if he were cursing at her for disturbing the peace of his forest. Or maybe he was just warning his friends —*Beware of the ghost and the weirdo talking to her.*

"It's just a squirrel," Charlie soothed.

"No. It's him." Her voice became panicked. She shook her head from side to side and took a step backwards. Charlie noticed that Trini's feet were transparent, but the pine needles snapped beneath them.

"Trini, no one is here except me. I promise." She took a step toward her.

"You shouldn't make promises you can't keep," Trini's voice caught on the wind and swirled around them. "It's mean."

Trini's gaze shifted to the space just behind Charlie. Her body flickered, faded. A sharp popping sound pierced through the woods. Trini turned and ran, becoming hazier with each step until she disappeared.

"Wait. Please don't go." The sound of crunching pine needles beneath running feet was her only answer. "Trini!"

Charlie crossed her arms and stared at the empty path before her. There was no point in chasing after a ghost. Especially one who didn't want to be found. Charlie turned back, disappointed. Every hair on the back of her neck stood up, and her skin broke into goosebumps. A cold finger traced down her spine, and from the corner of her eye she glimpsed the ragged sleeve of a black robe. Death. She had felt him before but had only seen him twice since the night she first called him. She'd gone unnoticed then, but now he stood beside her. She didn't want to look at him. Maybe if she pretended not to notice him, he would just leave. Her heart hammered staccato beats in her throat. She squeezed her eyes shut.

An icy trail scraped softly along her cheek.

Look at me — his voice was silky, almost seductive, and it echoed through her head.

"No." She pressed her lips together and squeezed her eyes tighter. She felt him shift from beside her. His robes created a soft, chilly breeze as he moved in front of her.

"Go away," she whispered.

Open your eyes — his words washed through her, chasing away the chill that had settled around her shoulders and penetrated her chest. *Look at me.*

Something sharp nicked the skin of her neck. Her hand found her throat, and warm sticky blood oozed between her fingers. Her eyes flew open, and she stared into the darkness of his hood, where his face should have been. All she could see were fiery amber-colored eyes. They fixed her to the spot. Her entire body froze as if she'd been dipped in liquid nitrogen. If he touched her, would she shatter into a million little pieces?

Where did the girl go? The smolder in the reaper's voice didn't warm her. Charlie wanted to ask him why he didn't know where the child went, but she couldn't stop shaking. He towered over her, his gaze unwavering. He tipped his head out of curiosity and leaned in. His warm breath washed over her face, and it smelled sweet, almost to the point of cloying. But then the scent of something else pushed through the veil of sweetness — rotted flesh mixed with moldy leaves and the sickly, sweet odor of a fresh corpse. The mixed scents coated her throat, making her gag. She fought the urge to vomit.

Hot tears pushed onto her cheeks, and she bent over, hands on knees, able to move again.

She turned and ran, pumping her arms. Logically, she knew there was no way to outrun death. If he wanted her, he would take her, but she couldn't just lie down and let it happen.

Something scraped across her ankles, causing her feet to tangle. The ground rushed up to meet her and a sharp pain spread through her tongue. The taste of fresh coppery blood filled her mouth. A black cloud blinded her for a moment.

His robes. She turned her head slightly and met his fiery gaze. Her skin broke into a cold sweat and a tremor shook her body. The reaper hovered over her. This was not how she wanted to die. There was too much left for her to do, and her eleven-year-old son Evan still needed her.

"Charlie?" Jason's voice cut through the haze of fear. The reaper shifted his gaze, crouching beside her for a moment, and a low growl rumbled through her head. Charlie closed her eyes and when she opened them, the reaper was gone.

Jason appeared on the path. Deep lines etched the space between his eyebrows and his usually intense glare zeroed in on her. He picked up his pace and kneeled as soon as he was next to her.

"Oh, my god, you're bleeding! What happened?" He pulled a clean white handkerchief from his pocket and pressed it against the wound on her neck.

"Nothing." She pushed his hand away and sat up. "I'm fine. It was stupid. I—" She thought about lying to him. He would believe whatever she told him. She sighed. "I just scared myself and tripped over my feet. I'm fine."

"Well, at least take this." He held out the handkerchief. Charlie sighed and took it, pressing it against her neck. "What spooked you?"

"Nothing. It was stupid, really."

"So, you didn't see Macey."

"No. I saw a different girl."

"A real girl? Or—"

"A dead girl. Her name was Trini."

"Great." He sighed and pulled a small notebook from his front pocket, along with a pen. He clicked the button on top of the pen and pressed it to the paper. "She didn't happen to spell that for you, did she?"

Charlie chuckled. "No. But she said it's not a nickname."

"Well," he said, scribbling. "I guess that's something."

"She also said there were other girls her age where she... uh... lives."

Jason gave her a side-eyed glance.

"You know what I mean." Charlie scowled.

"Did she say anything else? Like maybe an address?"

"No. Sorry. But—" Charlie bit her bottom lip and tried to call up the girl's face. "I think she's been here a long time. Maybe since the seventies."

"Why?"

"She was wearing high-waisted jeans and a rainbow T-shirt."

He suppressed a smirk. "Isn't that what they call retro-style?"

She chuckled. "Yeah, I guess, but I got the feeling she was from then."

"So, why were you running? Was she — you know? Scary?" His gaze intensified.

"No." She hesitated. This part of their relationship always seemed so fragile to her. Even though he believed in her, sometimes the things she told him were hard for him to swallow. Charlie offered a weak smile. "She seemed kind of lost. It was sad, really."

"Well, you scratched yourself pretty good. Your uncle Jack will not be happy with me."

Her lips twitched with a smirk. It was sort of cute that Jason worried about what her uncle might think.

"Don't you worry. I'll let him know it wasn't your fault."

"Good." Jason pushed to his feet. He offered his hand, and she took it, letting him pull her to her feet. Jason glanced around. "Come on, let's get outta here. This place gives me the willies."

Charlie nodded and the two of them headed back toward the house. The wind kicked up as they left the gloom of the woods. The soft breeze blew around them, and Charlie heard the reaper's silky voice whisper her name.

CHAPTER 2

Friday afternoon, Charlie pulled into the driveway of her ex-husband's house, parked her car, and growled a little when she didn't see her son Evan waiting for her on the porch of the three-story Victorian. This was Scott's doing. Anytime he wanted to talk to her, he made Evan wait inside. She really didn't have time to deal with her ex today. Friday nights were reserved for dinner with her three cousins, aunt, and uncle. She'd spent so many years without them when she was married, and after she and Scott divorced, she'd sworn she would not let any man come between her and her family again. She'd also promised her aunt she'd come a little early to help set up. Charlie honked the horn twice and waited.

Two minutes later, Scott stepped onto the porch.

His bare feet and casual attire, a pair of khaki shorts and a navy polo, did not soften the stern look on his angular face. He waved his hand, signaling for her to come inside the house.

She sighed and got out of the car. She was up the steps and at the glass-paned double front door within a minute. It was almost 4 p.m.

"What's going on, Scott?" Charlie asked, trying not to sound too irritated. "We're already running late."

"I understand," he said. "But I have something serious to discuss with you."

"What?"

"Will you please just not argue?" Scott snapped. "This is important."

"Fine." Charlie crossed her arms and stepped into the grand foyer.

Scott walked fast through the maze of the house they used to share toward his study. He led her through the formal living room—which was still decorated in gold and cream. Glistening crystal collectibles filled the room that her ex-mother-in-law gave her every year for birthdays and Christmas, even though Charlie hated them. She despised this room as much now as she did when they were married.

The living room had originally been decorated by her ex-mother-in-law's decorator when they were first married. Every inch of the space screamed 'do not touch.' The old biddy would've decorated the entire house if Charlie had let her, but after she'd finished with this room, Charlie had put her foot down and stood up to her mother-in-law. It was the hardest thing she'd ever done up to that point in her life. After that, her mother-in-law kept her distance, and Charlie believed that Marilyn Carver probably cheered when Scott told her their marriage was over.

Charlie's stomach flip-flopped as they approached the open carved walnut door of his study.

"Come on." Scott gestured for her to follow him. Some part of her shrank inside.

She reminded herself: *You are free. You are free. You are free.*

She scowled and followed him across the threshold.

"We need to talk about Evan. Close the door, please."

The spicy aroma of old books and tanned leather mixed with the slight scent of fresh lemon polish. The combination of odors tickled the back of her throat, and she couldn't resist the urge to rub the tip of her nose. She glanced around the room. It had been awhile since she'd been in Scott's office. Even when they were still married, she'd avoided the room. In the two years since she'd left, not much had changed.

He'd added a couple of new pictures of himself on whatever adventure he had oh-so carefully posed for, expanding the collection of pictures of him rock climbing, skydiving, hang gliding, water skiing, running the Boston marathon.

He was so handsome that he belonged in the pages of a magazine. It used to make her heart ache to look at him. He was so beautiful. There was a time when she wondered why had he ever chosen her? But those days were gone. The only feelings she had left for him were how she would deal with him until Evan was eighteen.

"What's going on with Evan?" Charlie asked.

Scott gestured to the chairs facing his desk, then he carefully lowered himself into the tall leather manager's chair, holding his right arm against his chest. He winced as he settled into it. The oversized mahogany piece gleamed, and it easily put five feet between them. Charlie took a seat in one of the leather armchairs facing the desk. Why did coming into this study always make her feel like she was sixteen years old again and had been called to the principal's office? Like she had done something wrong. She folded her arms across her chest.

"What's wrong with you?" Charlie asked, pointing to his arm.

"Bike accident. Hit a rock and flipped over the handlebars." He waved off her concern. "That's not what I need to talk to you about. I need your support." He said the words as if they were an order instead of a request.

"Okay," Charlie drawled the word and narrowed her eyes. She'd been here before, many times in their marriage. "I need your support" in Scott-speak meant "This is what I'm doing, like it or lump it." The knot in her stomach tightened. "Support for what?"

"Evan has not been paying attention in school. He's not doing as well as he should. I've talked to Mitch Holtz about this—you remember him, don't you? He thinks it could be chemical. Anyway, he's giving me a prescription for Evan. To help him focus. Evan doesn't want to take the pills. I need you to support me. He can't say no if you're on board too." Scott looked down his perfect nose. His hazel-green eyes narrowed, and he fixed his gaze on her.

Charlie dug her nails into the flesh of her upper arms and carefully controlled her voice as she spoke. "You took Evan to see a psychiatrist without calling me?"

Scott sighed. His upper lip twitched, and he gave her a why-must-you-always-question-me look, as if she meant to put him out with concern for her son.

"Charlie," he started, his voice full of warning. "This is not that big of a deal. There are plenty of kids in his class are on medication for ADHD."

"Well, that's just great if they actually have ADHD. But Evan is not hyperactive." Her bottom lip quivered. It took everything she had to remain calm. "He is a normal little boy."

"No! He's not." Scott placed his hands palms down on the desk and leaned forward. His nostrils flared like a bull readying itself to charge, and there she was waving a red cape in his face. Scott lowered his voice, using his most stern, authoritative tone. "He's going on medication, and that's all there is to it. I can't let this—this—thing he has take control of his life."

"What thing?"

Scott sat back in his chair and folded his hands on his lap. He studied Charlie for a moment. She had seen that look on his face before. It was the face he made when contemplating exactly how to go in for the kill. "You know what thing."

"What is going on, Scott? Is he really not able to concentrate, or are you just embarrassed because he happens to be a little more sensitive than other boys his age?"

"He needs to focus on his studies. He can't do that if he's having these—delusions."

"What delusions? What's happened?"

"Nothing specific." His eyes flitted to the window overlooking the marsh.

"Why are you lying to me?"

Scott's jaw tightened and his eyes sharpened on her. "We're not discussing this any further. I won't let this thing jeopardize his future just because you don't like the solution."

"I don't like the solution because it's the wrong solution. If he's having problems concentrating, maybe we should try, oh, I don't know, talking to him. Maybe there's something going on at school."

Scott's lips thinned into a disdainful line, and he met her attempts at information gathering with stony silence.

"No, of course not. Why talk when you can just get one of your cronies to write a 'script, right? I have read article after article about how American parents are too quick to jump on the medication bandwagon. And no, you do not get the last say in this. He's my son too."

"I am the custodial parent." There was something final and disparaging in those words. She could hear his heart speaking to her, his thoughts, even though his mouth didn't move again. *I am the responsible one, the sane one,* it said. *The one who didn't try to leave us all behind with a handful of pills.* She would always pay for her sin. He would make sure of it. Charlie's cheeks flooded with heat.

"I really hate you sometimes." She leaned forward in the chair and sat on her hands, to keep from picking up one of the paperweights up from his desk and chucking it at him. She fixed her gaze on him, trying to ignore the gold and green flecks in his hazel eyes and the way they shimmered in the light. She steeled herself as she spoke. "If you do this. If you give him medication against his will. Against *my* will. Without a second opinion of a doctor of my choosing, I will take you back to court and I will sue you for full custody of my son. Do you understand me?"

The corners of his mouth twitched, and the shadow of a smirk appeared. Icy dread wound its way around her heart and squeezed. How had she ever found his arrogance attractive? What was wrong with her?

"Good luck with that." He tapped one finger against the mahogany desk, smudging the fresh polish. "If you fight with me, Charlie, I will march out every doctor I know to declare you just this side of clinically insane. Is that really something you want to put Evan through?"

"You son of a bitch," she muttered. A trickle of cold sweat traced its way down her spine. The icy pang in her heart spread throughout her chest, chilling her whole body. "This isn't over."

"I believe it is. I'm sending his medication with you. And I will count the pills when he gets home. I will know if you don't give them to him. I'm sure a judge would love to hear how you refused to give him his medication."

"Screw you," she said.

"Don't fuck with me, Charlie." His hateful gaze fixed on her. A knock on the door broke their staring contest.

"Mom?" Evan's voice came from the other side of the door. "Are you in there?"

"I'm here, baby." Charlie hopped to her feet.

The doorknob turned and Evan poked his head into his father's study. "Ready to go?"

"I am. Come on. Let's get out of here." Charlie wrapped her arm around her son's shoulders, ushering him away. She smiled and focused on his sweet round face. "I can't wait to hear all about your week."

* * *

EVANGELINE STOOD BY THE STOVE WITH A MEAT FORK IN one hand. She stuck the sharp tines into one of the floured pork chops on the plate, lifted it and lowered it carefully into the boiling oil. The delicious aroma of fried pork filled the kitchen. Her long silver hair was wrapped in a neat bun at the base of her head. She wore a pair of denim Capri pants and a pale lavender blouse beneath the vibrant purple apron she favored, tied tightly around her slim waist. "Charlie, would you set the table please?"

"Yes, ma'am." Charlie looked at the stack of white china plates on the counter. She ran her thumb over the edge, counting to make sure she had the right number. "Are we expecting someone? There's nine plates here."

Her aunt's blue eyes twinkled, and a gentle smile stretched her lips. "Yes, I think so."

"Who?"

"I don't know." Evangeline poked her fork into one a chop frying in the black cast-iron pan and gently turned it over so as not to cause the oil to splatter.

"I don't understand. If you don't know who's coming, then how do you know somebody's coming at all?"

Evangeline's left eyebrow quirked up. Charlie knew that look well. It was the don't-question-me look.

"Broom fell earlier. Better do as she says," Lisa Holloway, Charlie's oldest cousin, said as she entered the kitchen. Lisa was an attorney by trade and spent her days in expensive suits and heels, poring over contracts, wills, and tax returns for her clients. But on Friday nights, she shed her lawyerly attire. Tonight, her long strawberry blonde hair fell over her shoulders in two loose braids. She had already changed from the smart white linen suit she'd worn when she first arrived into cut-off jean shorts and fitted red T-shirt that clashed with her hair. She leaned against the counter and wiggled her perfectly pedicured toes. "I sensed it too. There's definitely somebody else coming for dinner."

Charlie rolled her eyes and shook her head. She knew better than to argue with a couple of seasoned witches. She mumbled under her breath, "Well, I didn't sense anything."

"I don't think I'd brag about that if I were you. Especially since you've got paying customers now," Lisa teased. Charlie frowned and stuck her tongue out at her cousin. Lisa laughed. Charlie was only handing out the cards, offering her services on an as-needed basis. Although all her cousins had taken a stack to give out on her behalf.

"Is Daphne coming tonight?" Charlie asked.

"She's gonna be late," Lisa said, referring to their youngest cousin. "Mary Grace Whitten's daughter is getting married tomorrow. Daphne's making sure the mother of the bride's hair is absolutely perfect."

"Well, of course, she is." Charlie gave her oldest cousin a knowing look. Daphne was in high demand in their small town for her unique ability to make just about anyone look beautiful. Daphne liked to call it her super power, but it was just one more thing on a long list that fell into the category of witchy ways, and all her cousins had something about them that put their unique abilities on that list.

Charlie took the stack of dishes into the dining room, laid out the plates on the long cherry table that Evangeline had covered with a pale blue and white striped tablecloth. Charlie completed each setting with forks, knives, spoons, and iced tea glasses. Even though it was just Friday night dinner, Evangeline had also laid out blue linen napkins. Charlie glanced at the china closet and headed back into the kitchen.

"Do you think anyone will want a glass of wine—?" Charlie stopped and stared at the screen door.

Jason Tate was standing with his hand up, about to knock. Their eyes met and his fist opened into a wave.

"Hi," he said, offering a charming smile.

Lisa glanced at the door. She picked up the large wooden salad bowl and flashed Charlie an I-told-you-so smirk. Charlie ignored her cousin and pushed open the screen. "Hey, what are you doing here?"

"Manners, Charlie." Evangeline scolded from her post by the stove.

"I'm sorry. I meant hi, Jason. What the hell are you doing here?" Charlie used an exaggerated tone that she knew would irritate her aunt.

Jason chuckled. "Good to see you too."

"Jason don't pay her any mind. She's been ornery ever since she picked up Evan. You come on in."

Evangeline motioned him inside. For whatever reason, Evangeline had taken a shine to Jason. Maybe her aunt hoped somewhere deep in her heart that he and Charlie's relationship would bloom into something less professional and more romantic. Charlie kept a vigilant watch on her aunt's behavior when Jason was around, just to make sure the old woman didn't try anything, like slip a love potion into their drinks or cast a binding spell to bind them together.

"Thank you, Ms. Ferebee, I appreciate that. I can't stay long. I just needed to talk to Charlie for a minute."

"Well, according to the broom, you're staying for dinner, so you may as well just get comfortable," Charlie quipped

"Huh?" Jason's eyebrows rose halfway up his forehead and his gaze bounced from Charlie to her aunt.

Charlie rolled her eyes and shook her head. Her lips tugged into the first smile she'd worn since leaving Scott's house. "Nothing. Come on in."

"Jason, you're certainly welcome to stay. We have plenty," Evangeline said.

"Yes, and I don't think you've ever had my aunt's pork chops. They've been voted the best in the state by *Foodie Magazine*," Lisa chimed in.

"I don't know if I can pass up best in the state." Jason wiped his feet and stepped into the kitchen.

Evangeline gave him a wide smile. "I hope you brought your appetite. I've got lemon meringue pie for dessert."

"Ms. Ferebee, you're gonna make me fat." Jason's nostrils flared as he took a deep breath. "Smells delicious."

Evangeline winked at him and went back to tending the pork chops.

Jason touched Charlie's elbow, and she leaned in close. "S'there someplace private we can talk?"

Charlie nodded and pointed to the door. "Come on. I don't think you've ever seen my uncle's dock. Evangeline, we'll be back in a few minutes."

"Well, don't be long. Dinner will be served in less than ten minutes."

"Yes, ma'am." Jason gave her a nod and followed Charlie out onto the back porch.

Charlie settled on the bottom step and Jason sat down next to her.

"So much for seeing the dock," Jason teased.

"Sorry," she said. "We'll be late for dinner." Charlie wrapped her arms around her knees and turned her face to Jason. She could tell by the lines in his forehead, his visit was serious and not a social call. With Jason it was never really a social call, unless food was involved. "What's going on?"

"I've got a case. You up for it?"

"Another missing kid?" she asked. "So soon? We haven't even really solved the last one."

"No, this isn't a missing kid. It's a murder. Or a suicide. Or an accident. Nobody's sure exactly what happened."

"What do you mean?"

Jason glanced up the steps to the back porch. He hesitated, pressing his mouth into a thin line. His hazel eyes darkened.

"You don't want to say." It wasn't a question. She knew Jason had sensed something about her cousins and aunt, even though the word "witch" had never been uttered to him. He was always a little on guard when they were around. "You know they can't hear you, right? Even if they could, they wouldn't be listening."

"I know. It's just—" He sighed as if he didn't know how to finish his thought.

She patted his knee and gave him an understanding smile. "They can't do what I do. And I can't do what they do."

"What *exactly* is it they do?" Jason fixed his stare on her. Not too long ago the intensity of his gaze would have made her squirm, but now she didn't let it get to her.

"You really want to know?" Charlie quirked one eyebrow and lowered her chin.

Jason narrowed his eyes and opened his mouth,

but then closed it. "Maybe not tonight. So, will you help me?"

"Sure. When?"

"Now would be good."

"How 'bout you fill me in on the way over *after* dinner. My son is here."

Jason nodded and shrugged. "Sounds good."

CHAPTER 3

Charlie had never been to a fresh crime scene before. Most of the time when Jason brought her in, it was long after the forensics team had moved on to other cases and the yellow tape had been taken down.

The imposing iron fence surrounding the property had been cut, and the sharp spikes of bent metal reminded her of splintered bones. "Is that where she was?"

Jason nodded. "Yeah. It was the only way to remove the body." He gave her a supportive glance. "You ready for this?" Jason asked.

Charlie folded her arms across her chest and squinted one eye at the roofline. "So, this girl was on the roof during a thunderstorm? What was she doing up there?"

"Well, that's where it gets weird. I've got one neighbor telling me he saw someone on the roof with her. And I have another neighbor who said he saw her on the roof by herself."

"Who do you believe?"

"I don't know. Neither has any reason to lie, and they both seemed credible when I talked to them," he said.

"Okay. Well, which one was closer?"

"Mr. Baker." Jason pointed to the next-door neighbor's house and led her up to the victim's porch. He pulled a couple pairs of latex gloves from his front pocket and handed a pair to her. "It's still a crime scene."

"They didn't dust it already?" Charlie asked.

"They did. I'm just being cautious."

"So, you believe him?" She took the gloves and slipped them on more easily than Jason.

Jason sighed and rested his hand on the fancy bronze door handle. "I don't know who to believe, honestly. The next-door neighbor said he saw someone on the roof with the victim and that the person disappeared after charging the vic and falling from the roof with her."

"Is that why you think it was a spirit?"

"Maybe. We didn't find any hard evidence that there was someone. We found a couple of weird things though, and when it's weird, I defer to you."

"Great." Charlie's hand drifted to her neck and grabbed the round pendant hanging at the base of her throat. She brushed her thumb over the silver pentacle. "So, maybe we should make this quick. If it is a murderous spirit, I don't really want to be here if it comes back."

"Uh—" Jason's mouth twisted and his tan face paled. "What?"

Charlie chuckled. "Come on, I'll protect you."

* * *

"This way," Jason said.

Charlie followed Jason up the polished hardwood steps to the second floor. Nothing about the trendy decor and new furniture said haunted to her. In fact, the house looked more for show than everyday use. The rich cream and gold colors of the runner in the hallway and the subtle gold shimmer of the paint on the walls reminded Charlie of Scott's mother's house. Everything in its place and impeccably decorated. It all gave off the same do-not-touch vibe. The only thing out of place was the splintered door and jamb at the end of the hallway.

"The door was locked from the inside. We had to use force to get in," Jason explained. "This was her room."

Charlie stepped into the master bedroom, and all

the warmth from the rest of the house melted away. A chill settled around her shoulders, and the hair on her arms prickled. Something dead had been here and had left a tiny piece of itself from what she sensed.

Charlie stood in the middle of the room and slowly turned in a circle, taking it all in. The linen-covered duvet was wrinkled and pushed back to one side. Charlie closed her eyes and let the energy wash over and through her. For a moment, she could see Haley Miller waking suddenly. Her chest heaving, frightened as she glanced around the room. Charlie saw Haley in her mind's eye fixing her stare off to the right toward the open door. Charlie's eyes opened, and she glanced over her shoulder at the bathroom.

"What's happened in there?"

"Take a look." Jason walked into the master bath and flipped on the light.

In the spacious and spa-like master bathroom, cream and gold travertine surrounded the shower and extended behind the freestanding tub. The modern zebra wood cabinets floated above the stone floors, and all the fixtures had straight lines and a polished nickel finish. The whole room looked as if a decorator had lifted it from a page in a magazine.

"What did the victim do for a living?"

"Pharmaceutical sales."

"Well, she certainly had expensive tastes," Charlie

muttered. Her gaze settled on the large mirror extending over the cabinetry. A single handprint and the words *Sisters Forever* were still visible in the reflective glass over one of the sinks.

Charlie walked over and leaned in close. "Can I touch it?"

"Sure. It's not going anywhere."

"What do you mean?" Her eyes met his in the reflection.

"The handprint isn't on the outside of the mirror."

"Where is it?"

Jason shrugged one shoulder. "Forensics guy couldn't exactly find it. He had to scan it electronically."

Charlie hunched over the sink to get a better look. "You know, sometimes spirits can get trapped inside a mirror. They can use them to move from place to place." She touched the handprint and closed her eyes. Flashes of light filled her mind, but no specific image formed. She put her hands flat on the counter and frowned. "Weird."

"What?"

"I don't see anything useful."

"So, you think a spirit could have left an actual handprint?"

"Sure." Charlie nodded. "I've seen it happen before. Usually, though, that's within the spirit's boundaries."

"What does that mean, exactly?"

"Well, some spirits bind themselves to the place where they died. That's how most sentient hauntings occur."

"This entire neighborhood is new. I mean, I guess I can check for deaths in the area—" he said, focusing his gaze on the handprint.

"I don't think you need to do that." Charlie leaned against the counter.

"Why not?" Jason's gaze shifted to her, his eyes full of curiosity.

"I don't think the spirit is bound to this house. I think she was bound to the victim."

"Why?"

"That's what we're gonna have to figure out. It could be Haley wronged the spirit in some way when she was alive."

"She?"

"Yeah, I definitely sense a she." Charlie pointed to the shadowy palm print. "It's interesting that you can see the fingerprints."

"Yeah, we're gonna run it against our databases, but I'm not holding my breath. It's not like we can fingerprint ghosts."

"No, but maybe there's a Jane Doe out there stuck in some morgue drawer with no identity."

"We can hope, right? Are you getting anything else?"

Charlie pushed off from the counter and walked back into the bedroom. She made her way to the window. The carpet beneath it squished underneath her shoes, still wet from the rain. She glanced over her shoulder at him. "Don't worry, okay?"

"About what?" He gave her a puzzled look.

Charlie grinned and scrambled out the window before Jason could stop her.

The metal roof still radiated heat from the day, and any water from the rain had long since evaporated. The rubber soles of her shoes gripped the tin, and she stood up straight, just out of reach of the window.

"Charlie! What the hell are you doing? Come back in here," Jason ordered, sounding panicked.

"It's okay, Jace—just give me a minute. She was found on the fence separating the two yards. She climbed out through this window, right?"

Jason leaned out the window, holding his hand out. "Come on, Charlie, please—you're making me nervous."

"Well, answer my question," she said.

"Yes. We think she did."

"All right then." Charlie followed the narrow roof past a dormer and peered over the edge. She could see the fence and the hole where the victim had landed. There was no way she just slipped and fell and hit that fence. Something with strength had to have pushed her. The real question was, was it human or spirit?

Charlie turned back and headed toward the window where Jason's head protruded, carefully watching her. She flashed him a smile. "You said the neighbor saw her fall? Do you think I could talk to him?"

"Sure. I think I can arrange that. Now, will you please come back inside before something happens, and I have to explain why I let you out on the roof of an active crime scene?"

Charlie laughed and rolled her eyes. "Fine."

CHAPTER 4

Charlie sat across the round aluminum patio table watching Don Baker peel the label off his beer bottle. Two empty bottles stood next to the silvery pile of scraped paper. He picked up the bottle he was nursing and took a long swallow. Heavy black circles punctuated the skin beneath his eyes. He looked almost as someone had punched him. His dark brown eyes stared at the table, vacant.

"I really appreciate you meeting with us like this, Mr. Baker."

"You sure I can't get you folks something to drink? Water, maybe? Iced tea?" he offered.

"We're fine. Thank you." Charlie gave him a reassuring smile. "I know you've probably told this story a hundred times already, but it would be really helpful if you could tell me what you saw."

Don put the bottle down in front of him and leaned forward with his elbows on the table. He wrapped his meaty hands around the base of the green glass bottle.

"Well, it was raining pretty hard, and it was late. Well, after midnight." His eyes shifted toward the light streaming out through the patio doors of his house. "My wife likes to sleep with the windows open when it rains. Drives me nuts, especially when it's so hot. It just makes the house muggier, but happy wife, happy life, right?"

Charlie leaned forward and rested a hand on his wrist. The image of Don Baker standing at his window, watching Haley Miller on the roof popped into her head. "Can you tell me about the woman on the roof with Haley? Something about her eyes bothered you."

Don Baker stared at her for a long moment. He took a few carefully measured breaths and sat back, pulling his hands onto his lap, out of her reach. He didn't look at her. "I don't know what you mean."

Charlie steadied her gaze on him. "I think you do, Mr. Baker. I think you know exactly what I mean."

He laughed, but there was no humor in it. His hand scrubbed his chin, sounding like sandpaper, and he met her unwavering gaze. "It's gonna sound crazy."

"Not to me, it won't. I promise." Charlie folded

her hands in front of her and leaned toward him. "I'm all ears."

His eyes shifted from her face to Jason's and back to hers again. He let out a heavy sigh. "I heard a scream. I don't know how I heard it because it was thundering like a bitch the other night. At first, I thought it was one of my kids. But then, I realized it came from outside. That's when I looked out the window and saw her on the roof."

Charlie's head bobbed to encourage him, but the motion also mesmerized her a little, allowing her to slip into his words and view the scene inside his head.

"I saw something crawl out of the window after her." Don's smooth southern accent lulled her and Charlie could see the shape of the woman emerge from the shadows. Not quite solid.

Don rubbed the back of his neck. "It followed her. And at one point, Haley turned back around to look at it. To confront it, I guess, and I swear to God it threw its head back and laughed at her. Then it looked over at me, and I could see its eyes. Glowing red like fire. I know it sounds nuts…"

Charlie saw it in her head before he said the words. Saw the spirit snap its head in his direction. Felt him recoil.

"A minute later, it charged her. I thought for sure they both went off that roof. But when I went downstairs to check, there was only Haley. Hanging there..."

"It must have been terrifying and surreal." Charlie's mind filled with the image he saw of the victim suspended mid-air by the spikes of her fence. Her stomach churned, and she blinked several times until her head cleared it away.

"You know I hunt. I've killed more than my share of deer. Gutted and dressed them, but I'd never seen anything like that before. Made me puke."

One corner of his mouth tugged up, and his brown eyes became unfocused. "I always used to tease her—that she lived in a fortress. I guess even that fence and her security system couldn't really protect her."

"What do you mean?" Charlie asked.

Don shrugged. "When she moved in a year ago, there was a picket fence here. Like the other houses in the neighborhood. You know the type, white, idyllic. It really surprised me when the architectural committee approved that iron thing she put in."

"You said she has security cameras?" Jason asked.

"Yep. She had a ton of cameras installed along with one of the best security systems in the city. I should know because my company sold it to her."

"Do you know if that data is recorded and stored somewhere?" Jason wrote in the notebook on the table in front of him.

"Yeah. There should be a server in the house."

"Um, we didn't find a server. You wouldn't know where in the house, would you?" Jason paused his pen mid-sentence and glanced up at Don.

"I can call my company and find out where they installed it. It's usually installed inside a closet or a panic room."

"That would be great." Jason nodded appreciatively and glanced at Charlie. "Charlie? You have any other questions?"

Charlie forced a smile. She didn't want to tell him that mostly in her experience, spirits often wreaked havoc with electronics. She didn't want him to be disappointed when he pulled the video and found nothing. "No. I think that's all we need. It's getting late. We should let Mr. Baker get back to his family now."

Jason nodded and tucked his notebook into his pocket.

* * *

"YOU KNOW, I REALLY APPRECIATE YOU COMING WITH me tonight." Jason pulled his Dodge Charger into the driveway behind her uncle's pickup truck and put it into park. He shifted his body and looked at her, resting his hand on the corner of her seat.

"Any time." She smiled and put her hand on the

handle. She could see there were still lights on in the upstairs bedroom where her son was supposed to be sleeping.

"That was a really good call. About the eyes. You know he didn't share any of that in his original statement."

Charlie tipped her head. "Would anybody have believed him other than me, and maybe you?"

Jason chuckled. "Probably not."

"That's why you pay me the big bucks. To find out this kind of stuff." She smiled, but it faded fast when something behind Jason's head caught her eye. Something terrifyingly familiar stared into the car window — eyes of amber fire, floating in the dark shadows of a hood. Her heart hammered against her breastbone, traveling its way to the back of her throat. The curve of the silvery blade glinted in the moonlight. The reaper leaned down, and his bony fingers moved through the glass of the window and rested on the door. Charlie's breath caught in her throat.

"I guess I should get out of here and let you get some sleep."

"Don't move." Charlie's hand drifted toward Jason, dangling, palm up.

"Okay. What is it?" Jason's face shifted to concern. She closed her eyes, steadied her breath, and he took her hand.

"Just do as I say, okay?" she said, opening her eyes again.

"Oh-kay."

The reaper's fingers reached for Jason's head and Charlie yanked him forward toward her.

"You get out of here right now!"

"What?" Jason recoiled a little at the force of her voice and his fingers loosened around her hand. Charlie grabbed on tighter, not allowing him to pull away.

She fixed her gaze on his face and lowered her voice. "Don't move."

"You just told me to get out of here." Jason sounded irritated.

"I wasn't talking to you. Just stay here," she whispered. The reaper's other hand appeared on the car door and he leaned in. His gaze bounced from her to Jason and then to their joined hands. Charlie bolted straight up and pulled Jason so far over he was almost in her lap.

"You! Outside! Now!" Anger surged through her. The reaper's gaze met hers. Charlie held her breath. Would he raise his scythe and cut them both down in one swift motion? A silky laugh echoed through her head, and the reaper nodded and pulled his head out of the car.

Jason's mouth opened with shock. His brows

tugged together, forming a deep line between them. "Charlie, what is it?"

"There's someone behind you," she whispered.

Jason's eyes shifted right. "Do I need a weapon?"

"No," Charlie shook her head, "I need you to just stay here a minute, okay? If something happens to me…"

Jason still held her hand, and he squeezed it hard. "Maybe I should come with you."

"No. Stay here. If something happens to me, just run to my uncle's house and get my cousins."

"Charlie—"

She let go of his hand and scrambled out of the car, leaving him to gape after her. The reaper glided over the top of the car and loomed up in front of her. She stared up at him.

"What part of 'get out of here' did you not understand?" She pointed toward the road. He leaned in close, and she almost lost her nerve. The stench of his breath felt cool on her face, and his eyes fixed her to the spot. He raised his hand, which was not the skeleton often portrayed in art and literature. It looked almost human. The skin was paler than anything she'd ever seen, a bloodless gray, and it covered long thin protruding bones. There was a faded gray tattoo she couldn't quite make out stamped into the back of it. He brought his gnarled fingers toward her face and brushed them across her cheek. He nodded, gliding backward until he melted into the surrounding darkness of the woods.

Charlie's legs almost gave out as soon as the reaper left. Suddenly the air in her lungs burned. She'd been holding her breath. Her chest heaved, and she tried to take in fresh air, but she couldn't seem to get her lungs to work.

Oh, my god. Oh, my god! It marked me! It marked me!

Sharp, hot pain seared through her chest. Her hand flew out and found the car door. A moment later, Jason lifted her up by her elbow.

"Can't breathe—" Charlie choked on the words, pressing her hand against her chest. He slung her arm over his shoulders and wrapped his arm around her waist, supporting her. Her legs dragged on the ground as he tried to move her forward and he scooped her up into his arms.

"Help! Somebody!" Jason's shouts sounded panicked, but she couldn't comfort him. Tears squeezed from the sides of her eyes and a pebble formed in her throat, growing larger. The world around her grayed at the edges.

Jason carried her up the steps. The old screen door opened with a squeal.

"Jason?" Jen's soft voice penetrated the haze filling Charlie's brain.

"Call 911. She can't breathe."

"Daddy!" Jen shouted. "Something's happened to Charlie. Get your bag!"

"Bring her in here." Evangeline directed him to the dining room. He put Charlie in one of the large armchairs at the end of the table.

A moment later, her uncle Jack appeared with his black medical bag. He knelt in front of her and examined her.

"Charlie, can you tell me what happened?" her uncle said in a gentle and strangely dispassionate voice.

Charlie gulped in air and stared into her uncle's sharp blue eyes. How on earth was she supposed to explain to him she had just told off Death? And that for her impertinence, he marked her? She searched her aunt and cousins' faces. Charlie shook her head and continued to gasp for breath.

"All right, can you tell me where it hurts, exactly?"

Charlie tapped her fingers against her breastbone, just under her throat. Her uncle Jack nodded and pressed his mouth into a straight line. "Is this a sharp pain or dull pain? Is it throbbing? Does it radiate outward?"

"It's sharp," Charlie said between gulped breaths. "I can hear my heart in my ears."

Her uncle nodded his head. He gently took her

wrist and pressed his finger against her pulse. "Sweetie, you're not having a heart attack."

"I'm not?"

"Nope. You're having a good old-fashioned panic attack. Can you tell me what brought this on? What happened?"

Her shoulders slumped, and the pain in her chest faded to a dull throb. There were just some things that were better left unsaid when it came to her uncle. While he recognized that his daughters, nieces, and even his sister-in-law were all exceptional in inexplicable ways, there was an unspoken rule. Never tell Jack the truth about their unique abilities. Charlie glanced at Jason. His eyes pinched at the corners and he observed her carefully. "I don't know. Nothing, I guess. Nothing real."

Jack pressed his palm against Charlie's cheek and gave it a gentle pat. "You're gonna be okay, sweetie." He pushed to his feet and kissed her forehead. "Jason, I think the ladies here need to chat for a few minutes. I don't know about you, but I need a drink. I got some scotch and Jack. Pick your poison."

Jason knelt in front of Charlie. "Was it anything we talked about earlier?"

Charlie breathed easier now. She shook her head. "No. Nothing like that."

"You sure you're gonna be okay?" Jason asked.

"I'm fine." She gave him a reassuring smile. "Go on with Uncle Jack. I'm sorry I scared you."

"I'm just glad you're all right." Jason put his hand on hers and gave it a squeeze.

Charlie's fingers grabbed onto his hand, not letting him get up. "You're not driving, if you're drinking," Charlie said. "You'll stay here tonight. Okay?"

Jason opened his mouth to argue.

"Charlie's right," Jen said. "No drinking and driving. I'll make up the couch for you."

Jason offered a defeated smile. "Yes ma'am." He rose to his feet and followed Jack out of the room.

Lisa peeked around the corner, holding her hand in the air, signaling them to wait before starting their conversation. "Okay—door's closed. We can talk."

Jen, Lisa's sister, pulled up a chair next to Charlie. Concern etched lines into her delicate elfin face, and her large blue eyes darkened. "What happened?"

A breathy, nervous laugh escaped Charlie's lips. "It was stupid, really. A reaper appeared, and I thought he was going to hurt Jason."

Jen's dark eyebrows raised, and shock smoothed the lines of her face. "A reaper?"

"What do you mean?" All the color drained from Lisa's already pale skin. She folded her arms across her chest.

"I saw one a few days ago, when I was helping

Jason on another case. A missing child."

"Oh, good goddess," Evangeline muttered. She took a seat in the chair next to Jen.

"Is this the first one that you've seen since—?" Jen's voice trailed off, but Charlie finished the sentence in her head. In April, Jen had helped Charlie call a reaper to dispose of a tricky spirit. They'd all been on edge about the decision ever since.

"No," Charlie whispered. "I've seen it two other times. Once when I was at work and once when I was at the mall with Evan. Both those times, it was at a distance, and it didn't seem to acknowledge me at all."

"Well, it's acknowledging you now," Lisa said.

"I don't know what happened exactly. It was reaching for Jason, and I just snapped. I couldn't let it hurt him."

"What did you do?" Jen's usually gentle voice sharpened.

"I yelled at it. I told it to get out. To get off the property."

"And it just... did it?" Lisa asked, her tone incredulous.

Evangeline covered her mouth with one hand and grabbed hold of the small leather pouch hanging round her neck. "What were you thinking?"

"Evidently, I wasn't," Charlie said. "It touched me." Her hand drifted to her cheek where the back of the reaper's hand had brushed across her skin. Tears stung the back of her throat and she sniffled. "I think it may have marked me for death."

"I told you girls it was a bad idea." Evangeline shook her head. "I told you, you shouldn't be messing with such forces."

"It's gonna be all right." Jen wrapped an arm around Charlie's shoulders. "We're gonna figure something out."

Charlie let the tears spill on to her cheek and buried her face in her cousin's neck. "How? It's Death, for crying out loud. If it wants me dead, I'm dead."

"Okay, let's just think about this for a minute." Lisa raised her hands up as if to put a stop to their crazy talk. "You just said when Death comes for you, it comes for you." She paused and her green eyes squinted as if she were trying to think of the right words. "Death doesn't wait. If it wanted you dead, you'd be dead. That you're not speaks volumes about its intent."

"Spoken like lawyer," Jen muttered.

"'Cause I am a lawyer," Lisa shot back.

Charlie took in a deep breath and blew it out. Lisa was right. She had to be. "Then what does it want with me?"

Lisa hugged her arms around her waist, her face solemn. "I don't know. We'll have to figure that out."

CHAPTER 5

Charlie pulled her feet beneath the shade of the umbrella and shifted in her chair. The wood creaked, and she marveled at it. She ran her hand over the oiled teak arm of the steamer chair. It was smooth and reminded her of the chairs that her grandmother Bunny used to drag out to the beach. "You don't have to spend a million bucks to feel like a million bucks, Charlie girl," Bunny had said. Bunny would sit beneath a big red umbrella and watch Charlie play in the waves until the tide came in. Sometimes the old woman would bring a fishing pole and cast a line, and they'd have fresh fried whiting for dinner. Charlie smiled at the memory, halfway expecting her grandmother to show up. Sometimes Bunny visited her in her dreams.

Warm summer air blew across the beach, shifting

the sand a little. Charlie opened her mouth and breathed deeply. The taste of salt brine coated her tongue. She sat up straight and looked up and down the beach. There was no crowd, which was strange for a sunny summer day. She looked right and then left. A jetty of large granite rocks jutted out into the ocean. There were no landmarks to tell her which beach she was on. But since this was a dream, maybe it didn't matter which beach. She leaned back against the wooden slats of the chair and stared out at the waves crashing.

"Hey, Mom." Evan came up from behind her, startling her. He wore bright orange and navy surf trunks and a long-sleeved rash guard. Scott had taught Evan to surf on their last vacation together as a family in Hawaii. Surfing was possible off the coast of South Carolina, but the water was smooth as glass today. Evan picked up a boogie board leaning against the empty steamer chair next to her. He tucked it under his arm. She smiled and grabbed hold of his free hand. His blond hair glowed almost white in the sunlight, and his blue eyes glittered against his tan skin.

"You be careful."

He pulled away from her. "I will."

She blinked and Evan was already at the water's edge. *This is definitely a dream.*

The sand was whiter than any beach she'd ever

been on, and everything shined like she was looking at a glossy postcard. She breathed deep, inhaling the salt air. The muscles in her shoulders and neck relaxed.

"Don't get too comfortable." A silky voice came from behind her. A chill skittered across her shoulders, despite the heat of the afternoon. Slowly she turned her head and looked up to find a dark shadowy figure beside her. It glided across the sand, robes blowing in the wind, heading toward the water. Toward Evan. Charlie bolted upright, her gaze locking on her son as he stood up with his back to the ocean and waved at her. The ocean shifted from smooth to turbulent in a blink. A white-capped swell grew larger and larger behind Evan. If it crested and broke, it would knock him over. Evan was a powerful swimmer. He'd learned early and got into the water every chance he got, but it wouldn't be enough to combat the size of the wave or the swiftness of the current. Charlie jumped to her feet and raced toward the water's edge, waving her arms. "Evan, come out of the water!"

The reaper stopped between Evan and her, throwing a glance over his shoulder. Its amber eyes shimmered, crystalline fire in the shadow of his hood. A grin g shiny white teeth in a frightening leer. "Evan, come out of the water, right this minute! Ev—" His name died on her lips just as the waves broke over his head, knocking him forward. Her heart leaped into her throat, a hard rock of fear blocking her breath and voice. She launched herself toward him, but her feet sank into scorching sand, sucking her toes downward, making it impossible to move. Evan disappeared beneath the water, swallowed by the waves. The reaper's laugh slithered through her head, and she finally found her voice.

* * *

WHEN CHARLIE AWOKE, SHE WASN'T SURE IF SHE HAD screamed out loud or not. She sat up and listened to the room, to the house for any sign someone had heard her. There were no footsteps in the hall. No voices asking who had cried out. She placed her hand on her chest and breathed in deeply through her nose and out through her mouth. It was just a dream. A stupid, bad dream.

After a few moments, her heartbeat normalized. She glanced at the clock. The red numbers read 4:02 a.m. She heard something clank downstairs. The smoky scent of bacon drifted through her senses. *Jen.* Her cousin kept ungodly hours, but Charlie understood why. Jen would have to be at her restaurant soon to prepare for the breakfast crowd. The doors opened at 6:30 a.m. and there were customers to feed.

Charlie swept the quilts off her legs and got up.

She quickly made the bed, wrapped herself in a pale blue cotton robe and headed downstairs. Maybe she could catch Jen before she left.

Charlie peeked into the living room. Jason slept on the long plush sofa with one arm folded across his eyes. A soft snore escaped him. She smiled and moved on.

Charlie found her cousin sitting at the dining room table writing in a leather notebook. There was a shoebox-sized plastic container full of different colored pens on the table next to her. Charlie cleared her throat.

Jen glanced up and a wide smile stretched her lips. The blue tips of her short black hair glowed in the overhead light of the chandelier, and for a second, she looked almost like a tiny fairy. "Good morning. You're up awfully early. Couldn't sleep? I know that mattress is sort of lumpy. I guess it's a good thing you'll be moving into the cottage soon. Otherwise, I'd have to guilt Daddy into getting a new mattress."

"It's not the mattress." Charlie sighed and pulled out the chair next to her cousin. She sat down and peeked at Jen's notebook. Decorative script, doodles, and dates adorned the pages. "What is all this about?"

"It's how I keep up with all my lists." Jen returned the cap to the pen in her hand. She handed the book to Charlie. "It's my day planner, my dream book, my to-do list. My sanity."

"It's amazing," Charlie flipped through the pages, marveling at the exquisite hand-lettered headers, cursive handwriting, and neatly printed lists. "You have such pretty handwriting."

"Thank you." Jen shifted her gaze from the book to Charlie's face, her wide blue eyes full of speculation. "So, why are you up?"

Charlie's shoulders slumped a little. "Bad dream."

"Scott?"

"No—the reaper."

"Well, I can definitely understand that, after what happened last night. Seems like he's haunting you."

"Maybe he is."

"What happened in the dream?"

"It started out great—Evan and I were on the beach. The entire place reminded me of the beach Bunny used to take us to. Remember?"

"Aw, Bunny." Jen smiled. "I miss Bunny."

"I do too. She visits me sometimes—in my dreams. But she wasn't there this time. It was just me and Evan. He was playing in the waves and this huge swell drew up behind him. That's when the reaper appeared. I couldn't get to him in time, and the wave swallowed him up." Her chest tightened at the memory.

"Oh, sweetie." Jen rubbed the top of her arm. "It was just a dream."

"I know." Charlie picked up a red marker and popped the top off it. She clicked the cap back in place. "And I know he's not really going to show up and take Evan away from me."

"Good." Jen patted Charlie's hand.

"But it doesn't mean I won't see him again." Charlie met her cousin's gaze. "You know I wouldn't normally ask this, but is there something you can do? Some—spell, maybe?" She whispered the word spell as if it were a secret not to be spoken too loudly.

Jen's forehead wrinkled and the corners of her mouth tugged downward into a frown. She breathed out through her nose. "You still have your pendant, right?"

Charlie's hand immediately went to her throat, reaching for the silver circle. Two black tourmaline beads hung on either side of the pendant. She ran her thumb over the engraved pentagram. "Yes. I always wear it now."

"That's the best protection I can offer you against any danger. There is no spell or charm that can stand up to Death."

"Oh." Charlie stared down at the pen in her hands. She pressed her thumbnail against the bottom of the pen top, letting it bend the nail down.

"I'm sorry, sweetie." Jen gently removed the pen

from Charlie's grip and put it back in the box. She gathered the other pens and put them away, securing the box's plastic top in place.

"I guess I needed to hear that."

"I know Lisa likes to say it's Death's fault. The reaper, I mean. That it's his fault when people die. But honestly, I don't think that's the case. I think he's just doing a job. Like you and me. Your job is to provide customer service and help connect the dead with the living, and my job is to feed people. Speaking of which." Jen glanced at the old grandfather clock against the wall. The long black arm pointed to the two and the short arm to the four. "I really need to get going."

"Sure."

Jen rose from her chair and gathered her journal and pens. She tucked them into the olive colored messenger bag on the empty chair next to her. "You gonna be all right?"

"It was just a dream. Right?"

Jen gave her one quick nod. "Even someone like you is liable to have a plain old nightmare just like the rest of us."

Charlie called up a smile. "You're probably right."

"Of course, I'm right." Jen grinned and her blue eyes glittered. "Will I see you later?"

"I'll stop by for some breakfast on my way to work."

Jen gave her a wink and disappeared through the door to the kitchen. Charlie heard the old screen door squeal open. She touched the pendant hanging from the chain around her neck again and lifted it to her lips. She kissed it lightly before getting up and heading back to bed for another couple hours of sleep.

CHAPTER 6

Charlie pulled her blue Honda into the Givens' driveway and hopped out. It had surprised her that Mrs. Givens had been so accommodating when she asked if she could take another look at the property behind their house.

Charlie rang the bell and Marla Givens opened the door. "It's good to see you, Miss Payne."

"Please call me Charlie." Charlie smiled. "I really appreciate you letting me do this."

"If you think it will help you find my daughter—"

"I don't know what it will lead to, but there's something about those woods and I really need to take another look."

Marla Givens nodded and led Charlie in through the house to the back door.

"Should I stay here or do you want me to go with you?" Marla asked.

"It's probably best if you stay here. The spirit I encountered back there seemed a little skittish."

Marla's eyes widened a little, and she forced a smile. Charlie could see on her face she wanted more than anything to believe in Charlie's words, but there was just the tiniest bit of doubt in her brown eyes. Charlie smiled and gently pressed her hand against Marla's arm to reassure her.

"If I'm not back in an hour, text me on my cell. Okay?" Charlie knew Jason wouldn't like her coming here alone. If she could at least check in with Marla, maybe he wouldn't give her such a hard time if she came up with fresh information.

"I will. Should I call Deputy Tate if you don't come back or if I don't hear from you?"

Charlie bit her lower lip. She sighed. "If I'm not back in two hours, call him."

"Deal."

Charlie opened the back door and rushed to the expansive backyard. She held a steady gaze on the entrance to the woods, hoping the girl would come forward and greet her. When the child didn't appear, Charlie made her way into the gloom of the thick canopy. Leaves and pine straw crunched beneath her feet, and the chatter of squirrels and chirping of birds echoed around her, comforting her. When she got to the spot where she had seen the girl during her last visit, she stopped and glanced around.

"Trini?" she called. "It's Charlie. Can you come and talk to me? I promise I'm all by myself today." Charlie turned in a circle, making sure that the reaper hadn't followed her. Of course, he could materialize from the shadows if he wanted to. She shivered and pushed the thought out of her head.

"Please come talk to me," she called again.

The soft cooing of mourning doves came from someplace close by. Charlie sighed and continued walking deeper into the woods. She kept glancing over her shoulder just to make sure that the path was still there, and if a reaper was following her, she wanted to see him before he got too close.

The snap of a twig breaking, and the crunch of leaves sent Charlie's heart into overdrive. She spun around, ready to confront the noise maker. The path was clear. A little giggle escaped her mouth, and she shook her head.

"Stop scaring yourself," she muttered.

She almost jumped out of her skin when she turned to continue and found a man standing a few feet away, watching her. Her heart clogged her throat and blood rushed through her ears. The man watched her with wary golden-brown eyes. The most beautiful eyes she'd ever seen. He wore black pants that looked expensive and a crisply pressed gray button-down shirt. Not exactly the right attire for a walk in the woods. "Oh, my god," Charlie choked out. She pressed her hand to her chest. "You scared me."

"I'm sorry," he said in a lilting accent that she immediately recognized as proper Charlestonian. Her ex-mother-in-law had the same accent. She wondered how long his family had been in the area. "I didn't mean to frighten you. I rarely run into people out here."

He smiled, showing perfect white teeth that gleamed against his dark, well-groomed beard. His intense eyes fixed her to the spot. Something about the shine on his teeth made her uneasy. *The better to eat you with, my dear.* She pushed the thought out of her head. She was being ridiculous. He was just a man. Not a wolf. Not a reaper. Charlie forced a smile.

"I'm sorry. I was just visiting the Givens'." She pointed back the way she came. "Marla said it would be fine to take a walk here."

"I see." He quirked an eyebrow. "It seemed more like you were looking for someone."

"I—" She tightened her arms across her chest. *Lie. Lie now.* "I was just calling for my dog. Trini. Did you see her?"

"No. I didn't see a dog. Sorry."

"Oh. Well, if you see a German shepherd, stay

away. She's not friendly." Charlie hated lying, but his smile widened.

"What about her owner? Is she friendly?"

A chill skittered across her shoulders and down her back. "Not really." Charlie took a step backward. "I—"

Don't turn your back on him.

She glanced down at his feet. The fine black leather of his boots burnished even in the dim light. Not exactly the stealthiest footwear. Where had he come from? "I need to go. My friend will be waiting for me."

"Wait. I didn't mean that the way it sounded." He thrust out his hand. "I'm Tom. Tom Sharon."

"Um—" Charlie stared at his outstretched hand and hesitated.

"I don't bite. I promise," he said.

"I have a cold coming on. It's probably better if I don't—" She took another step backward. "Wouldn't want to get you sick."

"Right." His smile faded, and he dropped his hand to his side.

"I should get back." Charlie glanced over her shoulder. How long had she been walking? She hadn't been paying much attention to the time, only the landmarks. Her phone vibrated and The Twilight Zone ringtone interrupted. Jason's tone. Tom Sharon's gaze shifted to Charlie's hips.

"Your pants are ringing." He smirked and pointed. "Interesting choice of ringtones."

"See, there's my friend now." She forced a smile and pulled her phone from her pocket and glanced down at the screen.

Where R you? Marla Givens called me!! U OK?

"Sorry, I have to take this," she muttered and began texting him.

I'm OK. But ran into a weirdo in the woods.

Dead or alive?

Charlie clenched her jaw. Everybody was a comedian.

Creepy, but very much alive.

I'm on my way.

Unnecessary. Really. I can handle it.

Be there in ten.

"Dammit," she muttered.

"I hope you told your friend not to worry about you," Tom said. His deep tenor voice reminded her of someone, but she couldn't quite put her finger on who.

"I need to go," Charlie said abruptly and backed away nearly ten feet before finally turning and bolting. Something sharp clipped her ankle, and she belly-flopped onto the forest floor. She banged her head hard and laid on the path, breathing in the fumes of pine needles and dirt. A ringing filled her head.

"Miss!" Tom Sharon knelt beside her, placing his hand on her shoulder. He sounded panicked. "Miss? Are you all right?"

The warmth of his hand penetrated her thin T-shirt and a blur of images rushed through her mind along with the sounds of crying. Suffering. So much suffering. Charlie covered her head with her hands.

"Don't touch me!" Her voice shook when she heard the words come out of her mouth, but they sounded distant and nearly drowned out, as if someone else had said them. He lifted his hand and the clamor in her head stopped. She lay there for a moment, taking deep, heavy breaths. A cold fog of dread rolled into her chest, filling all the empty places.

"Miss, please let me help you."

Charlie opened her eyes and pushed up onto all fours. Alarm and concern filled his golden-brown eyes. He still held one hand hovering near her.

"I'm fine." The strident sound of her voice made her cringe. She didn't want to be the hysterical female that needed rescuing, and she didn't want Jason to come charging into the woods after her. Charlie called up a reassuring smile. "I'm fine. Really. Now, I really have to go. My friend is waiting."

He shifted his gaze to the path. "I should come with you. Make sure you get back safely. You hit your head pretty hard. That goose-egg will hurt."

Charlie sat back on her haunches and touched her hand to her forehead. She winced and sucked her breath across her teeth.

"Come on, let me help you," he murmured. "Please."

Charlie met his gaze. "No. I'm fine. I promise." She pushed to her feet and dizziness swirled through her head. She held out her arms to steady herself.

Tom quickly grabbed her by the arm. "Clearly, you're not all right. I don't have my cell phone with me; it's in my car. Perhaps I should take you there and call 911."

"Stop touching me." She yanked her arm out of his hand. "I told you I'm fine."

"Sorry." Tom lifted his hands in surrender. "I didn't mean to frighten you."

"I'm not frightened." She protested, but the words sounded hollow. A lie. "I just don't like strangers touching me, that's all."

"Noted. If you told me your name, then maybe we wouldn't be strangers anymore."

"Seriously? Does that line really work?" she snapped.

"I was just trying to be friendly, that's all."

Friendly. Of course, she lived in the friendliest place in the country. Her grandmother Bunny's voice popped into her head. *Don't be rude, Charlie girl.* She sighed. "Fine friendly Tom. I'm Charlie."

"It's very nice to meet you, Charlie. You sure you can get back on your own?"

"Yes." She didn't even try to mask her irritation.

He gave her a quick nod. "All right, then. I'll leave you to it."

He turned and headed away from her. She waited for what seemed a long time before heading back to the Givens house. Watching as he grew smaller before he disappeared among the trees.

* * *

JASON TATE WALKED ACROSS THE YARD TOWARD HER. Concern scratched deep lines into his forehead. "Are you all right?"

"I'm fine." Charlie tipped her head to the right and called up a reassuring smile. "I didn't mean to worry you. I'm sorry."

He was standing in front of her before she finished her sentence, stopping her in her tracks. He gently pushed the hair off her forehead. "No, you're not. What the hell happened? Did this guy hit you?"

"No. Nobody hit me. Except the ground. The ground hit me. I spooked myself. I'm fine now. Can we just go?"

"Yeah, sure. You didn't lose consciousness or anything, did you? Maybe I should take you to the hospital."

"Oh, for the love of Oprah. I'm fine." She batted away his hand.

Jason glared at her for a moment more, but he didn't push the issue any further. "Fine."

"Good. Let's get out of here." She nodded.

"All right. Let's go." The two of them headed back toward the Givens house.

"Can you do one thing for me?" Charlie asked as they walked up the steps to the Givens' deck.

"What?"

"Can you check someone out for me?"

Jason stopped and leveled his gaze on her. "Who?"

"The guy I met in the woods?"

"Sure—did he give you a name?"

"Yep. He sure did. Tom Sharon."

CHAPTER 7

Haley Miller's hand shook as she topped off her Diet Coke with a large splash of Jack Daniels. The lip of the bottle stuttered against the glass, and she steadied her left hand with her right. She set the bottle down and picked up her cell phone from her kitchen counter. Even after two drinks, her thumbs deftly found the contact she was looking for. She took a big gulp of the bubbly liquid. The ice rattled as she put it onto the counter. With both hands, she whipped off a text.

Charlie glanced around, trying to understand what she was seeing. This was a dream. She moved in closer and looked over Haley's shoulder. She got too close though, and her shoulder bumped into Haley's.

This is a dream. Charlie closed her eyes and took a

deep breath before stepping fully into Haley's body. She let herself feel the young woman's feelings and hear her thoughts. When Charlie opened her eyes, she read the text on the screen.

We need to talk. It's getting worse. I think I may have to tell someone.

Haley pressed the send button and waited. She took another gulp of her drink. The phone rang and vibrated in her hand. Haley jumped, startled by the quick response. The screen displayed a young woman with short brown hair and wide blue eyes, grinning on a beach with the ocean behind her and late afternoon sun lighting her perfectly tanned face. The name read Emma W. Haley pressed the green phone icon.

"What the hell, Haley!" Emma's shrill tone pierced the quiet of the house. "We took a vow. Does that not mean anything to you?"

Haley put the phone to her ear. "I know, but—"

"There is no but!"

Haley made an indignant sound in the back of her throat. "That's easy for you to say. You're not the one being haunted."

Emma sighed. "We have been over this. There is no such thing as ghosts."

"Do you know how many times I've had to replace my bathroom mirror this year alone because of her?"

"Haley—" Emma sighed, sounding impatient.

"She's touching me now. Waking me up." Haley put her head in one hand and leaned her elbow on the black granite counter. She closed her eyes. "She jerks my leg in the middle of the night, pulls off the covers. I haven't slept through the night in months."

"What are you talking about? She can't touch you, Haley. She's dead and buried right where we left her."

Haley's voice shook, and she took another gulp from her Jack and Diet Coke. "I know but—"

"Haley, how much have you had to drink tonight?"

"What does that have to do with anything? I've seen things. Okay? Weird, frightening things."

Haley could almost hear Emma rolling her eyes. "Haley. Come on now. You are spooking yourself."

"I know what I've seen."

"Sweetie, you need to lay off the Jack and Diet Coke."

"I can prove it. Just hold on a second." Haley thumbed through her pictures and found the one she needed. She attached the photo to a text and pressed send. A shiver crawled over her shoulders. "I just sent you a picture."

Haley heard Emma shifting her phone in her hand. The silence stretched between them.

"Is this a joke?" Emma's tone was sharp, but

Haley knew she was scared. At least she hoped it scared Emma. Maybe now she'd come. Maybe she'd help Haley convince the others to come too.

"No. It's not a joke. It's not photoshopped either. I took that not more than half an hour ago," Haley said.

"It's not real," Emma muttered.

"Yes, it is." Haley couldn't stop herself from being defensive.

"Sweetie, I don't know how you did this. Or why, but you need some help."

"That's why I am calling you. I need you to help me. Please, Emma. Help me."

"Fine. I'll have to rearrange some things at work," Emma whispered.

"Oh, my god, really? Thank you so much, Emma." Haley's shoulders slumped and her eyes stung with tears. Help was coming.

"I'll text you tomorrow," Emma said.

"Thank you. Thank you so much for believing me."

The line went silent, and Haley buried her face in her hands and wept.

* * *

CHARLIE AWOKE AND REACHED FOR HER PHONE. SHE SAT up in bed and quickly thumbed through her contacts for Jason's number. The phone rang twice before he picked up.

"Tate."

"Hey, it's me."

"What's going on? Everything all right?" His tone changed from grumpy to concerned.

"I had a dream about Haley Miller. She's not quite as innocent as we thought."

"What do you mean?"

"She was being haunted, and she *knew* who was haunting her."

"Okay." Jason's breathing evened out. "Who was haunting her?"

"Well, she didn't exactly say a name."

"All right. Anything else?"

"I can't explain it, but all her feelings about this spirit were ambiguous."

"What do you mean?"

"I mean she felt scared of the person haunting her, but there was also this underlying guilt."

"Guilt? Like she's responsible for this ghost?"

"Yes, and no."

Jason sighed. The phone crackled. She could almost see him rubbing his face, the way he did when he wanted to believe her, but what she was telling him was hard for him to embrace. "Oh-kay. Tell me why it's both?"

"I think she felt guilty. Remorse, even. But it's

almost like if she wasn't being haunted, then she wouldn't have given this person a second thought."

"Nice," he said, his tone dripping with sarcasm.

"Haley was talking to another woman. Someone named Emma W."

"Uh-huh." He sounded almost as if he were falling back asleep. "Emma is a pretty common name. I guess I can run Emma W's through my system, but it's not a lot to go on."

"No, I know. I'm sorry I didn't see more. I think they may have caused the spirit's death. Maybe that's why she's haunting them."

"Wait." He grunted, as if he were sitting up. "Did they say that?"

"Not exactly."

"What exactly did they say?"

Charlie recalled the dream for him, giving him as much detail as she could remember.

"Well, that makes sense now."

"What does?"

"We got the autopsy report back this afternoon. Haley's blood alcohol level was point one one, and for someone who was only thirty-one years old, she had an alcoholic's liver."

"Wow," Charlie whispered. "That's really sad."

"Yeah."

"So, do you think you have enough to go on? To find this Emma person?"

"I don't know. Maybe. I'll go back through her social media to see if I can find an Emma. Her phone was locked so I'm still waiting on phone records and texts from the carrier." He sighed. "Call me if you have another dream. Especially if you learn the name of the dead girl. The other dead girl, I mean."

Charlie chuckled. "I will."

* * *

CHARLIE STARED AT THE COMPUTER SCREEN ON HER desk, listening to the customer drone on. Her cell phone vibrated on the under-mount keyboard tray, distracting her from her phone call. She glanced down at it and could see it was a text but couldn't quite read it.

"Yes, ma'am," Charlie said into her headset. "Is there anything else I can do for you?"

"No, I think you've answered all my questions," the customer said.

"Well, thank you for calling and you have a wonderful day." Charlie pressed the end call button on her phone, making herself available to take another call. She looked up and glanced around the call center, noting where the supervisors were. Kaylee was at the supervisor-of-the-day tower feeding numbers into a spreadsheet for the hourly reports. Charlie didn't see any of the others. They may have been in their offices meeting with their reps about performance or any number of issues that came up daily. She picked up the cell phone and held it at an angle where she could at least see the text better.

Jason's name displayed across the top.

Call me when you've got a minute. I think I may have found Trini.

Charlie's heart beat a little faster. She hadn't stopped thinking about the girl since she first met her. If Tom Sharon hadn't interrupted her in the woods a couple of days ago, Charlie would've been able to contact her instead of having to rely on Jason. She quickly texted him to let him know she would call him on her break in forty-five minutes. She pushed her phone back under the cover of her desk.

"You know, one of these days you're gonna get caught." Brian gave her a wry grin. Charlie frowned and tipped her head to the left. She spotted his phone on his keyboard tray. The silver metal of his smart phone winked at her. She rolled her eyes.

"And that is the pot calling the kettle black," she muttered.

"Pot, meet kettle." Brian held out his hand like he would shake hers but jerked it away quick to answer his phone.

She heard a beep in her ear showing she had a call.

"Thank you for calling Bel-Com Credit Union. How can I help you today?"

* * *

"Well." Jason chuckled into the phone. "I think I found Tom Sharon."

"You did?" she asked. "That was fast."

"I just sent you a text with a photo attached. Let me know if that's him or not."

Charlie checked her texts and found Tom Sharon's driver's license photo staring at her. "Yep. That's him. So, is he wanted for murder or anything?"

"What?" Jason laughed. "Why would you ask me that?"

"Because when I met him, I sensed that death surrounded him."

Jason laughed again, harder this time.

"Oh, my god, it's not *that* funny," she grumbled.

"No, you're right," Jason said, trying to get himself under control. "It's just he *is* surrounded by death. Or at least dead people."

"Huh?" Charlie said, reaching into the large refrigerator in the break room. She pulled out her lunch bag and took it to a deserted table near the back wall. It was after 1:30 p.m., so she almost had the break room to herself. Only a couple of women from another department lingered near a vending machine, debating whether to get chocolate sandwich cookies or a granola bar. Charlie shook her head. Neither was a good choice, in her opinion.

"The Tom Sharon you just identified is one of the sons of Sharon and Sons funeral homes."

Charlie sat down hard in the plastic chair and put her head in her free hand. She could almost hear him smirking. "You have got to be kidding me."

"Nope."

"Well, no wonder he looks so damned familiar. That's where we had Bunny's funeral." Charlie made an indignant grunt in the back of her throat. She opened her lunch bag and pulled out her salad in a jar. Jen had whipped up a weeks' worth of salads for her. This one had buffalo chicken in it. At the bottom of the bag, she retrieved a small container of ranch dressing and a yogurt cup.

She twisted off the top to her jar and poured the contents onto a paper plate. "I still think it's weird that he just appeared out of nowhere."

"Maybe. But my guess is you were so engrossed in trying to find this girl you just didn't notice. I've seen you do that before when you're concentrating. Sometimes you don't even hear me."

Charlie frowned. "Was that all you had for me? I thought you had information about Trini."

"Yeah. I found one girl matching her description with the name Trini. Trini Dolan went missing in

1977 when she was thirteen years old. Went out on her bike one day and just didn't come home. The police thought she was a runaway."

"Why?" Charlie opened her yogurt and licked the creamy bit clinging to the top.

"It was a common assumption at the time. They never had a break in the case, that I could find. No one ever saw her again," he continued.

"Any chance I could get a look at the file?" Charlie stuck a plastic spoon in her yogurt carton and stirred up the fruit from the bottom.

"Sure. Are you gonna be home tonight?"

"Yes. But come to the cottage, not my uncle's house."

"Have you officially moved in there?"

"Mostly. Jen and I moved a bunch of my boxes last night."

"Great," Jason said. "I'll drop by tonight."

CHAPTER 8

Charlie walked into the Kitchen Witch Café and looked around. The small restaurant was already bustling with the dinner crowd. She spotted a table for two near the lunch counter and took a seat. She grabbed an unused menu from the nearby counter and began perusing the specials listed inside. She spotted Jen near the register and waved. Her pixie-sized cousin waved back and finished ringing up a customer, before picking up an order pad and heading toward Charlie's table.

"You know you don't have to eat here in the café every night," Jen teased and sat down across from Charlie. "You're still welcome to come eat dinner with us at the house."

"I enjoy eating here. I like the hustle and bustle."

Charlie glanced around and took a sip of her iced tea. She closed the menu and glanced at the clock hanging on the wall behind the lunch counter. "What are you still doing here? Don't you have to pick up Ruby?"

"Nope. Daddy picked her up. Evangeline's having to leave early this week so I'm staying later."

"Is everything okay?" Charlie asked.

"I think so. It's sometimes hard to tell. She wants to be all up in our business, but she doesn't want to share anything," Jen said.

"Well, it's probably hard for her to think of us as anything but kids."

Jen chuckled and rolled her eyes. "I don't think that's it. I think she has a boyfriend or girlfriend or something."

"You know everything doesn't have to be about boyfriends or husbands or girlfriends. Maybe she just needs some time to herself. She has a lot of demands on her between the business and the family. I mean, we're not easy," Charlie said.

"You're probably right," Jen said, frowning. "I just wish she would let me in. Maybe I could help."

"I know." Charlie tapped the top of Jen's hand. "We can do a quasi-intervention. But we have to get Daphne involved. She may know something we don't."

Jen looked up at her. The blue tips of her bangs

glimmered in the overhead light. "That's probably a good place to start."

"So, you gonna take my order or what?" Charlie teased.

Jen took an order pad from her apron and placed it on the table. The bell over the front door rang causing them both to look up just as Tom Sharon walked into the cafe. He stopped and glanced around as if he were looking for someone. His gaze settled on hers.

"Oh, crap," Charlie muttered.

"Well, hello gorgeous," Jen said doing her best Fanny Brice impersonation. Tom smiled, showing his gleaming white teeth amid his dark brown beard. He wore a navy pinstripe suit and a purple satin tie. Charlie frowned. There was something almost too perfect about him.

"What's with the suit?" Jen said under her breath.

Charlie whispered, "I think he's a mortician."

"Oh." Jen scrunched her nose. "Well, that's interesting."

"Hello, Charlie." Tom outstretched his hand as he approached the table. Charlie stared at it, and when she didn't return his gesture, he dropped his hand to his side. Had he not learned his lesson the first time? "Do you live here in town?"

"No." Charlie frowned. "Not exactly. What are you doing here?"

"God, Charlie," Jen half-laughed, half-scolded. "Please excuse my cousin. Evidently, she's saving her people skills for work. I'm Jen. Jen Holloway."

"Nice to meet you, Jen." Tom offered his hand and Jen hopped up from her seat and took it. "Tom Sharon."

"Oh—Sharon. Like Sharon and Sons?" Jen asked. "I saw the sign for the new branch coming to work."

"Yes." He smiled and Charlie watched Jen's face for any sign that she might sense something about him. When Jen returned his smile and then cast her gaze toward Charlie, her blue eyes full of expectation and a little scheming, Charlie's heart sank. Surely Jen could feel it too? There was something about Tom Sharon. Something she couldn't quite figure out. Something felt more than seen and it flitted around the edges of her brain, like vapor, disappearing completely if she tried to look at it squarely.

"Y'all just opened up, right?" Jen asked.

"Yes, we did. I'm running this office," Tom said.

"It's always good to meet another business owner," Jen said. "Make sure you join the Chamber of Commerce. I'm on the recruitment committee."

"This is your restaurant?"

"Yes, it is."

"Wonderful. I'm not much of a cook, so you'll probably see me here a lot."

"Great!" Jen said.

Tom shifted his attention to Charlie, his golden-brown eyes fixing on her. "I'm really glad we ran into each other. We got off on the wrong foot the other day and haven't been able to get it out of my head."

"Don't worry about it. It's not a big deal."

"I was rather hoping I could make it up to you."

Jen cleared her throat. Charlie glanced at her cousin. Jen's dark eyebrows rose, and a mischievous light filled her eyes.

"Well, since you're here, you may as well have dinner," Jen chimed in. "I'm sure that Charlie would love to have the company." Charlie's eyes widened, her cheeks filling with heat. "Wouldn't you, Charlie?"

"Sh-sure," Charlie stuttered and threw her cousin an I'm-going-to-kill-you glare. She called up a smile. "Of course, please join me."

Tom sat down across from her and placed his hands on the table. Jen picked up Charlie's menu and handed it to him. He opened it and smiled. "What's good?"

"Everything." Jen grinned. "But, of course, I'm a teensy bit biased."

"What would you recommend, Charlie?" Tom's gaze bounced from Jen to the Charlie.

"The jalapeno bacon and avocado burger is to die for." Charlie narrowed her eyes, waiting for him to take the bait. "If you can stand the heat."

"I can." Tom grinned and closed the menu. "Sounds great. I'll have that."

Jen's smile widened, but her eyes tightened. "You sure? It's pretty spicy. I can always make it without the bacon. Not everybody has Charlie's iron stomach."

Tom fixed his stare on Charlie. "If Charlie can stomach it, so can I."

Jen sighed and wrote down the order. "All right, then. Do you want fries with that?"

Charlie leaned forward and folded her hands on the table, weaving her fingers together. "Do you trust me?"

He narrowed his eyes. "I have no reason to distrust you."

Charlie looked at Jen. "Add the Cajun onion rings, extra spicy."

"Sounds perfect," Tom said.

"You sure about that?" Jen's voice arced, but the smile never left her lips.

He gave her one quick nod. "Yes. And some iced tea, please."

Jen scribbled it down the order, shaking her head. "Okay, but I'm adding them for you too, Charlie. I can't very well let him suffer alone. Now do you want your usual?"

"Yes, please," Charlie said.

"What's the usual?" Tom asked.

"Soft shell crab sandwich. It's dredged in hot sauce, breaded and deep fried and served with habanero pepper added to the tartar sauce. Can you add some extra sauce, please?"

"You got it. I'll bring a fire extinguisher in case you two burst into flames," Jen said. She turned and headed toward the kitchen with their order.

"So—" Charlie tapped her fingers against the back of her knuckles. "This is very weird."

"That's my fault, I'm afraid. I scared you."

Charlie pressed her lips together and stared at him. A fluorescent bulb buzzed overhead. Of course, she sensed death—he was a mortician, for god's sake. He was so handsome it almost hurt to look at him. Finally, she whispered, "Yes. You did. A little."

"Well, I am sorry for that." He drummed his fingers on the table, and the soft sound filled the awkward space between them. "So, how long have you lived here?"

"I grew up here. What about you?"

"My family has lived in Charleston almost three hundred years."

"A true Charlestonian. You're a rare bird. I take it you live downtown?"

"Actually, I just sold my house so I could be closer to my work. I'm renting a beach house in the meantime."

"Nice. I love the beach. So why Palmetto Point?"

"It just seemed like the right move. We've lost a lot of business west of the Ashley not having a branch here. My brother and I had talked about it for a while and finally just bit the bullet."

A petite young woman with blue hair approached the table and set down a very full glass of iced tea in front of each of them. A little tea splashed onto the table in front of Charlie, hitting her pinky finger. The young woman walked off unapologetically.

Charlie grabbed her napkin and wiped off her hand, then mopped up the iced tea. She sighed. "That girl still needs to learn some skills."

"Indeed, she does. Should we tell your cousin?" he asked, glancing around for Jen.

It struck her as odd how formal his speech was sometimes. Charlie gave him a wry smile. "No point. She already knows. But the girl's mother works here, so—"

"I see." He nodded. "Nepotism is rampant in my industry too."

"Sure. You just said you work with your brother." She nodded. "What do you do exactly?"

Tom leaned forward a bit. His intense gaze bore into her. Charlie's breath caught in her throat and heat crept up her neck into her cheeks. He was so handsome it hurt.

"I'm a..." a sly grin played at the corners of his lips, "mortician. Funeral Director. Unnnder-taker."

Charlie shifted in her seat but couldn't look away.

He laughed. "I have a question for you now." Tom leaned against the cushioned chair back, reaching into his pocket, breaking his spell over her. He pulled a silver engraved business card case and placed it on the table in front of him. His long nimble fingers lifted the metal flap, revealing business cards. His thumb brushed across the top one, sliding it out of the case. He closed the flap and pushed the case aside, then handed her the card. "That's you? Right?"

Charlie took the pale cream card and read it. The name printed on it in an unassuming script read—Charlie Payne—Psychic Medium. Lisa had helped her pick out the paper and font. "Go with simple," Lisa had said. "Direct. Classic. It will make you look serious. Put a ghost or a crystal ball on there and people will think it's a joke."

"Where did you get this?" Charlie picked up the card and stared at it.

"I was at the hair salon down the street. I overheard a lady talking about you, and the stylist handed her your card. I asked her about it, and she gave me one too. Said you were very good. The best, actually."

"Daphne," Charlie muttered. She would promptly kill her youngest cousin the next time she saw her. Daphne wasn't supposed to just hand these out to everybody.

"You know her?"

"Yes. She's one my cousins."

"I see. So it *is* you? Isn't it? There can't be two Charlie Paynes in a town this small, can there?"

Charlie sighed. "It's me."

"So much resignation in that tone." He chuckled. "Almost as if you don't want to be the girl on that card."

"I *am* the girl on the card," she said. *Whether or not I want to be.* Charlie looked him straight in the eye. "Usually when people hand me my card it's because they want a reading, but they don't want to say it out loud. Do you want a reading or are you looking to connect with a loved one who's passed on?"

His golden-brown eyes glittered, and his lips twisted into a wry grin. He scratched the side of his face, his fingers raking across the top of his well-trimmed beard. "I don't need to know my future, and there's no one I really want to talk to on the other side."

It was subtle—the lilt in his tone—but it reeked of skepticism. She scraped the short edge of the card against her fingers. Tom's face softened and the hint of smirk she'd seen a few minutes ago disappeared. He took a long sip of his iced tea and let his gaze drift around the restaurant, his expression indiscernible.

"It's okay if you don't believe. You wouldn't be the first person to doubt."

Tom brought his focus back to her. His eyes tightened, causing tiny wrinkles to appear, but he said nothing. He just stared at her and she wondered, was he trying to make her uncomfortable? He could try all he wanted. Charlie smiled, unafraid to meet his intense gaze with her own.

"You know, it won't hurt my feelings one bit if you'd rather not sit with me," Charlie said softly.

His brows tugged together, and a deep line formed between them. The wrinkles around his eyes deepened, making him appear older than he looked. "Is that what you want?"

Charlie shrugged. "I don't care either way. You're not the first to look at me like I'm crazy. Or worse."

He made an indignant noise in the back of his throat. "You don't have a very high opinion of yourself, do you?" Charlie opened her mouth to protest, but he cut her off. "It might surprise you what I believe in. The things I've seen would even make someone like you scratch her head."

Charlie stifled a laugh. "Really? I don't know. I've seen some really weird stuff."

"Tell me something, do you even have a dog?"

"A dog?"

"Yes. You said you'd lost your dog in the woods the other day."

Charlie thought for a moment. It had been stupid

to lie. She never remembered when she did and almost always got caught. She sighed.

"So, no dog," he said. A smirk played at the corners of his mouth. "Why were you in the woods? Were you looking for a ghost? What did you say her name was?"

"Trini," Charlie whispered.

"Trini." He nodded, recognition dawning in his eyes. "Yes. She's dead, right?"

"Maybe?" Charlie asked. His left eyebrow quirked, and his lips twisted with doubt. "Yes. So? What's your point?" Charlie glanced around. Maybe she should be the one to get up and move. The dinner crowd had already moved in, though, and the only empty seats were at the lunch counter.

"Why didn't you just tell me that?"

"Um, exactly how would that go? Hi, I'm Charlie, your local psychic. I'm looking for a little ghost girl, have you seen her? She's about yeah high." Charlie gestured the girl's height. "Oh, and by the way, are you a serial killer wandering around the woods looking for your next victim? That would've gone over beautifully, I'm sure."

His expression shifted, starting with his mouth. He bit his lips together, as if he were trying not to smile. Not to laugh at her.

"What?" Charlie snapped.

"You thought I was a serial killer?"

"I thought—" She clenched her jaw and blew out a breath. "Yes. I did. You appeared out of nowhere, looking like you'd just left a funeral."

His expression morphed again, becoming more solemn. "That's because I had just left a funeral."

"Oh." Her cheeks flooded with heat. "Isn't that your job?"

"Yes. But sometimes it's difficult. Sometimes I need to take a break. Which is what I was doing."

"What happened?"

A deep sadness rolled off him in a heavy wave, crashing over her. Being sensitive enough to see the dead and sometimes the future or past also meant being sensitive enough to feel what others felt. What the world felt. Her breath caught in her throat at the intensity of his emotion and she curled her fingers, digging her nails into her palms. For a second, the shadows beneath his eyes darkened, and his high carved cheekbones appeared sharper. If it had not been for his skin and beard, she would've sworn a skeleton was sitting across from her.

"Nothing. It doesn't matter now. Especially since you let me apologize and invited me to sit with you." A gentle smile curved his lips.

Charlie blinked and his face returned to normal, maybe even handsomer than before. She shifted in her seat.

"Are you all right?" he asked.

"Huh? Yes. I'm fine." She mustered a weak smile. "Just hungry. And I didn't really invite you. Jen did."

"What did Jen do?" Jen asked, placing Charlie's plate in front of her first.

"You invited Tom to eat with me."

"I did." A proud grin stretched Jen's lips. She put Tom's plate down and placed her hands on her hips. In her most cheerful voice, she said, "Now, is there anything else I can get you?"

Tom leaned over his plate and closed his eyes, inhaling deeply. "It smells divine."

"Well, let's hope your taste buds survive the heat and agree with you." Jen smirked and pulled a bottle of hot sauce from the front pocket of her apron, placing it next to Charlie's plate. "I'm not so worried about your taste buds. I know you burned them out long ago."

Charlie glared at her cousin. "I think that's all we need."

Jen ignored Charlie's pointed look. "Okay. Call me if you need me."

"We will." Charlie narrowed her eyes, trying to make it clear she knew exactly what Jen was up to. Jen grinned and walked away. Charlie shook her head. "I swear," she muttered.

"Everything all right?" Tom asked and unfolded his napkin. He placed it on his lap, pulled the top bun off the burger and reached for the ketchup.

"Yes, perfect." Charlie gave him a reassuring smile and unscrewed the cap of the hot sauce.

Tom squeezed a fair amount of ketchup onto his burger and eyed the hot sauce in Charlie's hand. "You know, I haven't known you very long, but you do that a lot. Can I have that?"

"Do what?" Charlie handed him the small bottle filled with dark, orange liquid and a habanero pepper and crossed bones on the label.

"Smile like everything is just fine."

"Everything is just fine."

"Is it? If your cousin's behavior upsets you, I'd like to hear about it." He put the top bun in place and grabbed hold of the burger, holding it up to his lips. "If you'd like to share, that is." He opened his mouth and took a bite.

Charlie leaned against the seat back and gaped at him. "I'm not upset." She protested, but it was a lie. "And what happens between my cousin and me is our business."

"Of course," he said apologetically. "I wasn't trying to pry. I'm just trying to tell you I find you fascinating. If you don't want to discuss it that's fine, but there's no need to placate me for the sake of politeness."

"I think my grandmother would disagree with you."

He swallowed his bite. A sheen of sweat appeared on his face. "Indeed."

"It's hot, isn't it?" Charlie smiled.

Tom wiped his mouth with his napkin and took a long sip of his iced tea. "It is. But it's good, although I think I will need more tea."

Charlie laughed. "You know, I appreciate your concern, I really do but I'm good. Really."

"Well, in case you change your mind. I'm an excellent listener. It seems you and I both deal in death. We may have more in common than you could ever imagine."

"I don't know about that." She dipped an onion ring in hot sauce and took a bite.

"Well, I bet we do, and honestly, I'd like to get to know you better to find out if I'm right."

"What do you mean?"

He put his burger down and wiped the corner of his mouth. "Have dinner with me."

"In case you didn't notice, I *am* having dinner with you."

"Yes, I know, but I mean—a date. You know. I pick you up, pay for dinner. We take a walk on the beach. Talk."

"Wait? You're not paying for dinner? Well, that's it," she teased, picking up her plate. "I'll eat at the counter."

Tom stared at her a moment, his eyes wary, as if he wasn't sure if she was joking or not. "What?"

Charlie chuckled and set her plate back down on the table. She leaned forward with her elbows on the table and looked him straight in the eye. "I really don't know what to say. The last time a man told me he wanted to get to know me better was my ex-husband, when I was twenty years old. I'm a little rusty."

"Me too." He smiled. "It's been eons since the last time I was interested in someone."

"Now that's just sad." Charlie picked up her burger and took a bite. Hot sauce dribbled from the corner of her mouth, scalding her face a little. She quickly grabbed her napkin and wiped away the burning liquid. Despite their first encounter, she had to admit, something about Tom Sharon was intriguing. "Well, I'm not saying yes. But—" She smiled. "I'm also not saying no."

"So maybe?"

Charlie nodded. "Definitely, maybe."

His dark golden eyes glittered, and he returned her smile. "Good."

* * *

JASON WAS SITTING ON THE FRONT PORCH OF THE

cottage when she arrived. She pulled her Honda next to his Dodge Charger and waved as she got out.

"Have you been waiting long?"

"No, just a couple minutes, really." He stood up and smoothed the fabric of his khaki pants. He pointed to the glass paned front door. "You should think about a dead bolt."

"Okay." Charlie chuckled. Her keys jangled in her hand. "I'll let my uncle know you think so."

"I could change it for you if you'd like."

"Thanks, but since it's my uncle's property…"

"Evangeline used to live here, right?"

"Yeah, she did." Charlie put the key into the lock and turned it. "After Jen and Lisa's mom died, she moved in here with Daphne to help take care of them." Charlie breathed in the cool air of the house and flipped on the light switch.

"Interesting." Jason followed her inside. "I've always wondered if there was ever anything between them."

"Between Uncle Jack and Evangeline? No way." Charlie dropped her tote by the front door and hung her keys on a small hook near the coat rack. "Why do you ask?"

"I don't know, just nosy, I guess. They seem pretty tight."

"They are. But trust me, there is nothing romantic between them."

Jason took a seat on the pale yellow armchair and put one leg up on the matching ottoman. He glanced around the room. "Your uncle did a nice job with the painting."

"Thanks. I love this color."

"It's cream." Jason said, a flabbergasted grin on his lips. "You don't get more vanilla than cream."

Charlie laughed. "I know. But it's a soothing shade of cream and during the day when there's light streaming in through the windows—" She put her hands on the top of the rocking chair on the opposite side of the old trunk she was using as a coffee table and glanced at the bank of windows behind the blue and white stripped couch. "It's bright and cheerful in here. Feels like a home."

Jason smiled. "Yeah, I can see that. So, how was your day?"

Charlie pointed over her shoulder toward the tiny kitchen. "You want something to drink?"

"Nah, I'm good." He put both feet on the floor and laid the folder he'd carried with him on the ottoman. Charlie sank into the couch and let out a heavy breath.

"That bad, huh?"

"Not bad exactly, just weird. I ran into Tom Sharon," she said.

"Really?" Jason's voice sounded funny, but she couldn't pinpoint why.

"Yeah. He said he was checking out eating places in town. You know they opened a new branch of their funeral home in Palmetto Point, which makes sense. I guess this way the islanders don't have to go very far." She shrugged one shoulder.

"Huh." Jason narrowed his eyes. "He told you all that?"

"Yep, over dinner."

"Huh."

She had never seen the expression on Jason's face before, and if she didn't know better, she would have thought he was jealous. "What?"

"You were terrified of him yesterday, and today you're eating dinner with him?"

"I was not scared of him," she protested.

"Uh-huh. Whatever you say."

"What is that supposed to mean?"

Jason scowled and shook his head. "Nothing. It doesn't mean anything."

"Are you mad at me?"

"No, of course not." He said the words smoothly, but Charlie sensed otherwise.

"You're lying to me. Why are you lying to me?"

"I'm not lying, Charlie. I'm glad you're not scared of the guy. By all accounts he's a clean, upstanding member of society."

"Good, because I gave him my number."

"Great. That's just… fantastic. So, are you gonna help me with my case or what?"

"That's what you're here for, isn't it?"

"Yes, it is."

"Well, let's look at what you've got. There's also something I'd like to talk to you about, something a little more personal, if that's okay."

"Sure, what about?"

"I want to take my ex-husband back to court for custody of my son."

"Good." Jason's face became serious. "It's about damn time."

"Well, now I have to find a good lawyer." Charlie leaned her elbow against the arm of the couch and propped up her head.

"I know somebody." Jason pulled his notebook and a pen from his front pocket and scribbled on a piece of paper. He ripped the paper from the notebook and handed it to Charlie.

"I figured I'd just ask Lisa." Charlie took the paper.

"Lisa's a corporate lawyer. You want somebody who knows the law for child custody."

"Kenneth Purdue?" she read aloud.

"Yep. Just tell him I sent you. He'll do right by you."

"Who is?"

"My cousin Kenny."

"I don't know if Cousin Kenny can really help me. I kind of screwed myself when I signed the stupid agreement in the first place."

"Tell me," Jason said. His intense face softened. "Please?"

Charlie folded her legs beneath her, getting more comfortable. She took a deep breath. Jason watched her face intently as she spoke.

"So, you know how I told you that my agreement with Scott was mutual."

"Yes. He told me the same thing. For the good of the child, and blah, blah, blah. Something about it never sat right with me though."

"Yeah, well, you're perceptive."

"I knew he was lying to me," Jason muttered.

"When I told Scott that I wanted to leave him, he had a total meltdown. I had tried to commit suicide only a couple months before, and after I survived and started going through therapy, I realized I couldn't stay with him. Being with him would eventually kill me, one way or the other."

"What do you mean?"

"Well, either I would die by my own hand or— I'm not saying he would kill me but being with him was killing me. Who I am, I mean."

Jason's gaze intensified, and he nodded. "I can understand that."

"Anyway, he tried everything to get me to stay.

Offered to take me away on an expensive vacation. Jewelry. Short of a flat-out sum of money, you name it, and he offered it. But then Evan started to show signs that he was more like me, if you know what I mean."

Jason nodded.

"So, I packed our bags, but Scott came home unexpectedly. We fought, and that's when he threatened to expose my abilities to the right doctors." Charlie held up both hands and made finger quotes. "Which was really just code for his friends. Friends who would listen to him when he said, 'my wife is crazy, help me.' He said he could have me committed long term if I tried to take Evan."

"Son of a bitch," Jason muttered through gritted teeth. He scrubbed the stubble on his face and leaned forward, putting his elbows on his knees. "He really does think he's God, doesn't he?"

"I don't know about God, but he likes to get his way. The only way he would agree to a divorce at all was for me to leave Evan with him. Told me if I tried to fight him, he'd spend every waking hour dedicated to keeping my son away from me. I believed him. So, to keep seeing my son, I gave up full custody." Charlie sighed and leaned forward. She stared down at her bare feet and wiggled her toes on the faded blue and tan wool rug. "God, I must sound like such a fool."

"No." Jason's hand landed on her shoulder and gave it a gentle squeeze. "You were just in a terrible situation. You know, just because he didn't raise his hand to you doesn't mean he wasn't an abusive prick. I'm sorry you had to go through that."

Charlie sat back and considered his words. It had never occurred to her that Scott's actions were abusive. Not really. She chewed on her bottom lip.

"You deserve way better. I'm glad you got out."

"I left my son so I wouldn't end up in an institution." A wide chasm cracked open inside her chest. The guilt she'd harbored for so long threatened to yank her into that expanse and drown her in the darkness.

"If the kid's sensitive like you, imagine what his life would be like without you in it. You think Dr. Dickhead would be supportive?"

"He's not supportive, even with me in Evan's life. He just had him put on meds for ADHD. Trust me, I've seen some of his friends. My son is not hyperactive. He's smart and can focus when he needs to. Scott just did it because Evan is like me."

"Please, talk to my cousin. Seriously. You make a good living. You saved enough for a down payment on your own home."

"Which I never bought."

"So what? It wasn't the right time. It still doesn't diminish the fact that you're the boy's mother. You have no criminal record. And even your own doctor has declared that you are no longer depressed anymore."

"How do you—" Charlie started but shut her mouth. She already knew the answer. Jason had been so wary of her when they first met, that he had investigated *her*.

"You know, he's not the only one who knows people. You know people too." Jason continued.

"I do?" Charlie quirked an eyebrow. "Who?"

"Me." Jason sounded indignant. "I'm an officer of the court, and you're a valuable asset to the Sheriff's Department. You've helped me solve many missing person cases."

"Many is a stretch. Three. I've helped to solve three."

"And a kidnap/murder case. There's no way I would've solved that one without you."

"Probably not a good idea to bring that one up since I was also one of the kidnap victims," she quipped.

"You helped solve that case and stop a murderer. You're good in my book. I'd stand up in court for you," Jason reassured. "Call my cousin Kenny. He'll take care of you."

"How expensive is he? I mean, Scott can afford the most expensive lawyer there is. I can't compete with that."

"You don't have to. Trust me."

"No. You are not paying for anything. I would ask my uncle Jack for money before I would let you do that."

"Sometimes he takes things pro bono. I can make sure that this is one of those things."

"How are you gonna do that?

"Don't worry about it. I want to do this for you. You deserve some happiness. I know you don't always believe that, but you do."

"Thank you." Charlie glanced at the paper still in her hand, then flashed Jason a grateful smile. "This means a lot."

"Well." He chuckled and shifted in the chair. Awkwardness crept up between them for a moment, and it dawned on Charlie that maybe Jason's feelings for her were more than just friendly.

"So." She blew out a breath and smiled. "Tell me about Trini."

Jason's expression morphed into relief, and he opened the folder laying on the ottoman in front of him. "Her mother's still alive. I think you should go talk to her."

"That's as good a place to start as any."

CHAPTER 9

Charlie floated above the scene. She watched as Haley Miller crossed an expansive marble foyer to a grand double staircase with a gallery overlooking the massive space. A crystal chandelier hung from the ceiling and gilded Greek letters hung on the bannister. *A sorority house?* The regal scale of the room reminded her of something out of a movie. Charlie zoomed in closer to keep up with the young woman who had climbed the steps and turned a corner. The lush color scheme reflected throughout the house, down to the cream-colored carpeting lining the hallway and crystal light fixtures. All the antique brass doorknobs gleamed. Charlie laughed as she flew through the corridor, keeping pace with Haley. She loved being weightless in dreams.

Haley stopped at the end of the long corridor in front of a pair of double doors. She knocked five times. Two short, one long, two short. It must have been a code. A moment later, another young woman dressed in a powder blue top and skinny jeans opened the door.

"You're late," she said.

"Sorry, I got hung up," Haley said.

Charlie followed Haley inside, staying close so she could get a look at things. She'd been interpreting her dreams long enough to know that sometimes she just had to follow along to get the message. Haley shut the door behind them quickly and turned the lock.

"All right, let's get this meeting started," the girl in powder blue said. She took a seat at a polished round mahogany table in the center of the room. Five other girls sat around the table. Lying on the table in front of the girl in powder blue was a manila folder. The young woman opened it as Haley slipped into the chair next to her. Charlie moved behind the girl in powder blue. She looked familiar. "Y'all know why we're here, right?"

"To take a vote on pledges?" the girl sitting across from powder blue said. She wore her strawberry-blonde hair in pigtails and a green tank top that showed her ample curves. Charlie bit her lip to keep from snickering at the vacuous look on the girl's face.

"No, Ashley," powder blue said. She pursed her lips. "We're here to talk about Brianna, remember?"

"Emma, I thought, we already decided this. We can't reject her because she's legacy," the brunette sitting next to Haley said. Charlie's ears perked up, and she scrutinized powder blue. She had seen her before. Her photo had popped up on Haley's phone. Charlie peeked over Emma's shoulder at the papers in front of the girl.

"No. Not true exactly. I've been looking into precedent, and I think I may have found a loophole. We can reject her if she doesn't meet our standards."

"She has a 4.0 and volunteers at a soup kitchen. And she's gorgeous. How is she not meeting our standards?" one girl argued.

"She also constantly argues with leadership and has no respect for our southern values," Emma countered. "If she was just a regular pledge, she'd have been out by now."

"It's not that we don't like her, Amanda." Haley leaned forward with her arms on the table. "But she's really not a good fit for us. That's all we're saying."

"Well, maybe if we worked with her—" one of the girls said.

"Jessica, please," Emma said. "Part of being in this sorority is knowing practically by osmosis whether you fit here."

"That's not really how osmosis works," Jessica

said. The other girls snickered, and Emma scowled and cleared her throat.

"Are y'all done? 'Cause this is serious."

The laughs and grins on the girls' faces faded fast, and they all resumed their focus on their leader.

"Sorry, Emma," Jessica said.

Emma straightened her back. "Regardless, it is not our policy to advise pledges on how to fit in. We are an elite group, and we can't accept just anybody off the street."

"Emma's right. Being here's a privilege, not a right. If a girl doesn't fit with us, she should be able to recognize that and leave on her own. If she can't do it for herself, then it's up to us to do it for her," Haley said.

"Harsh," Jessica muttered.

"Well, you know, just because she has an opinion about things—" Amanda started. Her long, straight blonde hair reached well past her shoulders, and she pushed one side behind her ear, revealing what could only be a one-carat diamond glittering in the yellow incandescent light of the room.

"If she wanted to have an opinion on everything, she should have joined Omega Tau," Emma snapped. "Now, let's get down to it. This has to be unanimous because of the potential liability involved. I need a show of hands, please." The girls all stared at Emma.

"All those in favor of doing the house challenge, raise your hand."

"Come on, Jess, you know this is better for everybody in the long run," Amanda said. "This is about sisterhood. The needs of the many must outweigh the needs of the few."

Jessica's forehead wrinkled and slowly she raised her hand.

Charlie glanced at Emma, who now wore a smug look on her face. This was the Emma who told Haley she was crazy.

"Let the record show that there is a unanimous vote for a night at the house," Emma said.

"Noted," Haley said, scribbling onto a notepad. "Do we have a date in mind?"

"I have just one question," Jessica said.

Emma's perfect full lips twisted into a scowl. "What?"

"What happens if she makes it through the challenge?" Jessica asked.

"Well, I guess," Haley began, giving Jessica a pointed look, "it's up to us to make sure she doesn't, isn't it?"

Jessica rolled her eyes. "I guess we'll just have to scare her to death won't we?"

* * *

CHARLIE'S EYES FLEW OPEN, AND SHE SAT UP. She reached for her phone and quickly jotted off the text to Jason.

Are you up? I saw Emma.

She pressed the send button and waited. After several minutes, she put the phone back down on the table next to her bed. The red numbers on her digital alarm clock read 1:30 a.m. Her phone vibrated, and she rushed to grab it. It surprised her when she saw her son's name and a text appeared.

Hi, Mom—are you awake?

She quickly ticked off a response.

What's going on? Did you have a bad dream?

No. I just can't sleep.

Charlie frowned at the phone. Reading the last five words over and over. What eleven-year-old couldn't sleep?

Want to talk about it?

Can I come stay with you this weekend?

I would love to have you, honey, but this is your dad's weekend.

I don't care. Please!!??

Charlie's heart wrenched. It was rare that her son uttered the words *I don't care*, even in jest. He was growing to be almost as sensitive as she was, and for him not to care about someone's feelings, especially his father's, gnawed at her heart.

Did you and Dad have a fight?

She stared at the screen, waiting for a response. After what seemed like too long, one word appeared—*yes*.

What did y'all fight about?
I don't like these meds. They make me feel weird.
Weird, how?
I don't know. Kind of like... nothing.
You feel nothing?
Yeah.

Charlie took a deep breath to fight the wave of nausea roiling through her belly. She hated Scott for trying to medicate Evan's sensitivity away.

How are you sleeping? Any dreams?
None since I started taking the meds.

So many things she wanted to say swirled through her head. More than anything, she wanted to tell him it would be all right. Somehow, she would get him off the meds. But she didn't know if she could make anything all right, didn't know if she could really stop Scott from making him take pills. She closed her eyes and counted to ten. The last thing she wanted to do was to pull Evan into the middle of a battle between her and Scott. He'd already been through so much because of her. She took a deep breath and opened her eyes. Her thumbs moved quickly over the keyboard.

I'll talk to Dad again about this. For now, you need to go to sleep. I love you. We'll figure this out.

I love you, too, Mom. Good night.

Night, night. Don't let the bedbugs bite.

A yellow-faced emoji appeared with Zz's floating above its head, and Charlie chuckled. God, she loved that kid. Her thoughts drifted to Scott, and she fought the hate growing there. Hating him was unproductive, but she couldn't stop herself. But more than hating Scott, she hated herself a little. Why had she ever signed that stupid custody agreement? *Because you thought you deserved it.*

Charlie sighed and stared at the ceiling. Sleep would be a long time coming tonight.

* * *

JASON SAT AT HIS DESK LOOKING THROUGH EVIDENCE gathered from Haley Miller's house. A bottle of pills. Pictures of two trashcans filled with empty Diet Coke and booze bottles, and the server had been exactly where Don Baker had said it would be. They'd pulled several days' worth of security video from the hard drive, and Beck was going through the footage. Jason volunteered to check out her social media and pictures from the crime scene. He had logged into Facebook and found her easily enough. Luckily, her profile was public. He started with her friends list, searching for anyone named Emma that she knew. Five different friends popped up. Great.

Charlie walked across the office and plopped down on the chair next to his desk. She opened her purse and rifled through it, pulling out a sheet of paper. "I had a dream."

"Good morning to you too." He picked up the paper and looked over the three symbols written there. "What is this?"

"I think it's a sorority." She leaned in close and lowered her voice. "In my dream, Haley walked into this house, and those three letters were everywhere. Then she went to a meeting room and met with several other girls, including our good friend Emma. It was very secret."

"Okay. Did they conspire to kill Haley?"

Charlie half-scoffed, half-laughed. "No, not exactly. They took a vote on getting rid of Brianna."

"When you say getting rid of—"

"I mean voting her out of the sorority."

"Why have a secret vote about it?"

"I don't really know the ins and outs of sororities; it wasn't my thing when I was in college. But from what I could glean, the girl in question wasn't getting along with everybody. Nobody really liked her."

"Why not just ask her to leave, then?"

"Something about her being a legacy."

"Legacy." Jason wrote the word down. "Did she have a name?"

Charlie shrugged. "Brianna. No last name. Sorry."

"Hang on a minute." Jason put in the name Brianna in the search field of Haley's friends.

"What are you doing?" Charlie asked.

"Searching through her friends on Facebook."

"They didn't like this girl," Charlie said.

"Yeah, well, I never really liked Tyler Cummings, either, but I still accepted his friend request," Jason said. "Maybe Haley did the same thing with this girl."

"You're friends with people you weren't really friends with?" Charlie gave him a puzzled look.

"Yep. Aren't you?"

"No. If I wasn't friends with you in high school or college, I sure don't have time to be friends with you now on Facebook."

"You know you look all soft and angelic, but you're really just a crabby old woman under that facade, aren't ya?" Jason chuckled.

Charlie laughed and nodded. "Pretty much."

"Well, thanks for the tip. I might head over to the college today, check out the sorority. Maybe something will pan out there."

"Wish I could go with you, but I've got two back-to-back readings this morning. I just wanted to drop that off."

"So, you're doing readings now?"

"Just a couple a week. I've been picky up till now, but if I'm gonna fight Scott in court, I need to make as much money as I can."

"I told you he'll take your case pro bono."

"I know." Charlie bit her lip and shifted in her chair. "I just worry is all."

Jason studied her face. Two black circles punctuated her eyes, even with her futile attempt at concealing them with makeup. "You doing all right? You look a little tired."

Charlie scowled. "Never tell a woman she looks tired. It's just a pleasant way of saying she looks like crap."

"That's not what I meant," he grumbled. "You just look like you haven't slept well, that's all. Maybe having you work on two cases is too much."

"No—it's not that, it's just Evan stuff. That's all. Sorry, I snapped."

"Do you want to talk about it?"

"Nope, no point. Nothing I can do about it. But thank you. You're a good friend." She glanced at the clock on the wall and stood up abruptly. "I gotta go. Text me if you get anything new."

"I will." He watched her turn and walk away. Something was on her mind, but until she was ready to share, he couldn't do much to help her. He picked up his notebook and looked at the words he'd scrawled at the top of the page.

"Legacy—Brianna," he muttered.

* * *

Jason sidled up to the information desk at Charleston College Library and flashed a smile at the pretty young librarian. She adjusted her wire-rimmed glasses up higher on her nose and smiled. "Hi, how can I help you?"

"Hi." He met her gaze and leaned forward on the desk. He pulled the piece of paper Charlie had given him from his pocket, unfolded it, and pushed it across the counter. "Any chance you could tell me what this means? Or point me in the right direction?"

The girl pressed the paper flat with her long, thin fingers. She clucked her tongue and looked up at him. "That's Mu Theta Chi. It's a sorority."

"Are they active on campus?" he asked.

She tugged her pale blue cardigan closed, and her gaze flitted over his badge, then to his face. "Are they in trouble?"

"Oh, no," Jason said in his most soothing, reassuring voice. "I just need to find some information about an alumnus. There was an accident and we're having trouble finding next of kin to notify."

"Oh, my god." She put her hand over her mouth. "That's terrible. Do you know what year she graduated?"

"She's thirty-one. So, maybe nine years ago?"

"I can pull yearbooks for you. There'll be pictures

of the alumni—and if she sat for a picture, then her affiliations would be listed too. If she was in a sorority, it would be there."

"That'd be great. Thanks." He smiled widely.

The apples of her cheeks filled with color. She smiled and adjusted her glasses again. "No problem." She took a slip of paper and a stub of a pencil with no eraser and pushed them across the desk toward him. "I just need you to fill out a request."

"Great."

* * *

Twenty minutes later, the librarian handed him three yearbooks and pointed him to one of the open tables nearby.

He flipped through the pages looking at the seniors under M. His finger traced through each name until finally it came to Haley Miller.

In her picture, she looked happy and young. Hopeful. In tiny print beneath her photo were the words Mu Theta Chi—Secretary. He flipped to the back of the book and glanced through the index. He traced his finger through all the sororities until he came to Mu Theta Chi. His heartbeat quickened, and he quickly flipped to page 280. A photo of fifty young women posed in front of one of the old restored mansions near to campus. He scanned through the list of alphabetical names. There were three Emmas, but no Brianna. He scribbled down the names of the girls named Emma and looked up their photos. One was a sophomore and the two others were seniors. Jason took out his phone and snapped pictures of the girl's photos and the group shot of the Mu Theta Chi sorority. He attached the images to a text to Charlie.

Which Emma?

A moment later, his phone vibrated in his hand.

Emma Winston.

CHAPTER 10

Marshall Beck sat on the corner of Jason's desk, watching as Jason searched for Emma Winston in the DMV database. The side of Beck's thigh brushed against Jason's elbow and he scowled.

"Can't you use the chair?" Jason snapped.

Beck smirked and folded his arms across his chest. He didn't move.

"Dude, seriously you're in my space." Jason held up his hands and glared at his partner.

"Fine." Beck shifted to the chair next to Jason's desk. "What are you working on?"

"I'm following up on a lead in the Miller case."

"You're wasting your time. The ME will rule this is an accident or suicide. Trust me."

"Maybe so, but until she does, I'm gonna do my damn job."

Beck shrugged. "What have you found so far?"

"She was a party girl, and she had lots of friends." Jason stopped himself from telling Beck anything about Charlie's dreams. He didn't need the hassle today.

"Even more evidence pointing to an accident if you ask me. Fifty bucks says that's the final COD."

"Don't you have other cases to follow up on?"

Beck sighed and got to his feet. "Fine."

Jason didn't look up to watch his partner walk back to his own desk. Instead, he focused on his computer screen. He made a printout of Emma Winston's license. Before he set off to pay her home a visit, he checked Haley's Facebook page one more time. He glanced through her photos again, looking specifically for Emma's face. The third picture tagged Emma, standing with Haley. Jason clicked on the link and it took him to Emma's page. Most of her privacy settings were in place, and all he could see was her profile pictures, but she'd listed her place of work. Jason quickly found the address for Danang and Winston orthodontics, scribbled it down and headed out. He dialed Charlie's number as he walked to his car.

"Hey," he said, "you finished with your readings?"

"Yep, just doing some laundry. What's up?"

"Wanna go play human lie detector?"

"Sure, for who?"

"Emma Winston."

He could almost hear her grin as she said, "What's the address?"

* * *

Jason flashed his badge at the young woman sitting behind the reception desk. Her dark brown eyes scanned the badge and widened. She bit her lower lip and got up from her seat.

"Wait here just a minute," she mumbled.

A moment later, a short, stout woman wearing purple scrubs and thick glasses greeted them. Her long hair was pulled into a messy bun. "Can I help you?"

"I need to see Dr. Emma Winston." His tone was stern, authoritative. What Charlie thought of as his cop voice.

"What's this about?" the woman asked.

"I'm afraid I can't discuss that with you. Now, would you please tell Dr. Winston that we are here to see her?"

A line appeared between her brows, and her lips pursed together, but she didn't argue. Instead, she spun and disappeared behind the door with a placard that said staff only. It warned of places he was not allowed. He tapped his toe against the faux wood grain of the wood receptionist desk and glanced at Charlie.

Charlie frowned at him and opened her mouth to tell him to just be patient, but a shadow from the corner of her eye caught her attention. A blast of frosty air blew across the back of her neck, and her body broke into goose bumps. Charlie looked toward the source, and her gaze trained on the mirror hanging behind the receptionist's desk. A young woman stood in the middle of the waiting room. Her pale skin was almost translucent, and sticks and dirt smudged her face. She wore a pair of pink plaid pajama bottoms and a white-T-shirt that was soaked in blood. Charlie's breath was harsh in her ears as she slowly glanced over her shoulder to the waiting room. All she saw was a mother and child. The woman sat against the wall, flipping through an ancient magazine, and the child sat next to her, playing on the tablet in his hands. Charlie shifted her gaze back to the mirror, and the young woman was now standing directly behind her. Charlie's heart slammed into the back of her throat.

"Charlie? Charlie!"

Charlie blinked hard and shook her head. "What?"

"You okay? You look like you saw a ghost or

something." Jason's tone was light, but his eyes flitted to the mirror and back to her.

Charlie let out a nervous laugh. "Maybe I did."

Jason scowled and his gaze shifted back to the mirror. "I don't see anything."

Slowly Charlie turned her head. The only thing reflected in the mirror now was the woman with her child in the waiting room. She blew out a heavy breath.

The door opened and the short, stout woman returned wearing a sour look on her face. She motioned for them to come behind the desk. Jason put on his game face—neutral but authoritative. Charlie and Jason followed the woman into the private office area. It was a short hallway with three offices on either side. One was a bookkeeper's office filled with filing cabinets and a desk with a computer and piled high with file folders. The door to the second office was closed, but the plaque read Dr. Katherine Danang. Dr. Emma Winston's office was next to it. The office manager knocked on the door and entered once she heard a woman's voice say to come in. She opened the door and motioned for Charlie and Jason to enter and pulled the door shut behind them.

Charlie glanced around the room quickly. Windows dominated one wall, and the other had floor-to-ceiling bookshelves with a smattering of books here and there and mostly collectibles gathering dust. A decorator had artfully arranged a long overstuffed couch in a soft gray fabric against the third wall while a fat white cat wearing a shiny rhinestone collar lounged across the top. As an eye catcher, however, a fine mahogany desk with curved legs and carved gold accents stood in the center of the room.

"Hello." Emma stood up behind the desk and walked around to greet them. She extended her hand to Jason and shook it. Charlie spied a suitcase jutting out from between the wall and one side of the sofa. A blue piece of fabric hung loosely across it, and it appeared the suitcase had been hastily zipped up. At the base of the sofa a large plastic cat carrier sat with its metal grate door ajar. Next to it was a litter box.

Emma shoved her hands into the white coat she wore over rumpled clothes. The circles beneath her eyes were so dark they looked almost like bruises. She guided them to the sofa. "Please have a seat."

Emma sat on the couch and Jason sat in the armchair and pivoted so he could look directly at her. Charlie took a seat next to Emma.

"So, how can I help you today?" Emma said, wearing a forced smile.

"We're just conducting a routine investigation. Did you know Haley Miller, Ms. Winston?"

Charlie glanced at Jason. He was focused intently on Emma, studying her.

"It's doctor. Haley and I went to college together. She's one of my best friends."

"Doctor, yes." A strange smile played at the corners of Jason's mouth. What was he up to? "When was the last time you spoke to Haley?"

"Um... I don't remember exactly. Is Haley in some sort of trouble?"

"I'm sorry to have to tell you this, Dr. Winston, but Haley's dead."

Emma's pleasant demeanor melted away. She shook her head as if she wasn't sure she'd heard him correctly. "That's... that's not possible." She pressed a hand to her forehead and tapped it lightly with one finger. She squeezed her eyes shut and sniffled. When she looked back up her green eyes swam behind a heavy wave of tears threatening to fall. Her voice cracked as she spoke. "Are you sure?"

"Yes, ma'am, very sure," Jason said.

"What happened?"

"We're still trying to determine that, which is why I'm here. Can you tell us if Haley had any enemies?"

Emma sniffled and wiped her eyes. "Enemies. No, of course not. Haley was—well, she was a Mu Theta. We don't have enemies. We have admirers."

Jason's eyes narrowed, and Charlie could almost see the gears of his mind whirring, taking in every twitch of her face. "So these admirers couldn't have been jealous or wanted to hurt her, then?"

Emma hesitated for a second before answering emphatically. "No. Everybody loved her." Emma glanced toward the enormous window. Her voice sounded shaky when she spoke. "Was she murdered? Is that why you're asking about enemies?"

"We have a witness who says that they saw someone push her off the roof of her house."

"Oh, my god." Emma sat up straight, horror marring her fine features. "What the hell was she doing on the roof?"

"That's what we're trying to figure out." Jason pulled his notebook from his chest pocket and flipped it open. "So, in going through Haley's communications, in one of her texts to you, she said, and I quote," and he read from the note. "'It happened again.' Can you tell me what she meant by that? What happened again?"

Emma's gaze flitted from Jason to Charlie and understanding dawned in her wide green eyes. "Haley was convinced that someone was stalking her."

"*Stalking* her?" Jason said. "So, she had at least one enemy, then."

Emma sighed and rolled her eyes. "I don't know. Sometimes I think she was her own worst enemy."

"How do you mean?" Jason asked.

"Haley was a party girl."

"You mean in college?" Jason asked.

"I mean, she liked to drink and to have a good time. In college and now. She brought home plenty of losers."

"Are you saying one of these losers could have been responsible?" Jason asked.

Emma pursed her lips and shrugged.

"Do you know if she ever reported the stalking?"

"No, not that I'm aware of. I don't think it was like that, exactly."

Jason tipped his head to the right and tapped the point of his pen against his notebook. "What do you think it was like, exactly?"

Emma took a deep breath and her gaze shifted down to her hands. "I think Haley may have had some mental problems."

"Why do you say that?" Jason asked.

"Because she was convinced that she was being stalked by a ghost."

"So, she was being haunted?" Charlie leaned forward and put her elbows on the table. "Do you know by who?"

Emma glanced up and her green eyes locked on to Charlie's. "Well, since ghosts don't actually exist, I can't say she was being haunted."

"So, you're not being haunted, either, then?" Charlie challenged.

"No," Emma brushed her off, chuckling. "Because that would be crazy."

"Right, crazy," Charlie echoed. "Is that why you're not sleeping? Because you think some of Haley's crazy has infected you?"

Jason's brow crinkled as he shot her a what-the-hell glance. His lips twisted into a scowl.

Emma's eyes widened and her voice shook as she spoke. "I don't know what you're talking about."

"I think you do. I think you know exactly what I'm talking about. Are you seeing her? Or just feeling her? Maybe she's making the lights flicker or experimenting with the radio or the TV. I know she was waking Haley up in the middle of the night. Jerking her leg. Pulling off her covers."

All the color drained from Emma's face.

"Is that what's causing those black circles beneath your eyes?" Charlie asked.

"You sound as crazy as Haley. Are you an alcoholic too?" Emma scowled and gave Charlie a pointed look.

Charlie's lips twitched into a smirk. This girl was good.

"Are there any other questions?" Emma shifted her attention back to Jason.

"Just a couple more." Jason pulled a photo from the pocket of his uniform shirt and handed it to Emma. "You were sorority sisters, right? Did Haley have any other sisters like you in the area?"

Emma picked up the photo, her gaze fixing on it.

"Where did you get this?" Emma asked softly.

"That was on the mirror in Haley's bathroom. Does it mean anything to you?"

"It's just something we always say when there's a group of Mu Theta's together."

"Was Haley still close with any of the other members?"

"Not really. Most moved on to graduate school or jobs or got married. There's a reunion every couple of years, but Haley hasn't gone in a while."

"Do you know why?"

"She said she didn't have time. Her job kept her pretty busy. She traveled a lot."

"Right," Jason took back the picture. He pulled out one of his cards from his breast pocket and handed it to her. "Well, we appreciate your time. If you can think of anything, please call me."

"Of course," Emma said wearing a cordial smile. She took the card and tucked it into the pocket of her white coat. Jason rose from the couch, and Charlie followed him. They headed to the door, but Charlie hesitated. She reached inside her tote bag and pulled out a small plastic business card folio. She opened it and pulled out one card and held it out toward Emma. "Call me if things get worse. I'd really like to help you before things get as bad as they did for Haley."

Emma took the card and scoffed. "A psychic medium? Seriously?"

Charlie met Emma's gaze. "Seriously. Call me if you ever want to talk about it. I'll be happy to listen. And if you need help getting rid of the spirit, I'd be happy to do that too."

Emma paused and for a moment Charlie thought for sure she would throw the card back in her face, instead Emma tucked it inside her pocket along with Jason's.

Jason didn't speak to her until they were at their cars.

"Well, that was interesting." Jason sighed. "Do you think she'll call you?"

"Oh yeah." Charlie nodded. "It's gonna have to get bad first, but I definitely think she'll call."

"Good. Till then, I'm gonna keep looking."

"I wouldn't expect anything else." Charlie touched her hand to her stomach. And it almost growled on command. "Now, I believe it's your turn to buy me some dinner, isn't it?"

He made an indignant noise in the back of his throat, but his lips curved into a half-grin. "No. It's your turn."

"No way. You ate free at the café the other day."

"Yeah, but that wasn't you paying, that was Jen."

She shrugged. "Same difference. Now, where are you taking me?"

Jason's mouth stretched into a Cheshire cat grin. "How 'bout a Happy Meal at McDonald's?" Charlie made a sad face and Jason laughed. "All right, you win. We're not that far from Shem Creek. Want some seafood?"

"Sure," Charlie said and hopped into her car.

CHAPTER 11

The next morning, Charlie parked her little blue Honda on the concrete pad next to the white mobile home where Trini's mother now lived.

Charlie opened the file folder, ran her finger over the original address that Elena Dolan had given when she filed a missing person report in 1977. She and her daughter had been living in a small house on Palmetto Island.

Charlie took a small pad of Post-it notes from her purse and wrote herself a note to run by the property where they originally lived. Sometimes spirits went home, especially if they didn't realize they were dead. Even though Trini knew she was dead, it might be worth a shot. Charlie closed the file folder and tucked it into the quilted tote that

Bunny had made for her when she left for college. She had recently found it when unpacking her things and couldn't remember why she had stopped using it.

Charlie got out of the car and glanced around the mobile home park. All the homes looked clean with neatly kept yards. Two boys on bicycles rode by, laughing and yelling at each other. She walked up the steps to the small deck and knocked on the metal door. A moment later the face of an elderly woman with short curly white hair and cloudy blue eyes appeared in the diamond-shaped window.

"Who is it?" the elderly woman asked, her voice muffled.

Charlie called up her most reassuring customer service smile. "Ms. Dolan, my name is Charlie Payne. We spoke on the phone, remember?"

"Oh, yes." Ms. Dolan nodded.

Charlie heard the clicking of locks, and finally the door opened. The elderly woman stepped back so Charlie could pass.

The stale smell of cigarette smoke and fried food assaulted Charlie's senses, coating the back of her throat as she breathed. The dark brown paneling combined with the brown plaid couch and coordinating tan chair that took up most of the space in the small living room made Charlie claustrophobic. She watched the bright sunny day disappear as the old woman closed the door. Charlie took a deep breath and faced her.

"Thank you so much for seeing me. I know you spoke to Lieutenant Tate. Did he explain what it is I do?"

"Please take a seat." Ms. Dolan guided her toward the couch. "All he said was that you sometimes help on cold cases."

"Yes, I do." Charlie took a seat on the couch, and Ms. Dolan sat in the chair. By the look of it, it was her regular seat. A blue plastic ashtray filled nearly to the brim with ashes and cigarette butts was next to the arm of the chair. A sweaty glass of tea with half melted ice sat on a cork coaster. The television was tuned to a talk show. Ms. Dolan picked up the remote control and clicked it off.

"So, that nice young man said that you would want to see some pictures of Trini, if you could."

"Yes, that would be very helpful."

Ms. Dolan leaned forward, grunting a little as she reached for two heavy photo albums on the bottom shelf of her coffee table. She placed them in front of Charlie and leaned back in her chair, panting. "Every picture I have of her is in here. I also clipped all the newspaper articles they did about her when she went missing and put them in there too."

"Do you mind if I—" Charlie pointed to the album on top.

"Not at all. Please help yourself. Can I get you something to drink? Some water or iced tea?"

Charlie smiled. "Iced tea would be wonderful, thank you."

The elderly woman got to her feet and headed toward the compact kitchen.

Charlie sat back on the couch, pulling the album onto her lap. She flipped open the first page and touched her hand to the photos protected by plastic pockets. Almost immediately, images danced through her head. Trini as a baby. Trini taking her first step in a different place with a green shaggy carpet under chubby baby feet. Charlie turned the page and there was Trini on the banana seated blue bike. She wore the same rainbow shirts she was wearing when Charlie met her.

Charlie started to turn the page when something dropped onto the photo. It landed on the plastic and Charlie stared at it for a moment unsure if what she was seeing was real or not. She touched her index finger to it and pulled it back, surprised that it felt so warm. She squeezed the red liquid between her thumb and forefinger. It was sticky. Another drop fell onto the photograph drawing Charlie's eyes up to the ceiling. She could find no obvious source. She glanced at the elderly woman who was pouring iced tea into glasses and arranging cookies from a tin on a plate. She wiped the blood on her jeans and a stain appeared. Would laundry detergent get out ghostly bloodstains?

Carefully Charlie fished the photograph from its protective sleeve. Trini sat on her bicycle at the end of a paved driveway. Behind her was a cul-de-sac and across the road was a trim split level house with a Buick parked in the driveway. Another drop of blood fell from the ceiling landing on the partial view of a shed peeking out from behind the house. The thick red liquid seeped into the faded matte paper, soaking the shed and warping the image.

A pebble formed in Charlie's throat, and she could hear blood rushing through her ears. She looked up and opened her mouth to apologize to Ms. Dolan for somehow ruining the picture. Ms. Dolan placed a glass of tea on the table in front of Charlie and glanced over her shoulder. "I took that the morning she disappeared."

"Where is this?" Charlie asked.

"That's at the old house. I lived there till hurricane Hugo hit. I couldn't bear the thought of leaving, you know, just in case she came home. But an old oak fell on the house during that storm and I lost everything I had. Those photographs were about the only thing I was able to save. Then I moved here. Been here ever since."

"Do you ever go back?"

"No, I don't really drive much anymore. I did stop

by once after the new owners took the property. They razed the house and put a great big new house on the land. I left one of the fliers that I had made of Trini and asked them to call me if she ever showed up." The elderly woman sat in her chair. She took a sip of her watered-down tea. Her cloudy blue eyes swam in tears that didn't fall. She cleared her throat. "They never did call."

"I'm so sorry, Ms. Dolan. Do you mind if I borrow this picture? I promise I'll be really careful with it."

The woman smiled, her face a relief map of wrinkles and sorrow. "Sure. That's fine. I've looked them over so many times, they're burned into my memory now."

* * *

CHARLIE HAD TO PLUG THE ADDRESS TO TRINI DOLAN'S old house into the GPS app on her phone to find the place. The cul-de-sac had changed a lot in the years since the picture was taken, but the split-level house across the street from the Dolan's former residence was still there. It was no longer pale green with dark green shutters. It had been painted a crisp white with black shutters and a red door. The shed which she could see once she pulled her car around the circle and parked, was still there, too, and it had been painted white to match the house. Charlie pulled a small pair of binoculars from her purse to get a better look at the shed. The black door had a padlock on the top and bottom. What could be in there that required so much security? Despite its updated paint and the bright yellow mums in planters on the front porch, a dark energy emanated from this place. Being this close to it made her skin thrum with awareness.

Charlie watched as a young woman emerged through the front door. She was slight in height and wore her dark brown hair in a tight ponytail at the base of her head. She wore blue scrubs and comfortable tennis shoes. A stethoscope dangled from around her neck. She stopped on the porch and pulled the stethoscope from around her neck and placed it inside her shoulder bag before heading to the silver Prius in the driveway. She got into the car, backed out into the street, and drove past Charlie's car without even a second glance her way. Did the young woman live there? Or was she treating the owner? Charlie pulled the picture of the house that Mrs. Dolan had let her borrow from her purse and touched her fingers to it. There was no way to know if whoever lived in this house when Trini disappeared even still lived here. Thirty-five years was a long time and people came and went. People died every day. Still, the shed was padlocked. It had to mean something, didn't it?

A flash of blue from the corner of Charlie's eye

startled her out of her thoughts, and she quickly found the source. A girl with long blonde pigtails rode past her car on a bicycle, rounded the cul-de-sac, and then headed back up the street.

Charlie pulled her phone from the front pocket of her purse and dashed off a quick text to Jason.

I met with Trini Dolan's mother today. We need to talk.

As she waited for an answer, her chest filled with icy dread and impatience. The child on the bicycle made another pass by her car, closer this time, following the same path as before. Her pale blonde pigtails floated behind her as if caught in a heavy wind. Charlie glanced at the trees in the neighborhood. There was no wind, and the child didn't appear to be going that fast. Charlie drew her attention back to the silent phone.

"Come on. Text me back."

Two more times the child passed her. Charlie pressed the window button on her car door and the motor hummed as the window retracted. "Hey!"

The girl stopped her bike and threw a look over her shoulder.

"Do you live around here?" Charlie asked.

The child glanced around before bringing her gaze back to Charlie. She nodded her head.

"Do you mind if I ask you a couple of questions?" Charlie asked.

"I'm not supposed to talk to strangers," the girl said.

Charlie smiled and an image of Tom popped into her head. She'd said something similar to her.

"No. You're right. That's a good thing," Charlie said. "Thank you anyway."

The child turned her bicycle around and pedaled back, stopping several feet away from Charlie's car—out of arm's reach.

"Are you lost?" the girl asked.

"Not really. I was just wondering if you knew who lived in that house?" Charlie asked, pointing to the split-level.

The child's gaze followed the line of Charlie's finger, and she stared at it for a long time before a visible shiver shook her little body.

"Are you all right?" Charlie asked.

"The monster lives there." The girl's hollow, high-pitched voice settled over Charlie's skin like a cold fog. Charlie stared at the child with a fresh set of eyes. The girl wore denim shorts and a pink T-shirt. Her pale skin was almost translucent.

"Dammit," Charlie muttered to herself. Of course. "How long has it been since anybody's talked to you?"

The child whipped her head around and fixed her eyes on Charlie. "I don't know. I don't remember."

"What's your name?" Charlie asked.

"Missy. What's yours?"

"Charlie."

"Charlie's a boy's name," the girl scoffed.

Charlie smiled. "It's short for Charlotte. But my family calls me Charlie. Missy, who is the monster?"

"Old Mr. Hatch. He poisoned my dog."

"Why did he do that?" Charlie asked.

The girl shrugged one shoulder. "Isn't that what monsters do? Kill things?"

"Yeah," Charlie mumbled. "I guess it is."

"He told my brother that if Lady got into his garbage one more time, he would kill her. Then we found her dead one day on the lawn."

"I'm sorry, honey. How long has Mr. Hatch lived there?"

"Longer than us."

"I appreciate you talking to me. Is there... anything you'd like me to tell someone? Maybe your mom? Or your dad?"

The girl shook her head. "I have to go now. He's awake."

"Who's awake?" Charlie asked.

The child took off without answering. She sped down the street toward the end of the cul-de-sac before making a hard left into the yard of the split-level house. Charlie watched as the child and her bicycle flickered, like it was just a bad video. A glitch in the system. The child stood up, pushing herself harder and completely disappeared into the wall of the padlocked shed.

Charlie's breath caught in her throat and blood thundered through her ears.

The phone vibrated in her hand, and she let out a little scream, dropping it into her lap. She reached for it and knocked it onto the floorboard.

"Shit," she muttered and bent down to grab it.

Jason's text read: *Where do you want to meet? When?*

The Kitchen Witch. ASAP.

Okay. See you soon.

Charlie cast one more look at the house and shed. She needed something concrete to give Jason. Something other than a ghost girl disappearing into the shed. He would believe her, but it wouldn't be enough. Warrants took actual evidence. Maybe he could give her some ideas, though, on how to get the evidence he needed so they could search the property. She didn't know or care how they made it happen. All she knew was she needed to get into that house. Needed to come face-to-face with the monster.

* * *

"BLOOD?" JASON SAID, HIS EXPRESSION A CROSS between disgust and incredulity. "Can I see?"

Charlie frowned and pulled the picture from her

purse. She pushed it across the table toward him. "You probably won't be able to see it."

Jason picked up the photograph and studied it. "Well, you're right about that. You say this shed had three padlocks on it?"

"Yep."

"Charlie, there's no law against somebody padlocking their shed. Especially in this area. There's a decent amount of crime. Maybe they've had lawn mowers or dirt bikes or whatever stolen, and this is just their way of being cautious."

"I know, but… there's something else."

"What?"

"I met another girl today."

"What do you mean, another girl?"

"I mean while I was looking at this house," Charlie leaned forward and lowered her voice, "A little girl on a bicycle rode past me. And she was dead."

"You sure?"

"Yes. Absolutely."

"Did you talk to her?"

"I did. Only I didn't realize she was dead at first. She seemed—more solid. It didn't really strike me as strange until I realized she was wearing short-sleeves and shorts."

"So?"

"It's only 62 degrees today. I wouldn't have let Evan wear shorts."

"All right, well, maybe her mother's not as good a mother as you are."

"I asked her who lived in that house and she told me the monster. She told me he killed her dog."

"Did she tell you her name?"

"Missy. No last name." Charlie fiddled with the paper napkin. "Sorry."

Jason's lips pressed into a flat line and he blew a breath out through his nostrils making them flare. "Anything else you can tell me about her?"

Charlie sighed and shook her head. "Not really. She was maybe ten. Blonde hair. Pigtails. Blue eyes. I think. Oh, and she rode into that shed behind his house."

"The monster's house?" Jason said, his voice full of skepticism.

"She said his name was Mr. Hatch."

"Well, at least that's something." Jason took out his notepad from his front breast pocket and scribbled down the name. "Do you have the address?"

Charlie nodded and rattled off the street number and name. He wrote it down and snapped the cover of the small notebook closed. He shifted in his seat, his lips tugging downward into a frown.

"What's wrong?" she asked.

"Nothing's wrong," he said.

"Must be really uncomfortable sitting there with your pants on fire." She challenged him. He blew out another heavy breath through his nose and clenched his jaw. "What?"

"Nothing exactly, I just—I got called in to my boss's office this morning. That's all," he said.

"Is everything okay?"

"Yeah, I just—unless we can prove beyond a shadow of a doubt that this case you've stumbled upon is somehow tied to Macy Givens, I've got to let it go."

"Why?"

"Because it's a thirty-five-year-old case. And as my boss ever so gently reminded me today, I have more pressing priorities than a thirty-five-year-old cold case."

"Macy Givens is a cold case."

"I know, but Macy Givens is *my* cold case. Trini Dolan's isn't, and neither is Missy no-name. I don't mean to sound harsh or—" The hand he had resting on the table clinched into a fist. "He's giving me a hard time about the Givens case and Haley Miller's case. The medical examiner hasn't signed off on it yet because they're still waiting for results of a full tox screen. But based on the evidence we have, it looks like an accident and that's the way my boss wants me to treat it. So, unless you have something new to offer, something real…"

"Real," Charlie scoffed and sat back hard against the cushion of the booth. She crossed her arms and frowned.

"Okay, tangible, then. Physical. Then he wants me to spend less time on the Givens case."

Charlie gritted her teeth. "You're the one who asked me to help you. This is the kind of help I can give you."

"I know. And it's not that I don't believe you. I do. But—"

"You're just giving up."

"No, I'm not giving up. Not totally. But I can't work it is hard as I'd like. I have to do what my boss tells me."

Charlie bit the inside of her cheek to keep from saying something she might regret. She knew what it was like to have a boss and she totally understood, but this wasn't about meeting some arbitrary metric for the number of phone calls she took in a day. This was about life and death. Maybe she was being dramatic, but she knew there was more to these three girls' stories. She felt it in her gut. They were all connected, and somehow, someway the monster was involved.

"So, what do you want to do?" she finally asked.

"I don't know just yet."

"Could we at least question him?"

"What would we ask him, Charlie?"

"I don't know—we could take one of the flyers of Macy Givens over there—tell him we're canvassing the neighborhood, that we had a fresh lead and ask if he's seen her, watch his reaction. I've seen you do that before."

"Maybe. Yeah. But I've got a few other tasks I need to take care of first, and I have to give testimony in court on Friday for another case."

"What if I ask?"

"I don't like it when you go off half-cocked. We've already talked about this."

Charlie sighed and narrowed her eyes. She hated this.

"Promise me you won't do anything without me, okay? Please? The last thing I need is for you to get hurt or worse, mess up my case."

"I will not get hurt." Charlie's shoulders deflated. "And you know I'll do whatever it takes not to jeopardize your case."

"We can question him next week, okay? I'll even let you go with me."

Charlie frowned.

"Listen, I don't mean to be cynical, but this case has been waiting thirty-five years. Another week won't make much difference."

"Fine," she relented.

"Good." He took the last fry on his plate and took

a bite. "I hate to eat and run, but I need to get back to the office."

Charlie glanced over her shoulder, looking for their waitress. Her aunt and cousin brought out two large cardboard boxes and placed them on the counter. Jen walked around and spoke to a woman with prim silver hair wearing a blue sweater over jeans and tennis shoes. Her cousin smiled graciously and nodded, and Charlie could almost read her lips.

When she spotted their waitress, Charlie waved her hand and a moment later an older woman with thick glasses and wild hair that had been dyed black approached the table.

"So, would y'all like anything else? Dessert, maybe? We got chocolate cake, and it is to die for."

"Oh, my gosh, Dottie, that sounds tempting. But I am full as a tick." Charlie patted her belly. Dottie looked at Jason.

"I'm good, Miss Dottie." He held up his hand. "Just the check."

Dottie shook her head. A smile played at the corner of her lips. "Now, Lieutenant, you know there ain't no check for either of you."

"Hey, Dottie, who's that woman with Jen and Evangeline?" Charlie asked, glancing toward her cousin.

Dottie threw a glance over her shoulder toward the counter. The woman was talking to Evangeline as two other women accompanying her worked at carrying the large cardboard boxes out of the café.

"That's Maureen Henley. She runs one of the senior programs down at the Methodist Church."

"Is that food?" Charlie asked, pointing. "In the boxes?"

"Yep," Dottie said. "On Wednesdays, Jen donates fifty box lunches and they deliver them to the seniors and shut-ins that go to their church."

"How neighborly," Charlie muttered.

"Yeah, well, your cousin is big on giving back to the community. You know how she is."

"I do."

One of the other patrons raised his hand, signaling for Dottie, and she headed off in their direction. Jason reached into his back pocket and pulled out his wallet. He rifled through it, taking a five-dollar bill. He laid it on the table.

"So, what's your plan for the rest of the day?"

"I have some overtime hours at four. So, I'll be heading into work," Charlie said.

"Sounds good." Jason took one last sip from his iced tea glass. "Let me know if anything new comes up."

"I will."

Jason stood up, stretched a moment, then smoothed out his tan pants. "See ya."

She watched as he left the café. Maybe the next

time she had a little free time she would show the man living in the split-level house just how neighborly she could be. She wiped her mouth with her napkin and pulled a few dollars from her wallet and laid them on the table with Jason's money before heading out into the afternoon sun.

CHAPTER 12

The faint clean scent of saddle soap clung to Charlie's nostrils, and the leather chair creaked when she shifted. She held a folder in her hand. When she noticed her knuckles had turned white and she'd creased the thick manila paper, she loosened her grip.

It turned out that Cousin Kenny was not quite the slime ball she had expected. He'd filled the office with expensive fine leather furniture, carved walnut paneling, and shelves lined with leather-bound books engraved with gold lettering. A painted portrait of Kenneth Purdue Esquire hung behind the receptionist's desk. An older woman who wore her silver hair in a graceful twist sat at the desk, furiously typing something on her computer. The woman had given

Charlie a distracted smile when she entered the office and directed Charlie to sit in the small waiting area. Charlie took deliberate breaths in through her nose and blew them out through her lips. She hated this sort of thing—telling strangers about her life and the choices she had made. She hoped more than anything Jason was right about his cousin. She was counting on it.

"Ms. Payne," the receptionist said in a soft southern drawl that sounded like it belonged to someone sitting on a front porch sipping a Hurricane or a Mimosa. She tipped her chin down and looked at Charlie over the top of dark blue framed glasses perched on the end of her long beak-like nose.

"Yes, ma'am," Charlie straightened, balancing on the edge of the seat.

"Mr. Purdue can see you now."

Charlie rose from her chair. "Thank you," she said and followed the receptionist down a short hallway to an office with the door open.

The receptionist knocked on the door jamb.

"Mr. Purdue," she announced, poking her head inside. "Your one o'clock is here."

"Thank you, Jane," Mr. Purdue said from behind a heavy mahogany desk.

Jane gave her a polite smile and stepped aside for Charlie to pass. "Go right in."

Charlie's stomach flip-flopped, and she stepped into the office.

Kenneth J. Purdue reminded Charlie of an English bulldog wearing expensive clothes. His large blocky head seemed to attach directly to his shoulders, and his crisp, white collar creased against his thick jowls.

There wasn't much family resemblance between Jason and Kenneth. Purdue's thinning blonde hair showed his scalp, and he looked like he'd spent too much time in the sun without sunscreen. But she recognized that he and Jason shared the same sharp hazel eyes, which now scrutinized her. He stood up, holding out a meaty hand. "How do you do, Miss Payne?" He pumped her hand up and down, and she fought the urge to wipe her palm on her pants once he let go. She wasn't sure whose hands were sweatier, hers or his. "I've heard a lot about you."

Charlie bit her tongue to keep from giving him a smart-assed answer. She called up a smile. "Jason's a good man. I think a lot of him too."

"Please have a seat." Kenny gestured toward the chair in front of his desk. "He tells me you're looking to renegotiate your custody agreement, is that right?"

"Yes, sir." Charlie set the folder down and pushed it across the desk toward him. "When my husband and I created the agreement, I was under duress and I may have," she sighed, her cheeks filling with heat,

"I may have allowed him to bully me into this agreement."

"Jason says you're doing some work for him, consulting for the Sheriff's Department."

"I am."

"He also said that the nature of your consultation can't be disclosed. Is that correct? Because you are, for lack of a better word, a psychic, and they can't officially acknowledge their relationship with you."

Charlie's face grew hotter beneath his sharp gaze. She clenched her jaw. "Yes. That's correct. Is that a problem?"

Kenny's lips twisted into an amused grin and he chuckled. "It's not a problem for me. Any chance you have the lotto numbers for me?"

Charlie forced a smile. *Why do people always ask that question?* "Unfortunately, it doesn't work like that."

"So, you're not a fortune teller, then?"

"Not exactly. I don't tell people's fortunes. I am highly sensitive. I often sense things that other people don't. I guess I'm what you would call intuitive."

"Intuitive." Kenny scribbled the word onto a yellow legal pad sitting in front of him. He sat back in his tall leather chair and folded his hands across his round belly. His sharp eyes fixed on her. "So, what do you sense about, Miss Payne?"

Charlie felt the smile she had been wearing fade, and she fidgeted. "A test? Is that really necessary?"

"Not really," he said. "But it will make going to battle for you a little easier if I can speak with some certainty."

"I thought lawyers were supposed to give a defense without prejudice," she said.

"Yes, they are, especially in a criminal proceeding. But you haven't been charged with anything. This is a civil court case I'm taking pro bono," he reminded her.

Charlie nodded, fully understanding now where he was going with this. "You want proof. That I'm somehow worthy of fighting for."

"Something like that. And who knows? You and I may just end up working together. I'm always looking for an edge."

Charlie took a deep breath and leaned forward with her hands out. "I need your hands to do this properly."

For the first time since she entered the office, Kenneth J. Purdue looked nervous. He cleared his throat and sat forward, stretching his thick tree-trunk arms across the desk. Charlie closed her eyes and exhaled slowly. Without fail, images flooded her mind—sights and sounds and smells from a life that she had never known before. A woman's face floated up—and Charlie immediately saw the resemblance.

What do you want me to tell him? Charlie asked the woman silently.

The woman's soft-spoken southern voice echoed in Charlie's ears. *Tell Scooter he better get to the doctor. Otherwise, he'll end up like his brother Jeffrey.*

Charlie opened her eyes. "You should go to the doctor unless you want to end up like your brother Jeffrey."

The doubtful grin that had stretched across his face faded, and he dropped her hands. A visible sheen of sweat rose on his forehead and panic filled his greenish brown eyes. "Did Jason tell you to say that?"

"No, Jason doesn't even know I'm meeting with you today. Your mother told me that."

"My mother?" His red face paled. "My mother's been dead for twenty years."

The woman appeared behind him, her short salt-and-pepper hair perfectly coiffed, and she wore a pink wool suit. Charlie wondered if it was her favorite outfit or if it was just what she had died in. His mother frowned at him and folded her chubby arms across her chest. "Scooter always was a hard-headed son of a biscuit."

"Yes, Scooter, she has," Charlie said dryly, irritated with this test. "She just said that you are hard-headed son of a biscuit. And I'm afraid I have to agree with her. Now, do you think you can help me or not, Mr. Purdue? Because I don't have all day to sit here and prove to you I'm worth your time."

"Oh, my Lord," he muttered. His eyes darted right and left. "Is she here now?"

"Yes, she is." Charlie let her eyes shift behind his left shoulder.

"You can tell him I think that portrait of himself is a little on the pretentious side."

"No, I want him to help me—" Charlie shook her head.

"Oh, he'll help you, honey. Tell him if he doesn't, then I'll definitely haunt him."

Charlie scowled.

"Go on now." She waved her hand in a brushing motion at Charlie. "Tell him."

"Fine," Charlie grumbled. "Your mother says that your portrait is a little on the pretentious side."

He looked around indignantly. His mouth gaped open and closed, reminding Charlie of a fish that had found itself stuck on the side of a bank, gasping for air.

"She said she'll haunt you if you don't help me."

Mr. Purdue turned his head and faced her.

"How's she gonna do that?" he croaked.

Charlie flitted her eyes toward Mrs. Purdue.

The old woman laughed and leaned over. "Watch this," she said and blew against the back of his neck. The temperature in the room dropped and his hot breath turned into a cold cloud, hanging suspended in front of his face.

"Make her stop," he said.

"Tell him to go to the doctor," his mother said.

Charlie sat up straight, trying to keep the shivers at bay. "She said go to the doctor and take my case."

His mother shifted her attention to Charlie. She stood up and put her hands on her ample hips. "Ooh, I like you," she said. "You're a smart cookie."

"Fine," he said, casting a wary glance over his shoulder. "I'll go to the doctor."

"And take my case," Charlie reiterated.

His thick lips flattened into a straight line. "And take your case."

His mother gave Charlie a wink and disappeared. Kenny took a handkerchief from his pocket and mopped his face with it, despite the chill still lingering in the air. He blew out a heavy breath. "You know, Miss Payne. I'm not gonna lie to you. This will be a battle, especially since there's a signed agreement in place. But—" He glanced around.

"She's gone," Charlie said.

"Good." His shoulders slumped a little as he relaxed.

"You were saying it would be a battle."

"Right, right. And it will be, but I think it's worth a shot. Now, are the records I asked you for in here?"

He laid his hand on top of the folder she'd set on the desk.

"Yes." Charlie nodded.

His face looked solemn as he flipped through the bank statements, tax forms, and paycheck stubs. "Very good," he muttered as he looked through the documents. His thick lips pulled into a reassuring smile, and he shifted his gaze from the papers to her face. "You pay your child support on time?"

"Yes, sir, every month."

"Surprised it's so much, considering what your ex-husband makes."

"Yes, sir," Charlie whispered.

"Do you know who your ex-husband's lawyer is?"

"I don't know his name off the top of my head. But I can call you back with it."

"No, that's no problem. Don't you worry about it. I'll find out who it is."

"What do we do first?" Charlie asked.

"First thing we do is we make a motion with the court. The court will then decide whether we can proceed. We must present a case to them that your ex-husband is not acting in the best interest of the child and that it's better for you to have custody of your son."

"How do we do that?" Dread coiled in a tight knot in her stomach. She'd hoped to leave here feeling better about the situation, but now she wasn't so sure.

"Well, the burden is on us to give the court a good reason to sign-off on the custody change."

"I think my ex-husband put my son on medication because he's more…" She paused, choosing her words carefully. "—intuitive. Like me. Scott should not be making medical decisions for our son without consulting me first. That *is* in the agreement."

"Did he write a prescription for your son?" Kenny picked up a pen and wrote something down on the yellow pad in front of him.

"No, he didn't write it, but he's a doctor, and most of his friends are doctors. He's done it before. Had a friend write a prescription without seeing a patient."

"He did this for your son before?" Kenny scribbled furiously.

"No, not for Evan. For me."

"What sort of prescription?"

Charlie looked down at her hands in her lap. Her fingers were woven together tightly, and her knuckles had whitened. "Anti-depressants."

"You're saying a doctor wrote you a prescription for anti-depressants, but didn't see you?"

"Yes."

"Well, that's something we can definitely work with." Kenny smiled. His fleshy jowls flapped as he sat back in his chair, his eyes scrutinizing her.

Charlie squirmed beneath his gaze. Her stomach flip-flopped. Why did she feel like a traitor? "So, Miss Payne? What would you think about coming to work for me? We could do a trade of services, so to speak. I think your talents might be useful."

"I don't know," Charlie said. "That sounds a little more like indentured servitude to me."

"I promise it wouldn't be like that," he said.

"Yeah, I don't think your mother would like it, if it was," she quipped.

Kenny laughed and sat back in his chair. "You know, I like you. You're a smart cookie."

Charlie shrugged and chuckled. "Yep, that's what they tell me."

* * *

THE HEAVY DARKNESS OVERWHELMED HER, AND THE heat and moisture of her breath made the bag over her head cling to her skin, heightening her fear even more. Screaming did no good and only left her throat raw.

"Here is good."

She jerked her head toward the familiar voice. Something tugged at the bag covering her head, and then she was free of it. She took big gulps of cool night air and blinked, trying to look everywhere at once. Finally, her eyes focused on Haley Miller and Emma Winston.

It took Charlie a minute to figure out what was going on. *This is a dream.*

Charlie walked around the three girls standing in front of her. They were so young—much younger than the woman she spoke with just the other day.

Yes. A dream. Charlie moved in closer so she could hear them a little better.

"God dammit, Haley. You didn't have to kidnap me." The girl standing in front of Haley and Emma folded her arms across her chest. She wore a white T-shirt and pink plaid pajama bottoms. "You could've just asked me."

She was pretty but not on the same level as Haley and Emma, who could be only categorized as homecoming queen pretty. There was a shrewd practicality in her expression and the way she held her body. Brianna gave off a don't-mess-with-me vibe that Charlie imagined was the real reason the Mu Theta's wanted to get rid of her.

"Well, what would be the fun in that?" Haley teased.

"Brianna, just lighten up," Emma scolded. "You want to be a Mu Theta?"

Brianna clenched her jaw and narrowed her eyes. "You know I do," she said, but didn't sound very convincing.

"Good. This is the last test. If you pass, then you are Mu Theta and we'll be sisters forever."

"You could've at least let me put on some freaking clothes." Brianna grumbled. "I'm gonna look like an idiot in my pajamas."

"Don't you worry about it," Haley said. "Nobody's gonna see you here."

"Except maybe the ghosts." Emma smirked and shifted her gaze to the house behind them.

Brianna followed Emma's gaze and her heavy dark brows tugged together. "Where the hell are we?"

"Are you up for it?" Haley asked, ignoring her question.

"You want me to go in there?" Brianna pointed to the dilapidated front porch. Most of the windows were broken and, like giant black eyes, they stared out blankly at the night.

"Yes. You have to spend the rest of the night there." Emma smiled her beauty queen smile.

"You have got to be kidding me," Brianna scoffed. "No fucking way. You guys are crazy."

Emma raised her eyebrows. "So, are you saying you want out, then?"

Brianna blew a breath out between her clenched teeth. A cold cloudy puff formed. "No," she said. "You know I don't. You know I need the Mu Thetas."

"Right," Emma said. "Being a Mu Theta can open a lot of doors."

"Yes, it can," Brianna said. "And I've already put in weeks of work. I know what you're doing." She turned and stared at the house. A soft groan echoed from somewhere inside. Brianna folded her arms across her chest and set her jaw. "All I have to do is spend the night?"

"Yes," Haley said. "Just be careful going upstairs. The floorboards are pretty rotted in places."

"Why the hell would I go upstairs?" Brianna sounded indignant.

"Have you never heard of Alice Brighton?" Emma said.

"No, why would I?"

"Alice Brighton is a tragic figure in the history of Mu Theta Chi. I thought you had done your homework, Brianna."

"If you can't even bother to learn the history of our great sorority, why on earth would you think we would accept you?" Emma chimed in.

Brianna raised her hands. "Now, wait a minute, just wait a minute. I don't remember anything about anyone named Alice Brighton in any of the literature I read."

"She was the daughter of the original founder of MTC," Haley said.

"In fact, I would dare say that she is the whole reason we even have a sorority," Emma said.

"What happened to her?"

"She died," Emma said.

"In this house," Haley said. "In 1917."

"It was tragic. She was waiting for her fiancé to come back from the war." Emma shook her head. "But, he died too. When she got word of his death, she went up to the attic of this house and hanged herself."

Brianna's expression shifted from curiosity to horror.

"Tragic, really. Which is why her mother founded the first chapter of MTC in the state so that girls just like her daughter would have a place to make friends and be with people who would support them in good times and bad."

"I thought the Jeffersons started Mu Theta," Brianna said.

"Well, they started the whole sorority, but the Brightons are the ones who brought it to South Carolina."

"Oh-kay." Doubt flashed across Brianna's face and crinkles appeared around her dark eyes.

"They say you can still hear her weeping." Haley shifted her gaze to the third-story window. Charlie glanced up into the dark hole, half-expecting to see a spirit standing there, but it was just an empty window. "If you hear her crying, tonight don't be scared. Okay?" A smile played at the corners of Emma's lips.

"Don't worry about me, honey." Brianna scowled and marched up the creaky wooden stairs. She turned around. "I'll see you when you get back."

Haley grinned, her blue eyes full of malicious mischief. "You actually have to go inside the house, Brianna."

Brianna stood there for a moment, glaring at them. Charlie let herself slip into Brianna's thoughts for a moment.

God, she hated these girls sometimes. If her mother hadn't been a member when she went to school, she never would have considered joining. The connections that her mother had made through Mu Theta Chi had helped her get a job after Brianna's father left them. They weren't poor, but they weren't rich, either, and her mother had sung their praises from the time Brianna was a small girl. Even referring to her sorority sisters as her saviors.

Brianna didn't see Haley and Emma as saviors—more like two mean girls who didn't like her and couldn't quite get rid of her as easily as they would like. They were trying to make her quit. But that's where they had underestimated her, because she never quit. She had her future all mapped out, and she wasn't about to let these two fashion dolls get in her way. She took a deep breath, put her hand on the crystal doorknob, and pushed open the front door. The rusty hinges squealed, setting her teeth on edge. She stepped inside and looked around the once-grand foyer. The silk paper was cracked and peeling in places, and vines had grown up through the floor. It was eighty degrees outside, but that didn't stop a shiver from skittering down her spine. Brianna turned back around to face them. "Happy now?"

Haley grinned wider. She held up one hand and wiggled her fingers in a condescending brief wave. "We'll see you at 6 a.m."

"If you survive the night." Emma laughed. The maniacal tone sent a fresh shiver through Brianna. She watched as the two girls climbed into Haley's BMW and peeled off, spitting dirt and gravel in their wake.

"Dammit," Brianna muttered. She had no idea where she was, but by the brightness of the stars in the sky, she was too far from the city to just hoof it.

She gritted her teeth. They would not win this stupid game. She let herself take in her surroundings. Grayish mold covered the walls. Cobwebs hung in every corner and shadows crept up the plaster, melding into the long swollen water stains. As if the walls had been crying. Brianna rubbed her upper arm to chase away the goose bumps.

"It's just an old house, Bree. There is nothing here

that can hurt you." The sound of her own voice comforted her. She folded her arms across her chest, hugging them tight to her body. An icy blast of air blew across the back of her neck and every hair stood on end. Something was watching her. The staccato beats of her heart grew faster in her chest, and she turned slowly in a circle, looking for the source. The sound of a woman crying echoed throughout the first floor. Brianna tightened her jaw. They were totally screwing with her.

"Very funny, Haley!"

The crying grew louder, focusing behind her. They probably had a fucking tape recorder with that noise on it. Brianna turned to face it. Her heart slammed into the back of her throat. Standing—no floating—in the doorway of the old parlor was a very pale translucent young woman. Her face etched with pain.

"Have you seen my Bartholomew?" the young woman asked.

Brianna shook her head and opened her mouth to say something, but the words died on her lips.

"Papa said he's not coming home. But he promised me he would. Even in death."

She didn't know why they were doing this. Did they really hate her this much?

"You're not real," Brianna muttered and took a step backward. The girl disappeared. After several moments, Brianna's heartbeat returned to normal. There had to be a projector in the house. It was the only explanation. "You bitches won't win!" She curled her hand into a fist and raised it, her face toward the ceiling. "Did you hear me? You will not beat me!"

The door slammed behind her, making her jump. Brianna's eyes tried to look everywhere at once. So that was the game, huh? Scare Brianna shitless. She gritted her teeth again. "Fuck you!"

A woman's wails echoed from above, and Brianna's breathing quickened. Slowly, she moved toward the staircase. She peered up through the stairwell that coiled through the center of the house to the third floor. She could see the sky in places where the roof had rotted away and fallen in. Bright stars twinkled against the indigo sky. Something shimmered from the corner of her eye, and she caught movement and whispering. Only there was nothing ghostly about it. They were trying to scare her. There was no such thing as ghosts. Brianna set her jaw. She would catch them in the act, confront them and be done with this shit. Brianna marched over to the stairs. She scanned them for signs of weakness. The wood looked graying old, but it didn't look rotted. She took her first step, and then another. The floorboards didn't feel spongy or loose.

"I hear you, you fucking bitches," she said under

her breath. Footsteps above her head made her stop in her tracks. She waited until her heart calmed down before beginning her ascent again. "I'm gonna catch you. You shouldn't have messed with this Jersey girl." Wailing echoed around her. They thought they could scare her. She would fucking show them what being scared was all about.

"Oh, Alice," Brianna called, "why don't come out and play with me?"

A woman dressed in an old-fashioned white dress with pale grayish make-up leaned over the banister. She was too solid to be anything other than Jessica Ellery. So, they were all in on it, huh?

"Leave me alone," she wailed, then stepped away from the bannister.

"Oh, no, you don't," Brianna muttered and ran up the steps. Her ears burned, the first sign she was in-your-face pissed. She didn't know what she would do once she caught up with Jessica and Haley and whoever else was up there fucking with her, but once she did, she would make sure they were sorry for this little stunt.

"Come out, come out wherever you are, Alice," she growled out the last word. She came to the second-floor landing and bent over the bannister and looked up. Something caught her eye in the empty room right off the landing.

Brianna looked around for a weapon. A loose

spindle that had cracked would do. She worked it out of the bannister and held the pointed end out like a sword. She made her way toward the darkened room. "Come talk to me. We'll have a girl's night. Braid each other's hair, paint each other's toes. Tell each other our secrets."

Someone giggled behind her, and Brianna spun, trying to catch them in the act. Something heavy landed on her shoulders and chest. Brianna screamed, beating at it with her spindle. Whatever it was, felt rough and ropey beneath her fingers. She ran out of the room and hit the bannister. The empty place where the loose spindle had been, cracked. The sound it made reminded her of when she was a kid. Her grandfather had worked in the forestry service and she had gone with him one day to watch as he cut down dead hemlock trees that had died.

"What killed them, Pops?" He'd hoisted her on his shoulder. "A bug, Bree. A nasty, invasive bug." The rangers had used chainsaws to cut the tall trees down, but some trees still cracked under their own weight. A sharp, thunderous sound that made her little girl's bones ache.

The bannister's cracking sounded like those trees, and for a brief second, she was free falling, just like the trees did once the crack was over.

"Oh, my god!" someone screamed above her. She wasn't sure if it was Haley or Emma or Jessica. When she landed on the floor, a sharp pain pierced her chest. All the color drained from the world and shadow people hovered above her. Whispering. Still whispering, only their whispers were no longer laced with teasing, only fear.

"What are we gonna do?" someone asked just before she sank into the dark.

CHAPTER 13

Charlie awoke with a horrible ache in her chest. She sat straight up in bed, pressing her hand against her sternum, gulping in air. Sunlight flooded through the window, and she blinked against the harsh light. It took a minute to orient herself. It had only been a dream. Several deep slow breaths later, she scrubbed her eyes with her palms, trying to erase the images in her head. She needed to text Jason to let him know, but dreaded the big question. The only question that really mattered to him—where's the body now? The body. With all the evidence. Her phone chirped, announcing a new text. Maybe he would beat her to the punch this morning with a text.

Meet for coffee at the café? My treat. :-)
Tom.

Her mouth curved into a smile almost against her will. She glanced at the clock. It was 7:07 a.m. Did she want to see him? She'd thought about him a few times since their last meeting, but had batted them away quickly. She had no time for romance. It didn't matter how handsome he was. Still... she enjoyed his company. She texted him back.

What time? I have to be at work at 11 a.m. today

Three dots appeared almost immediately, making her even happier.

As soon as possible. :-)

She brushed her fingers across her lips and smiled.

Okay. I'll meet you there in thirty minutes. I'm gonna want more than coffee though. She hesitated. Did that sound too sexual? Her face burst into flames at the thought of kissing Tom Sharon. Oh, god—she was a fifteen-year-old girl after all. She pressed the backspace key and tried again. *Okay. I'll meet you there in thirty minutes. I'm gonna want breakfast though.* There. That was better. She pressed the send button. The three dots appeared, followed closely by his response.

See you then.

She jumped out of bed and hurried to get dressed. Tardiness was one of her biggest pet peeves, and she had barely given herself enough time. Once ready, she jogged out to her car and peeled away, the dream almost completely forgotten by the time she turned onto the road heading toward town.

* * *

CHARLIE IGNORED THE SMUG GRIN ON JEN'S FACE AND scanned the menu in her hand while Tom engaged her cousin, much to Charlie's chagrin.

"Tell me about these peanut butter and jelly muffins." Tom pointed to the menu. "What sort of jelly?"

"Strawberry. They're delicious. They're one of my most popular muffin flavors."

"Can I substitute it for the blueberry on the Thursday scramble?"

"Yes, you can." Jen grinned, with her pen paused against her order pad. "Is that what you'd like?"

"Yes, I think I'll live dangerously." He winked at Jen and closed the menu. Jen picked it up and tucked it under her arm. "I'll have the Thursday scramble with bacon and a peanut butter and jelly muffin."

"Charlie?" Jen shifted her attention to her cousin and wrote something on the pad while she waited. "I don't know why you look at the menu at all. I know exactly what you want."

"Really?" Tom folded his hands together, placing his elbows and forearms on the table. The corners of his mouth curved into an intrigued smile. "Tell me?"

"She will order the banana pancakes with the chicken sausage," Jen said. "Very predictable. At least when it comes to her food."

Charlie laughed and her cheeks heated with embarrassment. "Is that your way of telling him I'm picky?"

"You said it, not me." Jen lifted one hand to her mouth and bent toward Tom, pretending to shield Charlie from hearing her words. "But she really is very picky."

Charlie frowned and shut the menu. "Fine. I'll have the banana pancakes with chicken sausage since you know so much."

"See?" Jen's right eyebrow quirked, she turned over her order pad and showed it to Tom. "Told you. Predictable."

Tom's gaze shifted between the two women. Amusement glittered in his eyes, and he was clearly enjoying the cousinly banter. Charlie gave Jen a pointed look. Jen winked at her, enjoying this way too much.

"All right, I'll get this in. Y'all just let me know if there's anything I can get for you." Jen walked away.

"I like your cousin. She seems nice." Tom smiled and Charlie felt a flutter in her belly.

"She's nosy and opinionated. But it's sort of in our genes so—" Charlie shrugged and traced a finger around the top of her tea glass. "What about you?

Do you have any family here who drives you crazy?"

"I don't know about crazy. I have a brother, William, and a sister, Joy. We all run the family business together."

"I imagine that's interesting." Charlie placed her arms on the table and leaned forward a little. She could not get over how beautiful he was. She had known handsome men. Her ex-husband could've been mistaken for a Ralph Lauren model, but there was something about Tom that struck her as almost angelic.

"Running a funeral home or working with my brother and sister?"

"Either. Both."

"I don't know about interesting. But it's definitely meaningful. At least to me it is."

"I imagine you couldn't do your job and it not be meaningful. You're offering people comfort in their worst moment. That's noble. I mean, except for the whole funeral home markup thing." She chuckled, teasing him.

"It is a business. I mean, do you charge for your services?"

"I didn't want to at first. It seemed sort of weird, you know? But once I got over my fear that I was somehow taking advantage, I gave myself permission to make a living using my gifts. It's not really any different from someone who can sing or write or paint. And what I give people has been meaningful to them. Or at least that's what they've told me."

"I can only imagine. Do any of your cousins share your talent??"

Charlie glanced at the counter where Jen was chatting up a customer and pouring coffee. "My cousins have their own gifts. But not like mine. My son seems to be showing signs that he may have inherited a little of what I have, though."

"You have a son? How old is he?"

"He just turned eleven in July."

Tom glanced at her hand and his brow wrinkled with curiosity. "But you're not married?"

"Not anymore. We divorced a couple years ago."

"I see." Tom fixed his gaze on her. Heat crept up her neck and into her cheeks, and the fluttering in her stomach moved to her chest. "I'd say I'm sorry, but I'm not. If you were still with him, you wouldn't be here with me today."

Charlie let out a breathy, nervous laugh. "I'm not sure exactly how to respond to that."

"Your response is perfect. I'm just going to throw this out there—get it out of the way. I like you, Charlie. I don't want to put you off, but I don't want you to be wondering either."

Charlie shifted in her seat. Her face grew hotter. "I… uh."

"It's all right. Again, I didn't mean to make you uncomfortable. Although you're adorable when you blush."

Charlie laughed.

"I just want you to know where I stand," he said.

"Wow. You certainly know how to make a girl feel wanted." She sat back and fanned herself with a napkin, unable to stop the grin taking over her face. "It's definitely flattering."

Her hands fidgeted with the napkin. "I haven't done this in a really long time. I was with my husband from the time I was twenty years old until I was almost thirty."

"And you haven't dated anyone since your divorce?"

"I haven't really had the time or inclination, honestly."

Tom sat back against the cushioned backrest of the booth. His eyes scrutinized her. "Not even that deputy you work with?"

"Jason? How do you even know about Jason?" Charlie tipped her head.

"Small town and people like to talk."

"Yes, they do." Charlie nodded. "Jason is my work partner, but that's about as far as it goes."

Tom's lips twisted into a wry smile. "Glad to hear it. Then maybe you'll let me take you on a proper date."

"Wait, this isn't a proper date?" Charlie said deadpan. She folded her arms across her chest. "Does that mean you're not buying breakfast? Because that's the only reason I came."

Tom feigned disappointment. "Oh, I see how it is now."

Charlie smirked and nodded. "Yes, it's all about the free food for me."

He chuckled. "Well, at least I'm going in with my eyes open."

"If you're gonna sweep me off my feet — I guess I'll have to go out to dinner with you on a proper date," Charlie teased

"Wonderful. Dinner with me. Saturday night."

Charlie's stomach flip-flopped and she smiled. "Okay. Saturday night it is."

* * *

"I don't have much time," Charlie announced as she sat in the chair next to Jason's desk. She put a small bakery box down on top of a pile of file folders.

"What's this?"

"Peanut butter and jelly muffin."

Jason flipped open the top and pressed his nose in close, taking a deep sniff. He broke the muffin in half and took a large bite, moaning a little. "Oh, my god, I love these things."

"I had another dream," Charlie said.

Jason said something to her, but it came out garbled. She tried not to laugh at the bit of jelly clinging to the corner of his mouth. She reached into her purse and pulled out a travel size pack of baby wipes. "Here."

Jason took the wipe and cleaned his lips. He swallowed before trying to speak again. "What was your dream?"

"Haley and Emma kidnapped Brianna, then they dumped her at this old haunted house."

"Okay… Did they kill her?"

"I—I don't know. Someone put a noose around her neck, and she ended up falling to her death. She never saw their faces."

"Did you?"

"No. I was in her head. I saw what she saw." Charlie frowned. "Sorry."

"So, what happened to her body?"

"I don't know. That's something we need to figure out."

"I'm still waiting on the missing persons reports from ten years ago," he said. "Any chance there was a flashing neon sign with the address?"

"Ha-ha. You're hilarious. Give me back my muffin." She held her hand out for the box. Jason picked up the last bit of the sweet pastry and scarfed it down. He washed it down with a sip of coffee and tossed the empty box into the trashcan next to his desk.

Charlie rolled her eyes. "What do you want to do?"

"Hard to bring Emma in without something more concrete than your dream, especially since it was so long ago."

"I wish we knew who the other girls were," Charlie said. "Then maybe we could tell her we have witnesses."

"What other girls?" Jason said.

"Emma and Haley didn't do this without a consensus from a group of girls running the sorority. Which means there were other people who knew exactly where they were taking her. Maybe they didn't realize what would happen to Brianna. I don't know, but as far as I'm concerned, they all got their hands dirty when they voted her out."

"Would you recognize the faces?"

"I think so."

"Great. What time do you get off work?"

"Seven-thirty. Why?"

"Maybe we could take a little trip to the library. I can show you the yearbook where I found Emma's picture."

"I can't tonight. I promised Jen I'd help her with something."

"Okay, what about tomorrow?"

"I'm working till six tomorrow. And tomorrow night I've got a date. Maybe day after?"

Jason's mouth pressed into a flat line. "You have a date?"

"Yeah. Tom Sharon's taking me to dinner."

"So, now you're dating Mr. Death?"

"Oh, my god, he is not Mr. Death," she said. "I am never bringing you muffins again."

"You're the one that told me death surrounded him."

"You don't have to be such a jerk about it."

Jason shrugged. "I'm not the one dating Mr. Death."

"Will you stop saying that!"

"Come on, you know I'm just teasing you. God, you're as bad as your cousin Lisa. Can't take a joke."

Charlie bristled. "It's not funny."

"It's a little funny," Jason muttered.

Charlie clucked her tongue and glanced at the clock. She stood up. "I have to go. My shift starts in less than an hour."

"Call you later to set up a time to go?" he asked.

"Fine," she said. "Talk to you later."

CHAPTER 14

Saturday night, Tom picked Charlie up at 7 p.m. on the dot. He wore black jeans and black Chuck Taylor's and a striped gray T-shirt. His dark brown hair fell in soft waves across his forehead, and when she opened the door, his warm brown eyes made her heart flutter.

"Wow, you look beautiful," he said, stepping inside the cottage.

She wore her long blonde hair in a loose ponytail, and soft tendrils curled around her face. The pink maxi dress she wore had faint orange lines around the bust. Lisa had teased her when she bought the dress, calling it strawberry and tangerine sherbet. Charlie didn't care, though. She loved the colors together, and she loved the cut of the dress. It was light, flowing, and feminine. If the evening had been even slightly cooler, she might have considered wearing a white sweater, but the low was only supposed to be seventy-five.

"I thought it would be fun to go for a walk on the beach. Maybe have dinner down at one of the restaurants."

"I think that's a great idea. I love the beach."

"Me too. Although I don't get to go often."

"No, I suppose you don't."

"No, unfortunately, death waits for no man." He used a light tone, and Charlie surmised it was his way of deprecating the darkness of his profession. "Shall we?"

Charlie nodded, and he led her to his car, a Black Ford Fusion sedan. He opened the door. She slid inside and settled into the soft black leather. "Nice," she said, running her hand across the edge of this seat. "Is this a hybrid?"

Tom turned the key in the ignition before fastening his seatbelt. "It is."

"I don't think I've ever ridden in hybrid before." She glanced around. Her ex had preferred BMW to almost anything else, and he didn't believe in hybrid cars. He was convinced they didn't really save much gas.

"Well, this will be a night of firsts, I guess." Tom smiled and put the car in gear.

The streets of Palmetto Point were still bustling

with people as Tom pulled into the parking lot of El Capitan restaurant on Conch Drive. Just because summer was over didn't mean the tourists had left; September meant long, warm days. The out-of-towners didn't really disappear until after Thanksgiving, when most of the beach homeowners closed up their houses for the winter. He took her hand in his as they walked into the restaurant, sending a thrill through Charlie. She couldn't stop herself from smiling. They stopped in front of a chalkboard sign with the specials.

"Anything tempt you?" he asked, tugging her a little closer.

His arm brushed against hers and she laughed nervously. She read over the sign. "Crab legs look good."

"You had soft shell crab for our first meal together. I'm sensing a theme here," he teased.

"Well, I grew up on an island. Loving seafood is kind of a requirement." She grinned and leaned in closer, letting her arm rest against his side. "Just for the record, crab is my favorite."

"Good to know," he said.

Several minutes later the hostess seated them, and Charlie scanned the menu.

"So, do you know what you want?" Tom asked, perusing the menu. "If you're starving, we could have an appetizer. Maybe some she-crab soup?"

"I love it, but it's too much food for me. I'm thinking I might try the stuffed flounder."

"I thought you were getting crab legs."

Charlie chuckled. "Too messy for a first date. Can't have you thinking I eat like a pig just yet."

"Right, can't see that side of you at least until the third date," he quipped. "Good thinking."

"There a lot of good things here though," she mused, glancing down at the menu again. "The low-country boil looks good, but I'm spoiled."

"Why is that?"

"My uncle makes a mean low-country boil. He always includes blue crabs."

"An anarchist," Tom teased.

Charlie laughed. "That's definitely my uncle Jack."

"So, you're close with your family."

"I wasn't for a while, but I am now." She paused, trying to keep Scott out of the conversation if she could.

"Was it because they didn't like your husband?" he asked.

Charlie fidgeted with her silverware. "It was more him than them. He didn't like my family."

Tom nodded and glanced down at the menu again. "That must've been difficult."

Charlie looked around. Where was an interrupting waitress when she needed one? "Sure. But we're all mended now, and I see my cousins all the time."

"What about your parents? Do you see them?"

"My parents died when I was little. My grandmother raised me."

"Is she still with us?" he asked cautiously.

"No." Charlie gave him a sad smile. "She died a few months before I got married."

"I'm sorry. Were you close?"

"Very. Looking back, I think it would have made her sad to think I got married to my ex."

"Why?"

"Oh, well, she hated him. Thought he was stuck up and selfish, and a few choice expletives that I won't share." She chuckled.

"Is he? Stuck up?"

Charlie sat her menu on the table and studied Tom's face, considering his question. It would be easy to paint Scott as the asshole he sometimes was. But he was also a good father mostly, and she knew that the actions he took were more out of fear than contempt for her—fear of the unknown. Fear of what he didn't understand logically. Was it fair for her to color Tom's ideas about her ex-husband? Did Scott just paint her with one solid brush of my ex-wife is crazy? She swallowed hard and feared he probably did, but she didn't have to do that.

"He's pretty much as flawed as I am," Charlie said.

"You don't seem very flawed to me." Tom leaned forward with his elbows on the table and smiled.

Charlie's face heated, and she opened to mouth to speak.

"What can I get for y'all?" The young waitress wore tight jeans and a tight red polo shirt with El Capitan embroidered just above her left breast. A clip held her straight brown hair back in a cute, messy bun. When she smiled, her white teeth almost glowed against her tan skin.

"Saved by the bell." Charlie let out a breathy laugh and looked him straight in the eye. "You know, I think I will have the crab legs."

Tom glanced at the waitress and handed her the menu. "Make that two."

He waited for the waitress to walk away. "So are these flaws why you divorced your husband?"

Charlie picked up her water glass and took a sip. "What makes you think he didn't divorce me?"

He leaned forward and his eyes smoldered as a grin stretched his lips. "For one thing, you're endlessly fascinating."

Charlie laughed and folded her arms across her chest.

"Seriously I'd like to know, if you want to share."

She took a deep breath and looked Tom squarely in the eyes. "He didn't believe in me."

Tom's intense gaze darkened. "In what way?"

"He doesn't believe in ghosts or psychics or anything outside of the realm of hard science."

"What about God? Does he believe in God?"

"He was raised in the Catholic Church."

"That didn't really answer my question."

"He goes to church on Christmas and Easter with his mother. Sometimes he takes Evan, although Evan hates it because it's stuffy and smells like old people."

Tom chuckled and took a sip of his water. "What exactly do old people smell like?"

"Pee and Ben Gay." She laughed and rolled her eyes.

"The musings of an eleven-year-old. Sounds about right then." Tom laced his hands together, and his eyes fixed her to the spot. "So, you were together for ten years. How could you be with someone for so long who didn't believe in you?"

Charlie's cheeks burned hotter and she glanced around the restaurant. There were still plenty of sunburned couples and locals who were enjoying the last of their happy hour Margarita after work. She sighed. "Isn't it bad juju to talk about your ex on your first date?"

His golden eyes glittered with mischief. "But it's

not really our first date. Technically, if I think about it, it's our third."

"How do you get that?"

"We've dined together two other times."

"Well, the first one doesn't really count, because I didn't even like you then," she quipped. Tom laughed, deep and hearty, at her assertion. The sound wrapped around her senses, warming her to her core. "And the second doesn't count, either, because you didn't pay for it."

He scoffed. "Neither did you."

"Exactly."

"Well, regardless of who paid, I think we're well into the territory where we bare our souls."

Charlie grinned and shook her head. "I'm not sure I'm ready to bare anything just yet." It felt so good to joke and be light.

Tom shrugged a shoulder and his lips stretched into a wry grin. "Can you blame me for trying?"

"No, I suppose, I can't."

"Well, hopefully, someday soon you'll tell me more." He stretched his arm across the table and held his palm up, beckoning her to take it.

Charlie could not take her eyes off his long, slender fingers. Those hands seemed to be built for playing a musical instrument, like piano or guitar. She slipped her hand into his and an image of his hands wrapped in latex, shoving a needle into a pale white neck and blood flowing into a long tube popped into her head. She squeezed hard, fighting the urge to jerk her hand back and blinked away the image.

Tom folded his fingers around hers. "What is it?"

"Nothing." Charlie smiled, but her stomach turned sour. Not even crab legs sounded good anymore.

"You saw something." He glanced from side to side, as if trying to find the source. "A spirit?"

"No." She shook her head. "Nothing like that. It doesn't matter. It doesn't matter what I saw."

"You sure?"

"I'm sure." Sometimes, she understood why Scott had worked so hard not to believe in her gift despite evidence to the contrary. Sometimes, she wished she had that luxury too.

* * *

CHARLIE COULDN'T REMEMBER THE LAST TIME SHE'D HAD such a good time. She looked down at their joined hands lying over the cup-holders separating the front seats of Tom's car. After dinner, he'd taken her to the beach, just as he promised, and they took off their shoes and dipped their feet into the cool ocean water. The smile on his lips had not weakened since their first touch. He pulled into the driveway that led toward her uncle's. The road split. The left road led to the house, and the right led to the cottage on her uncle's vast property. A small grove of trees formed a V where the road forked, but once he turned into her gravel driveway, the trees thinned and then gave way to a wide expanse of grass. Her uncle's big house glowed with life and light even at this hour. The security light on the cottage was on, and as they drew closer to the cottage, her heart leaped into her throat. Scott's black BMW sedan was parked behind her Honda.

"Is someone else here?" Tom asked warily as he pulled in beside her car on the concrete pad.

"My ex-husband," Charlie muttered.

As she and Tom got out of his car, Scott emerged. The security light lit up the yard, casting an eerie glow to the little white cottage.

"What the actual fuck, Charlie! You're suing me?" Scott snarled and waved a set of papers at her.

"Scott, you need to calm down." Charlie kept her voice steady. "I won't talk to you like this."

"Charlie? Who's your friend?" Tom stepped close, his elbow brushing against her. He slipped his hand into hers. There was something wary in his voice. She gave his hand a squeeze to reassure him.

"I'm her goddamned husband. Who are you?" Scott didn't hesitate to get right into Tom's face. Charlie's heart thudded against her rib cage. It had been a long time since she'd seen Scott be so ugly. Charlie moved between the two men.

"Scott," Charlie dropped her voice but kept it firm, "you need to go home. Now." She locked her gaze on his. "If you want to discuss this civilly, then call me tomorrow and I will meet you in a public place."

"A public—" Scott's eyes darkened and the lines in his forehead and around his eyes grew deep. "Are you fucking him?" Scott asked in a flat, icy tone that made her bones ache. Charlie's stomach coiled into a tight knot. Scott shifted his gaze to Tom. "Are you fucking my wife?"

"You and I must have a different understanding of what divorced means," Tom said calmly. He side stepped Charlie and moved closer to Scott. While Scott may have been short compared to Tom's tall slender figure, he also had a black belt in karate, was well muscled, and knew how to use his fists, something Charlie had learned early in their marriage. If Scott struck out at Tom, she didn't know how well Tom could defend himself. Tom took a step forward, almost chest to chest with Scott. A smile played on his lips. "Charlie has asked you to leave. You should do as she asks."

Scott ignored Tom and directed his words to Charlie. "I warned you what would happen if you challenged me. You should have listened to me."

Charlie's body went numb. What had she done? "Scott."

"Make this go away, or I will make sure that you never see your son again. Do you understand me?"

Charlie's voice shook and tears threatened to blind her. "Get out of here!" She pointed to his car. "Before I call my uncle Jack."

Scott narrowed his eyes and clenched his jaw, making the lines of his face even sharper than they already were. "I hope fucking him is worth it, because you will never see Evan again."

Tom lunged at Scott and Charlie grabbed hold of his arm by his elbow, pulling him back.

"No! It's what he wants!" she said, looking into his eyes. "He's just trying to control me. That's all."

Tom's entire body shook. His hands curled into fists and the well-defined muscles of his arms bulged. Rage rolled off him and washed through her. The sensations made her stomach roil, and she stepped back from them and pulled her cell phone from her pocket. She fumbled with the phone a second before finally finding the right number.

"I need you. Scott's here at the cottage." Charlie fought the tremor in her voice.

In less than a minute of ending the call, the screen door of her uncle's house screeched, and all six-foot-four of Jack Holloway emerged from the main house. In one hand, he carried his hunting rifle. Jen and Lisa trailed close behind him and the three dark figures hurried across the expansive yard.

Scott took one glance and backed away toward his car. Her uncle hated Scott, and although she knew Jack would never shoot him, he was not above scaring the crap out of him. Scott scrambled into his car. The electric locks clicked, and the brake lights pumped red just before the engine roared to life. Scott peeled out of the space. His tires ground against the gravel, kicking up dust and stone in their wake. He sped off and as soon as his car lights disappeared Charlie doubled over, feeling dizzy and sick. Tom put his arm across her back and knelt next to her.

"Are you all right?" he asked.

The vice-like grip of the adrenaline pumping through her body squeezed Charlie's chest, making it impossible to breathe. One phrase echoed through her head: *What have I done?*

Tom held his hand out for her, and she grabbed onto it, grasping it tightly. With his other hand, he rubbed gentle circles in the center of her back. Softly he said, "I'm here, Charlie, you're not alone."

"What the hell happened?" Jack asked as he approached.

"Scott was here. He threatened her," Tom explained as her uncle and two cousins surrounded them.

Jen knelt beside her. "Charlie, honey, what's going on?"

"Can't breathe," Charlie choked out.

"Come on, let's get her inside," Jack said, pointing to the front door of the cottage.

Charlie squeezed her eyes shut and tried to stand up, but her body wouldn't comply. Tears burned the back of her throat. She would lose Evan. She should have just kept her mouth shut.

"Charlie, honey," Jen's gentle voice cut through the thick haze. Jen slipped something cool and smooth into Charlie's palm. A sense of warm, calm spread up her arm, moving through her chest. Charlie squeezed the small flat stone tighter, absorbing its energy. Her shoulders and chest relaxed enough for her to gulp in a deep breath. She closed her eyes, breathing in slower.

"I am okay," Charlie whispered, mostly trying to reassure herself. "I'm okay." She looked up at the concerned faces of her family and Tom. Her heart wrenched again, but it didn't take her breath away this time. "I'm sorry, Tom, but you need to go."

Tom's eyes widened, and he looked shocked, but thankfully not hurt. "He can't keep your son from you."

"Was that the threat?" Lisa's mouth twisted into a disgusted smirk, and she put her hands on her slim hips.

"I went to see a lawyer about renegotiating our custody agreement. Scott was served with papers today."

"And he threatened that you would not see your son again because of me," Tom said.

"No. This is not because of you," Charlie whispered. "Not really. He's angry at me because I'm challenging him. But," Charlie paused, not wanting to say the words. "But you being here didn't help."

Jen's mouth fell open, and she pressed her hand against her lips. Jack's hands tightened around the rifle in his hands.

"Son of a bitch," Jack muttered.

"He can't do that. If he tries to keep Evan from you, he'll be in breach of your agreement," Lisa said. "That in of itself should be enough to get a judge to at least consider changing custody."

"He's already threatened to paint me as crazy. I don't need him throw slut into the mix." Charlie sniffled and turned her face away, wiping the wetness from her cheeks with the heel of her hand. "I'm sorry, Tom. I had a great time and I really like you, but…"

"It's all right, Charlie," Tom said. "Really. I understand." He leaned in close and kissed her on the cheek. Charlie squeezed her eyes shut, and she felt him slip away. The car door slammed, and his engine come to life, the sound of the tires driving across the gravel.

Jen slipped her arm around Charlie's waist. "Come on, sweetie, let's go in the house." Jen helped her to her feet and guided her back toward the main house. "I'll make you some tea. We'll figure out how to fix this."

Charlie glanced over her shoulder toward Tom's car one last time. His red taillights grew smaller as he drove away, then finally disappeared on to the main road. "How?" Charlie asked. "Y'all don't know Scott the way I do. Once he sets his mind to something, it's like he has tunnel vision, and it's all he can see or think about. Especially if he feels like he's right or deserving."

"Entitled son of a—" Lisa muttered but didn't finish her thought out loud.

CHAPTER 15

Charlie felt the warmth of the sun and turned her face toward the light, closing her eyes, letting it wash over her. She took a deep breath. The pleasant scent of pine straw filled her senses, and pine needles crunched beneath her bare feet. When she opened her eyes, she found herself on the path where she had first encountered Trini Dolan.

Charlie glanced around, looking for the girl, but the spirit was nowhere to be found. In the distance, the high joyous cries of children's laughter bounced off the trees, which was strange. Trini had been anything but joyful when they'd last met. Charlie turned in a full-circle, searching for the source. Tall pines stretched for as far as her eyes could see. Scrubby brush and fan-like ferns filled the spaces between the rough gray-barked trunks. Twenty yards away, between two trees, a child appeared, her red hair unmistakable.

"Trini!" Charlie called.

The girl moved away from Charlie but turned briefly and motioned for her to follow her. Charlie stopped and looked over her shoulder. The path she was on led back to safety. It beckoned her to follow it. Charlie shifted her gaze back to Trini, who was now even further away. Something wild raced through the underbrush, and Charlie's arms broke into goose bumps. Trini disappeared among the trees.

This is a dream—follow her. Nothing can hurt you here.

Charlie stepped off the path, following the girl deeper into the woods. "Trini, wait!"

Charlie broke into a run, scanning the trees for any sign of the girl. Ferns and small branches grabbed at her legs, snagging her pants.

Charlie stopped in her tracks. "Trini! Show yourself or I'm going back!" She waited for the child to answer. A crow cawed overhead, mocking her. Charlie glared at the large glossy blackbird staring down at her from a high branch.

"Come on!" Trini appeared beside her. Charlie's heart slammed into her throat and she cried out.

"Don't do that," Charlie scolded.

The girl paid no attention to her words and took

off again. A cacophony of giggles echoed on the breeze, and the hair on the back of Charlie's neck stood up.

"Show yourself!" Charlie demanded. A small girl with long blonde hair popped up about ten feet away from her. A young black girl with her hair worn in three neat twists stood up on the other side of the blonde. Another girl giggled behind her, and Charlie turned to see Macy Givens standing ten feet behind her. More giggles wafted through the trees, and Charlie counted five more girls, all standing in the ferns, surrounding her. Something touched the center of Charlie's back, sending a shiver crawling across her shoulders. She twisted to find Trini. The girl's faded blue eyes pleaded. "You can't forget about us."

"Who are all these girls?" Charlie said.

"They're me. And I'm them."

"Did the man across the street from you take you? Hurt you?" Charlie didn't want to say kill you. The thought alone sounded so harsh inside her head. A loud piercing foghorn sounded and Charlie winced, bringing her hands over her ears. The girls looked toward it.

"We have to go." Trini headed toward the sound, then stopped a moment, and threw a glance over her shoulder at Charlie. "Don't forget about us." She continued toward the other girls.

"Wait—stop!" Charlie called after them. But each

one disappeared into the shadows between the pines. She took off in their direction, trying to find where they were going and what the horn meant.

"Trini! Macey!" The surrounding forest grew dark. Something cold scraped across the skin of her shoulders and she turned to find the reaper staring down at her. Only he didn't look quite the same as he had before. This time, he wore a mask of Scott's face.

"I told you not to challenge me," he said, sounding too much like Scott. He raised his scythe and Charlie opened her mouth to scream, but nothing would come out.

* * *

CHARLIE'S EYES FLEW OPEN, AND SHE SAT UP STRAIGHT in her bed. Her eyes tried to look everywhere at once, and it took her a few minutes to calm down enough to remember where she was. A sunny yellow and white quilt covered her legs and lacy eyelet curtains let the early morning light flood into the room. She was at her uncle's house in one of the spare bedrooms. Jen had insisted that she stay the night. Charlie blew out a deep breath and covered her face with her hands. She rubbed her eyes and her stomach twisted into a knot and growled. The slight scent of cinnamon and the sound of voices wafted up the stairs and through the hallway. Charlie threw her legs over the side of the bed and touched her feet to the cold floor. She slipped off the oversized T-shirt her cousin had given her and put her dress back on, raking her fingers through her long blonde hair and twisting it up into a messy bun with a ponytail holder from her purse.

Ruby's high-pitched little-girl voice became louder as Charlie reached the kitchen. "Hannah said that fairies are stupid," Ruby said, sounding disgusted by the very notion. Charlie stood in the door watching the mother and daughter, reminiscing. She had always loved her time in the kitchen with Evan. The girl was a miniature Jen with long dark hair and wide blue eyes. She wore a pink T-shirt and a pair of denim shorts.

"Why did she say that?" Jen took a piece of French toast out of the cast-iron skillet and put it on a plate with a couple pieces of bacon.

"'Cause her mother told us they aren't real." Ruby sat at the long kitchen table in the center of the large kitchen. She leaned her head against her hand and her elbow resting on the yellow quilted placemat.

Jen put the plate in front of the child. "Here you go, baby. Well, her mother shouldn't have said that."

"You're telling me," Ruby quipped. Charlie bit the inside of her cheek to keep from laughing at the precocious girl. That child definitely had being a Payne down. One day it would get her in trouble.

Ruby grabbed the bottle of syrup on the table and upended it. Jen turned her back for just a second to put another piece of French toast into the pan.

"Whoa." Charlie stepped in quickly and gently took the bottle out of the girl's hands before she emptied it onto her plate. "I think you're good on the syrup, Rubes. Unless you're planning on swimming in it later."

Jen glanced back at her daughter and sighed. "Ruby."

Ruby pulled a piece of drenched bacon from the plate and popped it in her mouth, not seeming to care about the disapproving adults. Sticky syrup dribbled down her chin. Charlie grabbed a paper towel, wet it in the sink with some warm water and handed it to the girl.

"Wipe," Charlie said.

Ruby stuck her tongue out, trying to lick the sweet stickiness from her chin, but couldn't get it all. She looked up at Charlie sheepishly and did as she was told.

"Thanks," Jen said.

Charlie shrugged and sidled up next to her cousin by the stove. "Hey, it takes a village. Where's Jack?"

"He's having breakfast with one of his fishing buddies this morning, and then they're gonna go out in his friend's new boat."

"Smells good." Charlie grabbed a piece of bacon

from the plate and chomped on it. "Can I have a piece?"

"Of course," Jen said. "Get a plate, this one's yours."

Charlie opened the cabinet and pulled out two plates, one for her and one for Jen. She watched as Jen plopped two pieces of golden brown French toast on the plate and topped it with a couple of slices of bacon.

"Here ya go," Jen said in a chipper tone. Charlie marveled at her cousin's ability to be so positive most of the time. Sometimes Charlie was sure she'd walk into the kitchen and find her cousin dancing around, singing to a bunch of little animated forest animals and birds, like she was Snow White. Charlie took a seat next to Ruby and poured a drizzle of syrup over her French toast. Jen served herself and sat across the table from Charlie.

"Did you sleep okay?" Jen asked, dousing her toast in syrup. Charlie smiled. Like mother, like daughter.

"So-so." Charlie cut into her breakfast and took a bite.

"Bad dreams?" Jen asked before taking a bite of bacon. Charlie gave Ruby a sideways glance. "It's okay. Sometimes Ruby has bad dreams too. Don't you, babe?"

"Uh-huh." Ruby nodded as she chewed.

"Not bad, exactly, I guess. More like weird," Charlie said.

"Can I be excused?" Ruby asked. Jen glanced at her daughter's empty plate.

"May I," Jen corrected.

Ruby sighed. "May I be excused?"

"Yes. You may." Jen smiled. Ruby jumped up, put her plate in the sink, and ran out of the kitchen, her shoes clacking as they went.

"Is she wearing tap shoes?" Charlie asked.

"Yes, she's taking tap lessons at Miss Fancy's."

"Miss Fancy's School of Dance," Charlie said with real nostalgia in her voice. "Is she still alive?"

"She is."

"She was old when we took lessons there," Charlie said, chuckling.

"Well, that's what you get when you make deals with the devil," Jen quipped.

Charlie laughed. "Does she have class this morning?"

Jen shook her head. "Nope." Charlie gave Jen a puzzled look and Jen shrugged. "She likes the sound they make."

Charlie laughed. "Well, let me know when they have a recital. I'd love to come."

"I will make sure you're invited."

"You don't have to work today?"

"I do not," Jen said, sounding happy and sad at the same time. "We hired a weekend manager."

"That's great."

"Yes, it is," Jen agreed between syrup-drenched bites. "This is the first day off I've had in maybe six months."

"Well, you certainly deserve it," Charlie said.

Jen looked up from eating her fork hanging in mid-air. "So, you had weird dreams? Another reaper dream?"

Charlie sighed. "Sort of. It started out about this missing girl's case. But it morphed into a reaper dream. Only this time, he had Scott's face."

"Oh, honey," Jen said. "This one's gotten under your skin, huh?"

"I guess it has. One of the girls told me not to forget them."

"That's horrible—for the girls, I mean."

"I know." Charlie pushed her plate away, not wanting to finish the last few bites of her breakfast. She suddenly wasn't hungry anymore. "I just wish I knew what to do for them."

"Were they, you know—" Jen grimaced.

"Dead? I know at least two of them were. I don't know about the other girls."

Charlie got up and emptied her plate into the trash bin under the sink. She turned on the hot water and gave the plate a soapy swipe with the dish brush before rinsing it and placing it in the drainer on the counter.

"What are you going to do about it? These possible dead girls?"

Charlie turned and faced her cousin, leaning against the counter. "Not much I can do, really."

"You could do as they ask and not forget about them. I mean, you're coming at it from the perspective of somebody who's in law enforcement. Somebody who's looking for a missing child. Maybe you should look at it from their perspective. Maybe they just want someone to care what happened to them."

"I care about them. A lot," Charlie muttered. "Maybe I am thinking about everything too hard from Jason's point of view."

"What d'ya mean?"

"Every time I come up with a lead, I think I can't do this or can't do that because I don't have a probable cause or a warrant."

"But you're not a cop. Would you need those things?"

"Yes and no. I think it's more complicated because I consult for them."

"Would it be complicated for someone like me?"

"No, probably not. Police get evidence like guns and drugs from civilians a lot, and Jason told me once it's almost never suppressed."

"Hmmm." Jen twisted her lips, and she stared off into space for a moment.

Charlie folded her arms across her chest. "What's going through that head of yours?"

"I was just thinking about how I could help."

"What do you have in mind?"

Jen got up and washed her plate, placing it in the drainer behind Charlie's. "Maybe we should drive over there and take a look."

"Look at what? You can't see the girls."

"No, but that doesn't mean I can't help you. If nothing else, I can keep you company."

"I appreciate that."

"I also may have a trick or two up my sleeve, but I'll need to consult the book."

Charlie nodded. It had been years since she'd seen the grimoire that had been passed through her family's women, and that her aunt and cousins kept and consulted. It held their most treasured spells and incantations. Charlie didn't expect there to be much magic that would help her find these girls or know what happened to them, but she'd also learned a long time ago that sometimes the most magical thing a person could do was to have faith in the people she loved.

CHAPTER 16

On Monday afternoon, Jason stared at Emma Winston through the two-way mirror of interrogation room 2. She sat at the table in the middle of the room facing him but didn't look up. Instead she stared at her clasped hands, her knuckles white.

"So, tell me again why you think this woman is attached to the Haley Miller case?" Beck asked. He stood next to Jason with his arms across his chest, leaning back. Jason had seen that expression before. A mix of skepticism and curiosity.

"She and Haley went to college together. There were in the same sorority. She was the last person to talk to Haley before she died."

"I thought you interviewed her already?"

"I did, but I've got a few more questions." Jason focused on her. Finally, she glanced up at the mirror.

"She'd be kinda cute if she didn't look like somebody'd hit her in the eyes," Beck said, referring to the dark circles.

"She's a little out of your league." *And possibly a murderer.* But Jason didn't say that out loud. Truth was, he didn't know what she was.

"Well, she sure looks as nervous as a long-tailed cat in a room full of rocking chairs."

"Yeah, well, that's what people look like when they're hiding something."

Beck scowled. "What exactly do you think she's hiding?"

Jason held up a manila folder. "That is what we are about to find out."

He stepped out of the box and headed for the interrogation room.

Emma jumped a little when he threw open the door. She pressed her hand against her chest.

"Sorry about that," Jason said, chuckling. "I didn't mean to scare you."

"Well, you sure have taken your sweet time." She folded her arms across her chest and sat back in her chair, glaring at him. "You said on the phone this wouldn't take long. I've got patients this afternoon."

"Yeah, I apologize for that. It's been busy around here this morning." Jason took a seat in the chair across the table from her. He placed the folder down in front of them.

"So, Dr. Winston, I came across something curious during my investigation of Haley's death."

"Okay. So, it's not an accident?"

"We haven't ruled out anything yet. But I have two different witnesses that said they saw a woman on the roof with Miss Miller the night she died. One of them said she saw the woman push Miss Miller off the roof. Which is consistent with some of our forensic evidence. The way she fell, the distance from the house, that sort of thing."

Emma's hand drifted to her throat and her eyes flitted to the mirror behind Jason. All color drained from her cheeks.

"So, you think she was murdered, then?" Emma asked softly.

"It's possible. But I'm not really here to ask you about that night."

Emma didn't take her eyes off the mirror. "What are you here to ask me about?" Her voice cracked as she spoke.

Jason opened the manila folder and pushed it across the table. "Do you recognize this?"

Emma shifted her gaze to the paper in front of her. "It looks like a missing person's report."

"It is. For a young woman named Brianna Fiorello. A pledge of Mu Theta Chi, right?"

"I—" She played with the diamond heart pendant hanging around her neck. "I don't remember. Maybe."

"You don't remember?" Jason asked.

"No, I don't. This is dated ten years ago. I don't remember every pledge," Emma snapped.

"Not even the ones who you file missing reports for?" Jason said.

"What?" Emma shifted in her chair.

"Yeah." Jason flipped the stapled pages, pointing his finger at the signature field on page two of the report. "See here? Emma J. Winston. That's you, right?"

Emma fixed her gaze on the report. She hesitated before finally answering, "Yes."

"Still don't remember her?" Jason asked.

"Um, vaguely, I guess."

"Why don't you cut the crap and tell me what really happened the night she went missing?"

Emma's fake smile faded. "What does this have to do with Haley?"

"It may have nothing to do with her." He leaned forward with his elbows on the table. Emma breathed in deep and blew it out in a huff.

"You told me Haley fell off her roof."

"No," Jason said, his voice firm. "I told you we were investigating her death, and that we had a witness who saw a woman push her from the roof."

"Well, I didn't do it, if that's what you're implying," Emma snapped.

"Oh, I'm not implying that you killed Haley."

"What are you implying?"

"Nothing at this point. I just need to understand more about Brianna's disappearance."

"Brianna. Why are you asking me about something that happened almost ten years ago, when it's right here in this report?" She pushed the report back toward him.

"It is in the report, but I'd like to hear it from you. If you wouldn't mind."

Emma's nostrils flared as she blew out her breath through her nose. She leveled an angry gaze on him. "Everything you need to know is in that report. The pledges had tasks we gave them to perform. One of them was to go to an old house and get an artifact we had planted there and bring it back."

"So, you're saying that you and Haley didn't take Brianna to this old house and just dump her off as part of the test?"

Emma's eyes tightened and her cheeks and neck reddened. She pressed her lips together into a flat line. "No. Of course not."

Jason opened his mouth to ask his next question, but before he could, Emma jumped as if something had startled her. Her gaze had moved off behind Jason, her eyes widening, staring at the mirror behind him. Jason threw a quick glance over his shoulder. Only the room reflected in the silvered glass. He turned back to her and snapped his fingers in front of her face, making her jump again.

"You okay, Dr. Winston?"

She blinked several times and bristled. She cleared her throat. "I'm fine. Is that all? Can I go?"

"No," he said flatly. He took the report back and read it to her. "You gave the addresses for these houses where you sent the pledges? Is that correct?"

"You know we did. They're right there," she snapped.

"All the addresses?"

"Yes, of course. We were concerned."

"Interestingly, this address doesn't lead to anywhere. It's not real."

"What do you mean?"

"I mean, I looked it up, and it's not an actual address. Are you aware that lying on an official police report is crime? A felony, actually."

Emma narrowed her eyes. "I want a lawyer."

"Okay, fine—although technically you haven't been charged with anything yet." Jason closed the folder and rose to his feet. Emma stared at the mirror again.

"No, wait. Don't leave me here alone." She sat up straight.

"Then answer my questions."

Emma rolled her eyes and scowled. "Fine."

"Were you and Haley the only people who knew about these old abandoned houses where you placed these artifacts?"

"No. We had a pledge committee. They determined the tasks."

"So you and your committee had no problem with hazing, even though it's illegal?"

Emma's mouth pressed into a straight line. "This was not hazing. The tasks were innocent. All the artifacts had historical significance to the sorority. No one was humiliated or threatened."

"But if they didn't complete the tasks then they could be disqualified. Is that correct?"

"No. Not exactly the way it works. If one of the girls had not gone through with it for some reason, maybe they were scared or something, they could do some community service. Because that's what Mu Theta is really all about—serving the community."

Jason smiled. "Sisters forever, right?"

Emma scowled. Her gaze flitted to the mirror and then glanced at the gold watch on her wrist. "I have to go, and unless you're going to charge me with something, I know you can't hold me." Emma rose to her feet and threaded her arm through the handles of her purse. The expensive red leather bag hung from the crook of her elbow, brushing against her hip.

Jason hopped up. "Sit down, Doctor, or I will charge you with obstruction."

Emma's chest heaved with anger. "If you're gonna play it that way, I want my lawyer."

Jason hated playing chicken. In a case like this, he had no reason to hold her. She stepped forward, looking him directly in the eye. It took all he had not to force her to sit her ass down and stay. She still hadn't given him what he needed. "Is there anything you'd like to add to your statement? Maybe a different address. One you forgot."

"No," she said. "I gave the deputy in charge of the case ten years ago all the information I had."

"I'll let Brianna's family know you were so cooperative."

"Brianna's family? What do you mean?"

"Well, sometimes on missing person's cases, especially old cases like this one, every once in a while, the family will call us just to make sure nobody's forgotten about their loved one. We periodically go through cold cases too. This one just sort of fell into my lap because of the Haley Miller case."

"Well," Emma's cheeks flushed pink. "If you talk to Brianna's mother, please send her my best. Let her know that she's still in the thoughts and prayers of the Mu Thetas."

Jason gave her a pointed look, his tone dry

enough to peel varnish from wood. "I'm sure that will bring her great comfort."

"Is that all, Deputy?" Emma scowled.

"It is. For now." He stepped out of her way. Emma marched past him, without a second glance at the mirror.

Jason bent over the table and put the report back into the folder before thumbing it closed. A chill skittered down his spine, and for a moment he felt like someone was watching him. He scowled at Beck. Slowly he looked up at the mirror ready to sneer at his partner. The sight of the young woman standing in the mirror staring back at him made him drop the folder and take a step back.

Her dark wavy hair was full of pine needles and dirt. Her white T-shirt was soaked with blood. His breath caught in his throat, and his heart hammered in his ears. He didn't blink and couldn't look away. My god, was this how Charlie felt every time she confronted a spirit? And why was it he could see her? He opened his mouth to speak and the door opened. Jason glanced away.

"Well, you just gonna stand there all day or you want to get some lunch?" Beck said. Jason looked from his partner back to the mirror. She was gone.

"No," Jason blew out a breath. "Come on. You're buying."

* * *

"Now, I know why you like to come here so often." Beck looked over the top of his menu toward the lunch counter where Jen Holloway stood talking to a customer. She wore jeans and a blue floral blouse. Wrapped around her waist was a green apron. "Who's that hot little number at the counter? I wouldn't mind cooling my bread on her rack."

"Jesus, you are such a pig." Jason made a disgusted sound in his throat. "That's Charlie's cousin. You mind your manners. She's a nice lady. And she has a kid. Not exactly your type."

Beck closed his menu and laid it on the table. "Eventually all the women your own age will have kids. That's why I only date twenty-five-year-olds."

"Right, like any twenty-five-year-old would touch you with a ten-foot pole," Jason scoffed.

"Well, hey there, Jason," Jen said as she approached the table. God, he hoped she had heard none of their conversation. A wide smile crossed her lips, and her large blue eyes sparkled. Beck was not wrong. Jen definitely was a looker.

"Hey, Jen," Jason shifted in his seat. "Good to see you."

"Good to see you too. What can I get for you guys?"

"I'm gonna have your special today," Jason said, handing her the menu. She tucked it under one arm.

Beck looked her up and down. "You wouldn't happen to be part of the special today, would you?"

Jen laughed and her cheeks reddened. "No, sir, but thanks for asking. I will let my five-year-old know that her mother's still got it."

Jason glared at Beck. "Gimme a break, man."

"No, it's all right, Jason. I can take care of myself. What's your name?"

"Beck. Marshall Beck. I'm a lieutenant with the sheriff's department."

"I see. That's all the information I need. That and —" she leaned in close "—you have a little something on your shoulder there, Lieutenant." She pinched a clump of hair between her thumb and forefinger. "Oh. Looks like you're losing your hair." She made a tsking sound. "You know, you should see my cousin Daphne. She's the owner of the salon down the street and she can do wonders on thinning hair. Make you look ten years younger."

"Uh." Beck reached for his scalp, pulling out another clump of hair. "What the hell?"

Jen wiped her hand on her apron, and Jason saw her slip the hair into the pocket. "Now, what can I get you today, Lieutenant Beck?"

Beck scratched through his scalp. "I'll have what he's having," Beck mumbled and got up from the table, heading toward the bathroom. "I'll be right back."

Jen bit her bottom lip, fighting a smile. "Good choice," she mumbled and wrote down his order. She picked up his menu and tucked it under her arm. "I know you want tea. Do you think your friend does too?"

"Sure," Jason said, watching her carefully. He opened his mouth to ask her what she knew about his partner's sudden hair loss but thought better of it. He didn't really want to know. Jen headed back to the counter, and Jason got up and followed her, watching curiously as she pulled a napkin from a holder on the counter and pulled Beck's hairs from her apron. She folded the hair into the napkin and put in the front pocket of her jeans.

"Are you collecting hair these days?" Jason asked.

Jen flashed him a smile. "As a matter fact, I am. I use it to cast my voodoo spells."

Jason laughed, but it felt cold and brittle. He liked Jen and her sister Lisa a lot, but sometimes they could be just downright strange, and he wasn't sure if she were joking with him or being for real.

"I guess I should be glad it wasn't me, huh?"

"Yes, you should." Jen stood on her tip-toes and put the ticket on the wheel at the pass-through window and spun it. "Order up!"

Jason took a seat at the counter and leaned

forward. "Hey, Jen, you mind if I ask you a question?"

Jen put herself right in front of him and leaned forward on her elbows. She smiled widely. "You just did." She chuckled. "No I don't mind. What's going on?"

"Well, I had something strange happen today. And I tried to call Charlie, but I think she's working so—"

"So, you just thought you'd ask me. Being her nearest relation and all." Her tone was light and jokey, but there was something darker beneath it. "You know, I don't see what she sees."

"I know," he said. "But you've been around the sort of thing she can see before." He didn't really want to come right out and say it in the middle of her bustling restaurant. *Hey, I think I saw a ghost today. How do I know for sure?* No, that was not what he wanted to say out loud.

"I have been around Charlie my entire life and I have sensed my share of unusual things," Jen said.

"I can't really go into the specifics too much, but I had a weird thing happen during an interview today, actually it was after the interview."

"All right," Jen said, the lightness gone from her tone. Her usually sparkling eyes darkened. "What did you see?"

"I think I saw—" How did he put this delicately?

"I think I saw something that Charlie would normally see. But that doesn't make any sense to me, because to put it bluntly, I'm totally *not* sensitive, if you know what I mean."

"I know what you mean." Jen nodded. "Do you still have that pendant I gave you? The one I made you wear that night at your mother's house?"

"Yeah. It's at my house."

"You need to find it, put it on, and wear it. It will protect you." Her gentle voice was soft but intense. "You also need to buy some salt."

Jason laughed. "Any particular brand?"

"Nope. It's all the same. I want you to pour it in front of your doors and windows and mirrors. The salt is a deterrent for the thing you saw. It can't cross a line of salt."

Jason straightened in his seat, an uneasiness settling into his belly. "You're serious."

"I am."

"You're kinda freaking me out."

She cocked her head. "Did you really expect anything else from a conversation of this nature?"

"Well, I was kind of hoping you'd say 'don't worry about it. I'm sure it was nothing.'"

Jen nodded. "I wish I could say that. Unfortunately, if somebody like you is seeing what Charlie would see, then we're dealing with something dangerous."

He blew out a heavy breath. Why did he feel like she'd just punched him in the gut?

"It's gonna be okay. Just make sure you do what I say and let Charlie know too. She's got tons of experience with these sorts of things. Maybe she could offer you some advice." She smiled, and the shadow lifted from her eyes. "Now, go on. Sit back down, and I'll bring you guys some iced tea."

Jason hesitated a minute before he gave her a brief salute and headed back to the table.

CHAPTER 17

Charlie pushed aside the lacy curtain covering the window of her front door. Jen stood on the little stoop holding a grocery bag in her arms. Her cousin gave her a wide smile and a brief wave. Charlie waved back and quickly opened the door, standing to one side so Jen could enter.

"I probably should have called," Jen said. "But I saw your car in the driveway and thought maybe you'd want to hear about what I discovered."

"Sure. Come on in." Charlie guided them to the small bistro-sized table where she and Evan ate breakfast on the days he stayed with her. "What's in the bag?"

"A craft project." Jen put the bag down on the table. "If you're up for it, that is."

"Sure," Charlie said. She peeked into the paper bag. Inside were skeins of yarn and embroidery thread. "You weren't kidding. You gonna teach me to knit?"

Jen laughed. "No. We're making a spirit trap, and then I will teach you how to use it."

"Okay," she said. "What exactly are we talking about here?"

"A spell," Jen started. Charlie opened her mouth to protest, but Jen cut her off. "Now, before you say anything, it's a very simple spell. Anyone can do it. Even a child."

"Then maybe you should teach it to a child," Charlie teased.

"You're hilarious," Jen said, putting her hands on her hips. "Charlie, you can do this. I know you think you don't have an ounce of magic in you. But basically, with this, the magic will already be in the object. You'll just act as a catalyst and as long as you believe the words, they will work. A tiny seed of faith in yourself and in the spell is all the magic you'll ever need."

Charlie fought the smile trying to emerge. Her cousin's belief in her made her heart swell. "Fine," Charlie relented. "But it's on your head if I blow up something."

Jen laughed. "I promise you're not gonna blow

anything up. Now, come on, we need to go find some sticks."

Charlie gave her cousin a strange look. "What kind of sticks? Like popsicle sticks?"

"Nope. The kind that mother nature made." Jen headed toward the door. She threw a glance over her shoulder. "Well, don't just stand there. It's getting dark."

Charlie quickly caught up with her cousin, and they headed out into the yard. The sun sank low in the sky, grazing the tops of the trees. They walked together across the broad expanse of freshly mown centipede grass. Charlie wore no shoes and the short stiff carpet of grass pressed sharply against her toes and the skin on the sides of her feet.

Jen explained that they needed to find several hardwood tree branches. Pine wouldn't cut it and oak was the best, but hickory or pecan would do too. Her uncle's yard had several large trees meeting the criteria, and they set out toward them.

"Something interesting happened today." Jen ambled and kept her eyes focused on the ground, scanning for twigs that had fallen in the last storm.

"Yeah?" Charlie asked. "Did Dottie get a new tattoo?"

"No, not exactly. Although she got one a couple months back, that was kind of interesting. I'll have to make her show it to you next time you come in. No,

Jason Tate came in with his partner and had lunch today."

"Yes, I'm sure that was interesting. Marshall Beck can be a little much. I hope you put him in his place."

Jen smirked. "Oh, don't you worry about me. The good lieutenant may not be back."

"What did you do?"

"Nothing really." She shrugged. "But he may lose some hair for the next week or two."

"Jen!" Charlie said.

"Don't worry, he won't go bald."

Charlie laughed for a long time. The image of Marshall Beck's hair falling onto his shoulders without explanation made her sides ache.

"That wasn't the strange thing though. Jason was worried about something." Jen stopped dead in her tracks and picked up a twig.

"What?"

"He saw something and he wasn't sure if it was real or not."

"What did he see?" Charlie spotted a branch on the ground from one of the old oak trees scattered across her uncle's property. She picked it up and broke off several of the smaller limbs and handed them to Jen. "Will these do?"

"Those are perfect," Jen said, taking the branches from Charlie. "He didn't say exactly. Talked in Hypotheticals, really. Asked me if I'd ever seen anything the way you see things."

"What d'you mean? Like if you've ever seen a spirit?"

"I think so. But again, he was being vague." She shook her head.

"I'll call him later," Charlie said. "Do you think we have enough? Or do you want more?"

"Let's just get a couple more," Jen said.

Charlie headed toward one of the old oaks covered with silvery beards of Spanish moss. A fine sheen of sweat broke out across her bare shoulders and trickled down her back. The soft fabric of her sundress swayed in the breeze coming off the river and the leaves whispered in the wind. This was her favorite time of day, just before the night swallowed up the land. In the dark shadows of the woods, the cicada had already started to sing, and crickets chirped. The grass thinned beneath the old oak and pine needles crunched beneath the soles of her feet. Charlie found another fallen branch and broke off several of the smaller twig limbs.

"I think that should be plenty," Jen said.

They headed back toward the cottage. A light came on in the kitchen of the main house, glowing warm and yellow in the milky gray twilight. A sense of safety washed through her.

Jen took the twigs and peeled some bark and any

lichen growing on it. "I want it to be as clean as possible," Jen explained. "So, it doesn't snag the yarn or the floss."

"Yeah, I'd also like to keep the bugs out of the house," Charlie chimed in.

Jen chuckled. "That too."

Once the twigs were clean enough, they took them inside and Charlie spread a piece of newspaper across the trunk she used as a coffee table. Jen placed one twig over another to form a square cross and then took a red skein of yarn from the paper bag and tied a tight loop around the twigs where they touched. She crisscrossed the yarn back and forth until it stabilized the twig cross, forming an X with the yarn.

"See?" she said, holding it up. "It's a cross. Now, we're gonna make it a trap." Jen coiled the thread around one arm of the cross, pulled it tight, pushing the yarn close to the center, then wrapped it around the next piece of wood. She continued around the entire cross, several times, until the shape of a yarn square formed. "Now, we just keep expanding it until it forms a nice solid web. Once it's the size we want, we'll tie it off and then I'll teach you a spell that you can say in a spirit's presence so you can trap her."

Charlie picked up the cross and held it in her hands. Bunny had tried to teach her spells when she was a child, and she had always failed miserably. She wasn't sure that Jen would have any better luck. Charlie called up a dubious smile. "Okay. All I can do is try, right?"

* * *

JASON PUT THE BAG DOWN ON THE TABLE NEXT TO HIS front door and walked through the condo, heading straight for his bedroom. He had taken off the small silver pendant Jen had given him several months ago and put it into a carved wooden box that had once belonged to his mother. Charlie had an identical pendant, but she had several stone beads strung on either side of it. She had told him what each stone did, but he couldn't remember what she'd said now. Maybe he should've paid more attention and not been so dismissive.

Something pricked his finger and a sharp pain permeated his fingertip. He drew his hand out of the box. Blood drizzled down his finger, and he stuck it in his mouth, sucking away the pain. A slight metallic taste coated his tongue, and he pulled his hand from his lips. The bleeding had stopped, and he carefully examined the contents of the box. He confronted the culprit—his twenty-five-year-old Boy Scout pen. The brass had gone almost green. He lifted it out and placed it on top of the dresser. He should've gotten rid of the damn thing years ago, but his mother had instilled a bit of sentimentality in him for such things. Finally, the silver pendant glinted in the overhead light. He held it up on the long black silk cord.

A loud thud came from the dark bathroom, drawing his attention. Jason hovered his hand over his firearm holster. He unsnapped the leather strap that held his weapon in place, just in case. The skin on his arms prickled as he slipped into the darkened room. He flipped on the light. The shower curtain rustled, and he unholstered his weapon. With his heart hammering in his throat, he swept the opaque blue curtain aside, half-expecting to find the ghost of Brianna Fiorello standing in his bathtub. Instead, his cat stared up at him with wide green eyes. The tuxedo cat perched over the drain and a bottle of conditioner laid on its side on the floor of the tub next to her.

"Watson? What the hell!" he scolded. "What are you doing in here? You've got a water bowl in the kitchen. Go on, get out of here." It was not the first time he'd had to chase her out of the tub. The cat stood up, stretched her back, and gave him a disdainful glance before jumping over the side of the tub. Jason holstered his gun, feeling stupid. Seriously, what if Brianna Fiorello's ghost had been standing there? What was he going to do, shoot her?

"Good move, Jason," he said aloud. He turned

around and faced the sink. His stomach dropped like a brick of ice. Brianna Fiorello's ghost stood behind him, staring. Her dark eyes were murderous. She gritted her teeth and tightened her jaw. Jason shook his head and slowly glanced over his shoulder. He could not see ghosts. That was Charlie's job. There was no one there. He closed his eyes for a second and took a deep breath before finally looking back to the mirror. Brianna glared at him, her expression full of hate.

"Brianna?" he muttered. "What are you doing here?"

"You stay out of it," she hissed. "Do you understand? Emma is mine."

"Brianna," he started. A banshee's scream issued from her mouth as she charged forward through the mirror. The high-pitched sound drilled into his head and he covered his ears with his hands, dropping the pendant. Brianna scrambled over the sink.

Out of the mirror. How could she come out of the mirror?

Jason pointed the gun at her and stepped backward. His calves connected with the side of the tub and he grabbed for the shower curtain, trying to keep his balance. Something hit him hard and his knees buckled. Pain seared through the back of his head and his vision went gray around the edges. The last thing he saw before everything went black was Brianna's angry face hovering above his, and he felt her icy fingers on his throat.

* * *

An unpleasant fishy scent filled his nostrils, exacerbated by an uneven warm air blowing across his lips. *Tuna?* His eyes fluttered opened. All eleven pounds of Watson—the black and white cat that he'd rescued from behind the dumpster of his building when she was a kitten—sat on his chest. Her legs tensed and her paws pressed hard against his sternum. Her black fur formed a mask over her green eyes. She blinked, long and slow. She purred so loudly it made the ache in his head worse.

"It's okay, girl," he muttered and scratched her behind her ears to put her at ease. Gently, he pushed the cat off him and tried to sit up. Sharp pain shot across the back of his head, down his neck. He took a deep breath and cradled his head in his hands. What the hell had just happened? Jason remembered the feel of Brianna's icy hands on his neck. His heart thudded against his ribs and his gaze shifted to the mirror. The image of her emerging from the glass sent a shiver skittering down his spine. He almost fell on his face as he fought with the torn shower curtain, still clinging by two silver rings to the rod. Finally, he made it to his feet.

The salt.

Not even five minutes later, he poured a long thick line of fine white grains in front of the bathroom mirror. Then he went into the bedroom and took down the mirror hanging on the back of the door. He had to dig out a screwdriver to remove the one attached to his dresser, and his fingers shook the entire time. What if she came back? Finally, the last screw fell to the floor, and he hoisted the heavy-framed glass over his head and took it into the bathroom. He leaned the two mirrors against the wall inside the linen closet attached to the bathroom, lining them up side by side. Then he poured a straight line of salt in front of them and poured another line of salt in front of the threshold of the closet for good measure. He traced his steps backward and found the pendant on the floor behind the toilet. He fastened the black silk cord around his neck and dropped it inside the collar of his shirt.

He pulled his cell from his pocket and quickly found Charlie's number in his recent calls. The phone rang three times before she finally picked up.

"Hey," Charlie said. "Were your ears burning? Jen and I were just talking about you. She told me about your unusual experience."

"Yeah?" His voice shook. "About that—I think I know exactly what happened to Haley."

"How?"

"Brianna Fiorello just attacked me."

"Oh, my god. Are you okay?"

"I'm not hurt—well, not too bad anyway." He ran his fingers through his hair. "I just poured a whole container of salt in front of every mirror I own, though, which is crazy."

"No, it's not," she breathed. "She's dangerous. You stay put. We're coming over."

Jason sighed and pinched the bridge of his nose, squeezing his eyes shut. He leaned against the wall of his foyer and slowly slid down until his butt finally hit the cold tile floor. "How am I seeing these things, Charlie?"

"We'll talk about it when we get there, okay?" Charlie said.

"I don't know what to do," he whispered.

"I know, but we do. She's a powerful spirit. One of the strongest I've ever encountered. But it doesn't mean we can't stop her. Jen and I will be there in half an hour tops. We'll cleanse the house and make sure you're protected."

Watson pushed her head against Jason's elbow and meowed. "Okay," Jason said. "Good."

* * *

THIRTY MINUTES LATER, CHARLIE BANGED ON THE DOOR.

When Jason opened it, Charlie and her three cousins filed into the tiny foyer of his condo.

"Well, I didn't expect the entire clan," Jason said. "I'm surprised you didn't bring Jack and Evangeline too."

"Now, you know very well that Uncle Jack doesn't do this sort of thing, and Evangeline's working tonight. Otherwise, she'd probably be here too. She thinks the world of you," Charlie said.

Jason's cheeks heated from her gentle rebuke. He laughed nervously. "All right, then." He raised his hands in surrender. "Let the cleansing begin."

* * *

JASON FOLLOWED THE FOUR WOMEN INTO HIS LIVING room and watched curiously as they formed a circle. Lisa's strawberry blonde hair was still coiled and pinned against the back of her head, and her pale gray skirt hugged her slim hips. She looked like she'd just come home from work and hadn't had time to change. Charlie was more casual, dressed in a pink sundress. Daphne had changed her hair color again since he'd seen her last. The tips of her short brown bob were bright pink and matched the short skirt she wore.

"Come on, Jace—" Charlie said, gesturing for him

to stand next to her. He fell into the circle and joined hands with her and Jen.

"Blessings be upon us now as we cleanse this place of all those above and below who would do harm," Jen said. "So, mote it be."

"So, mote it be," Charlie and the other two women echoed.

Jen opened her eyes. "So, we all have our assignments?"

"Let's do this," Daphne said, sounding gung ho. They dropped hands and paired up. Jen and Daphne took the downstairs and Charlie and Lisa the upstairs. Jen lit a bundle of ash colored sage and moved through each room, swirling the smoke around. Daphne placed small polished black stones in every corner of every room.

"Those won't stay put," Jason warned. "Soon as Watson finds them, she'll think they're toys and bat them around."

"Don't worry about it," Daphne flashed him a smile and pushed her pink-tipped hair behind one ear. The cat rubbed against Daphne's leg and she bent over and gave her a good rubbing behind the ears. "You're not even going to see these, are you, girl?" Watson closed her eyes and purred loudly.

"Trust me, she'll see them. She's extremely curious," Jason countered.

Daphne leveled her gaze on him and smiled, her

hazel eyes boring into him. "Trust *me*, when I say she won't."

Jason's arms broke into goose bumps. Just one gaze from these usually congenial women could set him on edge.

The word witch danced on the tip of his tongue. But weren't witches just something in fairy tales? The other word that came to mind was powerful, but it did not quite seem to fit either, although they *were* powerful. They knew things more easily than others without a lot of information. Charlie constantly told him they can't do what she does and that she couldn't do what they did, whatever that meant. He crossed his arms, thankful when Daphne shifted her attention back to her work. Jen and Daphne moved on to a different part of the house, and Lisa went from window to window pouring a line of salt in front of each one, then placed what looked like ash on top of it.

"Should I even ask?" he said. He liked Lisa. She was tough and shot straight from the hip.

She offered him a conciliatory smile and patted his arm as she passed him. "Nope. You don't want to know. Don't worry about the mess, we'll clean it up once the danger's passed. Although you may have to re-do some of it, if your cat sits in the windows."

"Great," he said, his tone full of sarcasm.

Finally, when they finished, the four women

joined him in the living room. He sat in the leather recliner that faced the room entrance. Charlie was the last one in, and she walked straight over to them and stooped down in front of him. Jason sat up straight, shifting a little.

"What?" he said.

"Where did she hit you?" Charlie asked. "You said she touched you. Where?"

Jason's gaze flitted from face to face. All of them stood around Charlie with their arms crossed, staring down at him. Jason scowled. "For crying out loud, ladies, have a seat. You're making me nervous."

Daphne and Lisa took a seat on the couch, and Jen stooped down next to Charlie. Gently, she placed a hand on top of Jason's.

"Sorry about that. But we need to know how she entered you. Where she touched you."

Jason looked from Charlie to Jen and back to Charlie before blowing out a heavy breath. "She charged out of the mirror and hit me on the chest. I —" he cleared his throat. "I felt her fingers on my neck. I couldn't breathe."

Jen gave Charlie a knowing look.

"What?" Jason snapped. "At least she didn't kill me."

"No, she didn't—this time—but it doesn't mean she won't try again," Charlie said softly. Jen reached inside her pocket and pulled out a black stone wrapped in silver wire and attached to a piece of leather. She took Jason's hand and wrapped the leather bracelet around his wrist, binding it in place.

"What's this?" he asked.

"It's black tourmaline," Jen said. "It'll protect you against negative energy and any more psychic attacks."

"Psychic attacks?" Jason rubbed the center of his chest. "It felt real. This is not all in my head."

"Nobody said it was." Lisa leaned forward, her hands clasped together, her elbows resting on her knees. "She can get to you physically and mentally. That's what the stone protects you against. I didn't have time to stop and get a dream catcher from my house. Charlie, I'll get it to you, then you can give it to him."

"I didn't think about that either," Jen muttered softly. "Dammit."

Jason laughed. "Okay, I think that's enough. I'm fine with the salt and the stones, and I appreciate your concern. I really do. But I'm drawing the line at a dreamcatcher."

"That's your choice," Lisa said. "But don't think she can't still get to you in your dreams."

"Well, isn't that what this is for?" He held up his arm with the bracelet now attached.

"It'll help," Jen said. "And it's powerful, but it's not foolproof. She's already proven that she's strong enough to make her presence known to someone like you."

"She's gonna kill Emma." Charlie leveled her gaze on him. "We need to do whatever we can to stop that from happening."

"Agreed," Jason said. "But she's adamant that nothing's going on with her. How do we make her let us help her?"

"We go after the source," Charlie said. A chorus of yep and she's right, came from Jen, Lisa, and Daphne.

"How?"

Charlie sighed. "We find Brianna and we trap her."

"Okay, great. How do we do that?" Jason asked.

"Don't worry about that," Jen said. "We've got the trap handled."

"Great, how do we keep Emma safe till then?"

"I'll talk to her," Charlie said. "We're gonna have to find Brianna's body, and Emma's the only one who knows where it is."

"No offense, but she's not admitting anything, and she doesn't even believe in you," he said. "I'm not sure what good talking to her will do."

"I have to at least try," Charlie said.

"How do you know Brianna won't kill her before you can convince her?" Jason asked.

"That's easy." Charlie sighed. "I think Brianna's having too much fun torturing her."

"That's messed up," Jason muttered.

"Yep." Charlie nodded. "You know, when I was a little kid, my father used to tell me that people turned into angels when they died, but in my experience, people's souls don't transform into angels. At least not the ones still stuck here on earth."

"What do you think they turn into?" Jason asked.

Charlie shrugged. "Sometimes, they become so consumed by their last emotions that they turn into monsters."

Jason's cheeks went numb, and he sat back in his chair. He'd become a cop to fight the bad guys and monsters of the world. He wrapped his hand around his wrist and centered his palm over the stone Jen had strapped to him. "How the hell do we fight that?"

Jen offered a comforting smile. "With a little magic and a lot of faith."

CHAPTER 18

Charlie picked up a file folder from her desk and fanned herself with it. She hung up with her last customer and let her phone go into a not ready code. A little twinge behind her eye threatened to turn into something worse, and she reached for her purse inside the file drawer. She searched around blindly until she found what felt like the right bottle. When she was sure she had the right bottle, she shook two caplets into her palm.

"Another headache?" her coworker Brian asked.

She nodded and washed down the two caplets with some water from the large cup on her desk. "I think I need to get my eyes checked. They've been achy lately."

"Yeah, that's what happens when you get old," he teased.

"Watch it, buddy. You're not that far behind me." She swept her gaze across the call center, stretching her neck right and then left. A man materialized right in front of her and she froze. She looked right and then left with her eyes. Had anyone else seen him or was he—"Charlie?"

She scrutinized him and her heart leaped into her throat. Scott. It was Scott. He was only four feet away from her and he looked around, confusion on his face. Finally, his gaze met hers and he smiled wide like he was happy to see her. It had been a years since she'd seen him smile at her that way.

"Charlie! Oh, my god. How did I get here? What's happening?" Scott took a step forward and moved right into the desk.

"Oh, god," Charlie muttered. Dread coiled around her heart and squeezed hard. As much as she hated Scott, especially right now with their custody issues, she had never once wished him dead. And that's what he must be, wasn't it? Dead.

Scott looked down, shock marring his pale face when he realized he was now part of the desk. The computers buzzed and flickered.

"Charlie? What's happening to me?"

"Scott—" The back of her throat tightened, and she couldn't get the words out.

Scott took a deep breath, his chest expanding. "My god," he muttered. "This is amazing. So amazing. It's like you see everything and know—everything." He raised his face and closed his eyes, as if he were basking in sunlight. "It's so bright."

Charlie glanced at her coworker, not wanting to panic him, and not wanting to speak out loud to Scott, but she had so many questions for him. Like what had happened? Why was he here? A shadow filled her peripheral vision and Charlie brought her gaze back to Scott. The reaper loomed up behind him. Scott jolted and opened his eyes when the creature put his hand on Scott's shoulder. Scott slowly glanced down at the bony fingers, terror marring the lines of his face. "Charlie? What's happening?"

Charlie screamed as the reaper dug his fingers into Scott and raised the scythe in his hand. She jumped to her feet. The scream building in her chest died on her lips.

The reaper disappeared, taking Scott with him. Dizziness swirled through Charlie's brain, and the world around her grayed at the edges just as her body struck the floor.

* * *

"I WISH YOU'D LET ME CALL FOR AN EMT." JOAN, THE manager of the call center, handed Charlie a cup of water. Charlie took it and sipped the cool, tasteless liquid. When she'd come to, Joan had insisted she come to her office. It was bigger than the supervisors' offices and had a window overlooking a green lawn and a cement path that led to a walking trail.

"I am so sorry I disrupted the call center," Charlie said for the hundredth time. "I'm fine, really. Please don't."

"All right. If you're sure," Joan said.

Charlie nodded. She fidgeted in her chair and looked at the phone on Joan's desk.

Joan turned her head, following Charlie's gaze. "You keep looking at that phone almost like you're expecting a call."

"I… um," Charlie started. What was she supposed to say? Why, yes, Joan, I'm expecting someone to call me and tell me that my ex-husband is dead. How do I know he's dead? Because his ghost visited me out there on the call center floor. Yeah, that would go over well.

"Charlie." Joan paused, and Charlie could almost feel the question coming. "I don't know how to ask this without sounding, well…"

Joan hesitated and shifted her legs. Her fingers fiddled with her hair before finally pushing the long silver strands behind one ear. She looked Charlie squarely in the face. "Does this have anything to do with that thing they talk about?"

"I'm not sure what you mean. What thing?"

Joan frowned and wrinkles around her lips deepened. "You know." She didn't finish her thought. Aloud.

Charlie fought the inexplicable urge to laugh. She knew people talked about her. Sometimes, they stopped talking when she entered the break room or when she passed people talking in the hall.

Charlie took a deep breath. She really didn't have time for this. "I'm not sure what *they* say about me. I'm not even sure who *they* are."

"Nothing, really, it doesn't matter. Are you going to be all right?"

"Yes. I'm fine." The phone on Joan's desk rang, and she gave Charlie an apologetic look. "I just need to take this. Sorry."

"Sure." Charlie leaned forward in her chair and put her elbows on her knees.

Joan reached for the phone on her desk. "Yes? Of course, put her through." Joan cast a glance at Charlie. "Hello? Yes. Yes, she is. Can you hold just a moment?" She smiled and held the receiver away from her ear. "Charlie, it's for you."

Charlie straightened up in her chair, and her heart leaped into her throat. Her hand shook a little as she took the dull black handset from Joan and put it to her ear. "Hello?"

"Mom?"

The fear in her son's voice sent a chill through her. Oh, god. What if Evan had been with Scott when he died? Charlie choked out the words, "Baby, what is it? Are you all right? Are you hurt?"

"They just took dad away in an ambulance."

"Is Miss Cora there with you?"

"Uh-huh." Evan sobbed.

"It's gonna be okay, Evan. I'm gonna come get you. Can I speak to Cora?" A shuffling noise came from the other end of the line.

"Ms. Payne, this is Cora," her warm voice soothed. "I just want you to know Evan is safe. Mr. Scott's been taken to the hospital."

"What happened?" Charlie closed her eyes and listened carefully. Images flooded her mind as the woman told her what she knew.

"Well, he came home early, complaining of some pain in his left shoulder. I told him he should go rest, but he went for a run. Twenty minutes later, Evan comes screaming into the kitchen that his dad is dying on the driveway. I called 911, and they came right away."

"Thank you, Cora. Thank you so much for being there for Evan. I'm gonna come get him and take him home with me. All right?"

"Yes, ma'am," Cora said. Charlie was grateful the housekeeper didn't argue. "I think that's a good idea. You should prob'ly know that I called Mr. Todd too."

Charlie tightened her jaw. "That's fine. Don't worry about it."

"I just wanted to make sure you knew, in case he got mad about you taking Evan with you."

"Don't you worry, I can handle Todd." Charlie suppressed the urge to spit after saying his name. She'd had a contentious relationship with Scott's brother for most of her marriage, and it had only gotten worse since the divorce. Todd Carver never believed Charlie was good enough to be part of his family because she didn't come from old money—or any money, for that matter.

"Yes, ma'am."

"If you could pack Evan a bag and make sure he has everything he needs for school, I'd really appreciate it."

"Yes, ma'am."

They said their goodbyes, and Charlie looked up to find Joan watching her intently.

"Everything all right?" Joan asked warily.

"No. My husb—my ex-husband was just taken to the hospital with chest pain, apparently. I need to go pick up my son."

"Oh, my gosh, of course," Joan said, her voice full of concern. "I'll let your supervisor know."

"Thanks." Charlie rose from her seat.

"Call me and let me know if there's anything we can do."

Charlie ducked into the call center through the back entrance and quickly gathered her things without a word. If they took Scott in an ambulance to the hospital, that meant he was alive—at least for the time being.

* * *

Charlie sat next to Scott's bed holding his hand, ignoring the old man in the hospital gown sitting in the chair in the corner watching them. When had he died and how long had he been hanging out in this room?

"He'll be okay," the old man said. Charlie shifted her gaze back to him. "I hate to see such a pretty girl like you worry."

Charlie bit the inside of her cheek. If she revealed she could see him, he might not leave her alone, or worse, he might raise the flag for any other spirits wandering the hall who wanted her to pass along a message to those left behind. She blinked.

"Did you hear me?" The spirit sounded astonished. He sat up and his gown raised higher on his thighs. Too high. Charlie blinked and shifted her focus back to Scott. She really didn't need to see an old ghost man's junk today. Scott's pale, wan body had tubes running into his arm and electrodes disappearing into his gown. When asked if she was family, she'd lied and told them she was his wife. It was stupid, but it got her into the ICU ward.

His eyes fluttered and his hand tightened around her fingers. He reached with his free hand, touching the cannula resting just below his nose.

"Hi," she said, placing her other hand over the top of his. "I was thinking I might miss you."

"Miss me?" he said, his voice scratchy. "Water?"

Charlie stood up and fetched some ice chips from the nearby nurse's station. There were actual doors in the cardiac ICU, but they were not closed for the most part.

Charlie spooned some ice into his mouth, and he closed his eyes and wrinkled his brow. "What happened to me?"

"You had a pulmonary embolism. The doctors think it's because of the fall you took off your bike last week. Something about it causing a blood clot."

Scott's eyes widened, and his gaze fixed on her. "I saw you," he whispered. "God, it was so real. You had on headphones and you stood up and stared at me." He swallowed hard, but the words still sounded like he'd pulled them across a rasp. "It was probably just a dream. Neurons dying, maybe."

Charlie poked the spoon into the cup of ice. She didn't want to look at him. What if he opened his eyes and saw the truth? That some part of her wanted him to acknowledge that he'd been dead. If only for a few minutes. And he'd seen her, and she had seen him. Charlie's heart sank to her belly, an icy rock of disappointment. "Yes, a terrible dream."

"Evan found me."

"I know. He's pretty shaken up. I don't want to start a fight, but I'm taking him with me until you're better."

Scott sighed and reached for her hand. "No. I think that's a good idea."

"You do?"

"He should be with you. I'm sure it was terrifying to see me that way."

"Yes, I'm sure it was." Tears stung the back of her throat and clouded her eyes.

"You'll take care of him, won't you?"

"Of course."

"You're a good mother, Charlie."

She sniffled and laughed. "I wish I had a recording of that."

"I've never questioned your skills as a mother."

Charlie brushed the hair off his forehead and leaned over, giving him a kiss. "Thank you. You have no idea how much that means to me."

"What is she doing here?" A familiar voice came from behind her. Charlie turned just in time to see the disdainful glare of Scott's older brother Todd. He shared Scott's chestnut colored hair, hazel-green eyes, and sharp angles of his face. He still wore his white coat and his I.D. badge with his photo and his title, Dr. Todd Carver. He pressed his thin lips into a straight line. "Nurse!" His voice was too loud, and the nurse scurried over, shushing him as she approached.

"Doctor, you're going to have to keep your voice down."

"This woman should not be here. She is no relation to my brother."

"Todd," Scott said weakly. "Shut up."

The nurse glared at Todd and then shifted her gaze to Charlie. "Ma'am, if you're not family…"

"It's fine." Charlie picked up her purse and slung the strap across her body. She patted Scott on the upper arm gently. "I'll be back tomorrow."

"No, you won't." Todd put his hands on his hips. He meant business. He aimed his comments to the nurse. "No, she won't."

"Todd, shut up." Scott raised his voice and winced.

"See what you did?" Todd gestured toward his brother. "As usual, you're causing him more pain."

"I'm leaving, Todd. There's really no need to be such a dick about it," Charlie said.

Todd made an indignant sound in the back of his throat and glanced at the nurse. She raised her eyebrows, but her lips twitched at the corners, fighting against a grin.

"I'll see you later, Scott. Don't let him give you too much grief." Charlie directed her words to the nurse.

The nurse smiled at her. "Oh, don't you worry, honey. I won't have any problems throwing him out. Even if he is a doctor."

Charlie gave her a quick nod and patted her on the shoulder. "You take care of him, okay? He's the father of my son, and boys always need their father."

"We will do our best," the nurse said.

* * *

CHARLIE FOUND EVAN IN THE WAITING ROOM PLAYING A game with Lisa.

Lisa stood up as Charlie approached. "I saw Todd. I hope he didn't give you too much crap."

Charlie folded her arms across her chest. "Did he say anything to you?"

"He knows better. I think he's scared of me." Lisa sounded almost proud.

Charlie's lip twisted into a half grin. Evan tucked the game into his backpack and stood up. "Can I see Dad?"

Charlie brushed her fingers through Evan's soft blond hair. "Not today, sweetie. I'm sorry, but you have to be thirteen or older to go in. They'll probably move him out of ICU in a few days, and when they do, I'll bring you to see him, okay?"

Evan nodded. His rounded cheeks had thinned over the summer, and like his father, his jaw and chin were becoming sharper and more angular. He was the perfect mix of them. He had her blond hair and blue eyes and Scott's chin.

"Okay," he said. "He'll be okay, right?"

"Of course, he will." Charlie pulled her son into her arms and held him close, gently stroking his hair. He wrapped his arms around her waist and hugged her tight. "We'll talk about what happened when we get home. Okay?"

Evan nodded. He let her go and shifted his gaze to her face. "I'm hungry. Can we get some food now?"

"Sure. We'll stop someplace and get dinner, then run by your house and grab your things. You're gonna stay with me for a while."

"Really?" Evan said.

"Really."

"Do I have to take the medicine when I'm with you?"

Charlie gave him a weak smile. "We can talk about it when we get home. Okay?"

Evan frowned. "Okay."

"Come on, let's get out of here before the spirits figure out I'm here," she said.

* * *

Charlie peeked around the corner into the dining room where Evan and Ruby were playing Chutes and Ladders. Jen stood at the sink washing up the last of the supper dishes. Charlie took the damp dish towel from her shoulder and picked up a dish, drying it thoroughly before placing it inside the cabinet in front of her.

"Well, I'm glad he let you take Evan. Who knows, maybe this whole thing will soften him up a little," Jen said.

"I love your optimism. But I know Scott, and he's not gonna go down without a fight."

"You never know." Jen stopped mid-swipe, with a soapy plate in one hand. "Traumatic events like this change people. Maybe he'll surprise you."

"I would love to be surprised, but I'm not gonna hold my breath."

"Well, just don't discount him yet. He could still come through." Jen finished cleaning the dish, gave it a good rinse, and placed it in the drainer.

Charlie picked up the clean, heavy stainless steel pot resting on the counter and dried it. She placed it on the stove top and moved on to the plate in the drainer.

"You know Mabon's coming up," Jen said. Something in her voice sounded a little strained. "Next month."

"Uh-huh," Charlie nodded and picked up a

partially dry pot lid. She swiped the dish towel over it.

"Lisa and I thought that it'd be great if you joined us."

Charlie stopped drying the pot lid in her hand and met her cousin's gaze. "I'm not a witch."

"I know, but it doesn't mean you couldn't enjoy the ritual. It's more about prayer and community than anything else. You used to go with Bunny."

"And that's exactly how I learned that I don't have a stitch of magic in me."

"There are plenty of pagans who practice Mabon who don't have a stitch of magic."

"I'm not pagan either. Not anymore."

"Well, if you change your mind, we'd love to have you."

"I appreciate that, but with this custody thing, I don't want to give Scott any more ammunition. I already have things stacked against me. I don't need some judge deciding

'Hey y'all, she's a witch. Let's burn her at the stake'."

Jen scoffed. "They don't burn witches anymore."

"Maybe not physically. But it's not the predominant religion in this state. I just—" Charlie threw the towel over her shoulder. "I just don't want to ruin my chances of at least getting joint custody of Evan."

"You know if you want, I could cast a spell…"

"No. Please. Don't do that." Charlie crossed her arms. "I appreciate your intentions, I really do, but I just… don't want to risk anything."

Jen's elfin face pinched with frustration. "Okay. If that's what you want."

"It is."

"Well, you have our support no matter what. You know that."

"I do. And I love you for it."

Jen reached for the towel resting on Charlie's shoulder. She took the red and white linen, folded it, and hung it up on the rack next to the sink. "Well, I've got to get Ruby to bed."

"Yeah, I should get Evan settled too." Charlie picked up her purse, then set it down again. She looked at her cousin squarely.

"Is there any chance you could take tomorrow afternoon off?"

"I think so. I'd have to check with Evangeline. Why?"

"I need to do a little ghost hunting, and I don't want to do it alone."

"Which ghost? The one who attacked Jason?" Jen's voice pitched up, and she bit her bottom lip.

"No. The little girl I told you about. Trini."

"Oh, um," Jen cocked her head. "Lemme call Evangeline. If she says yes, I can definitely help you."

"Great. Any chance your dad could watch Evan after school tomorrow?"

"Of course."

"Great. That's a big help until I can get this childcare thing figured out. I'll call you tomorrow morning and we'll set things up." Charlie slung her purse over her shoulder. "Evan, come on, son. We've got to go."

Evan appeared at the dining room door with his backpack in hand. The two of them set off into the dark to cross the wide expanse of perfectly mowed grass to the little white guest cottage.

CHAPTER 19

"I really appreciate this." Charlie stepped into the foyer of Marla Givens' house and smiled.

"No problem. I'm happy to let you look," Marla Givens said.

"Do you need me to wait for a text again? I was going to run out to the grocery store."

"No. We should be fine. I have my cousin with me. Marla, this is Jen Holloway."

"Hi." Jen gave Marla a reassuring smile.

"All right, then. I'll leave you to it." Marla walked them to the back door. Her thin wan face looked more weathered and tired then anyone her age should have. She drew in a stuttered breath. "If you see my Macey." The woman's glassy gaze locked onto Charlie. "Tell her that her mama loves her, and that it's okay if she wants to go to heaven. She doesn't have to wait anymore."

Charlie placed a gentle hand on Marla's shoulder and gave it a squeeze. "I will definitely tell her you love her if I see her."

Two fat tears spilled onto Marla's cheeks as she called up a melancholy smile. "Thank you. My husband is still holding out hope, you know, but I know she's gone."

Charlie's heart wrenched. "One way or another, I'm gonna find her. And whatever happens, you need to know the truth."

"Thank you," Marla whispered. She sniffed and cleared her throat.

Jen, who stood beside Charlie, stepped forward and wrapped her arms around Marla, giving her a big hug. She didn't say a word—no, it will be okay. No promises she couldn't keep. It was one of the best things about Jen, in Charlie's opinion, she knew when to keep her mouth shut and she understood that real comfort never came from words. Jen's loving presence often pulled people into her orbit. Marla wrapped her arms around Jen and gladly took the hug, choking back a sob. After a minute or two, Charlie put her hand on Jen's back to signal that they needed to go. Jen released the woman but held on tight to her hands.

"Peace be with you," Jen said.

"Thank you," Marla answered, swiping the tears off her cheeks.

Charlie and Jen headed out through the back door across the large backyard to the tall grove of trees. They walked a long time in silence, listening to the sounds of the woods. Birds sang above their heads and squirrels leaped from tree to tree. Charlie constantly scanned the path, looking for some similarity to her dream.

"Maybe it's me," Jen finally said.

"I don't think so."

"Maybe we should get off the path, then. Isn't that what you did in your dream?"

"It is but—" Charlie stopped and faced the thick grove of trees ahead of her. "The woods were different in my dream."

"Maybe it wasn't a real place, then. Maybe it was just symbolic." Jen picked up a stick and broke it in half.

"Symbolic of what?"

"I don't know. Fear. Death. New growth."

"Or maybe a cigar is, you know, just a cigar," Charlie teased.

Jen chuckled. "Maybe. So what do you want to do? Go back? Keep walking?"

Charlie stared into the thicket. "Maybe you're right. Maybe we should get off the path. But we should probably use a marker. The last thing I want to do is get lost out here." She glanced at Jen, who was grinning. "What?"

"Breadcrumbs. Maybe we'll find a candy house."

"Let's hope not. I mean, you're a witch. Do you really want to end up in an oven somewhere?"

Jen laughed out loud. "No, thank you. In this story, I think I'd much rather be Hansel and Gretel than the witch." Jen reached into the messenger bag slung across her body and pulled out a handful of small white stones.

"I don't think we'll be able to see those very well. I mean, they just look like any other rock on the ground."

"Not for long," Jen smiled. She took one rock into her palm, held it tight and closed her eyes. Her lips moved silently, and then she opened her fingers one by one. The milky white quartz glowed with a bright white light, casting back the gloom and shadows of the woods.

"Well, that's one way to leave breadcrumbs," Charlie said. "I guess we don't have to worry about the birds gobbling it up."

"Nope. We also don't have to worry about anybody else coming across it and pocketing it."

"We don't?"

"No. It has a deterring spell on it, so if someone gets too close to it, it will immediately cause them to turn away."

"Wow, will they even know what's going on?" Charlie asked.

"No. They'll get a little prickle on the back of their neck and think, 'I shouldn't go that way.'"

"Cool," Charlie said. Jen foraged around for several sticks. She stuck the first one into the ground and hovered the stone over it. Charlie admired her cousin's handiwork. It looked almost exactly like a torch.

"Come on, let's keep going," Jen said.

* * *

THEY WALKED A LONG TIME, STOPPING EVERY TWENTY-five to fifty feet to put a stick in the ground and hover a glowing stone above it. Charlie could see a clear path leading them back toward the Givens' house. It was slow going, though. Saplings and rough brush grew thick between the trees, making it impossible to pass in a straight line. Sometimes they had to walk perpendicular to their path to get around the obstacles. After much zigzagging, the trees thinned before finally opening into cleared plots of land that looked to be part of a subdivision under construction.

Charlie pulled the map she'd brought from her back and opened it. They followed a dirt road until it turned into a paved road that had a road sign. Charlie quickly found it on the map.

"The Givens' are here." Charlie pointed to another road. "You have a pen?"

Jen dug through her purse and pulled out a purple washable marker. Charlie raised an eyebrow. "What? They're Ruby's."

Charlie put a purple X over the place where the Givens' lived. "This road leads to this road." She followed it with her finger. "It looks like they built this whole subdivision in phases. This area here," Jen said, pointing to the map, "was built in the late-seventies."

"Right. There's a park here." Charlie touched a small patch of green surrounded by nearby streets on the map. "I wonder how long it's been here."

"At least since the late-eighties. Maybe longer."

"How do you know?"

"Well, because I went to elementary school with a girl who lived in this subdivision, I came over here a couple times after school with her." Jen pointed to a neighborhood on the map. "We played in that park."

"Do you remember what year?"

"Oh, well, I must've been ten or eleven, so ninety-three? Ninety-four?"

"That's good. You don't remember anything about kids going missing from this area, do you?"

"Well, when I was fourteen, I remember Brittany Hazel going missing. I think she lived in this area."

"That's great. We can look that up. There were

several girls in my dream. Which makes me think there must be several girls who are dead."

"And you're sure Macey Givens is one of them?"

"Yes. Trini's the real catalyst though. If I could just find her, I think the rest of it would kind of unravel itself."

"Do you want to keep walking? We're not that far from the subdivision where she lived."

"Do you mind?"

"No, of course not." Jen smiled. "Lord knows I could use the exercise."

* * *

JEN AND CHARLIE MADE THEIR WAY PAST THE PLACE where Trini Dolan's house originally stood. A new house had been built in its place, which made sense from what Mrs. Dolan had told her about the house being destroyed in Hurricane Hugo. It was a little salt box style house that didn't fit with the rest of the ranch houses and split levels lining the street. But the yard was trim and well kept, and a bright fall wreath hung on the dark green front door. Charlie pulled the picture of Trini from her backpack and stopped at the end of the driveway of Trini's old house.

"There's blood on that picture," Jen said. "That's a real shame." She took the photo from Charlie's hands and stared at it and looked up at the house catty-cornered to it. "That's the house, isn't it?" Jen asked.

"Yep," Charlie said. "It is. You can see the blood?"

"Yeah. It's just a smudge, but I can see it."

"Jason can't see it. Neither can Ms. Dolan."

"Well, that's good. At least it's not ruined for them," Jen handed the photo back to Charlie. "What do you want to do?"

Charlie tucked the photo back into a pocket inside her backpack. "I want to get into that house."

"Okay. How are we to do that?"

"I think we'll have to kill him with kindness."

* * *

"You want to do what?" Lisa asked, looking at Charlie and Jen as if they had both just suggested that they were going to walk naked down Market Street.

"I told you telling her would be a bad idea." Jen took a seat on a barstool at her sister's breakfast bar. Jen glanced around. "New couch?"

"The only reason that I'm even telling you anything," Charlie said as she stared into Lisa's shocked face, "is because if this does not go well for some reason…"

"Oh, you mean like if he's a psycho killer? You

want to make sure someone knows to come looking for your bodies?" Lisa chimed in.

"I don't think he's a psycho killer, at least not to us," Charlie said.

"What?" Lisa scoffed. "All you have to do is watch any true crime show to know that if you force a psycho killer into a corner, he will kill you! And bury you in his backyard!"

"Or shed, in this case," Charlie said.

"That vein on your forehead is bulging." Jen smirked. Lisa rolled her eyes and scowled.

"I think you should at least tell Jason," Lisa said.

"No, I can't. He hates it when I do this kind of stuff."

"Well, I wonder why?" Lisa said, her tone full of sarcasm.

"Honestly, this case is not one of his big priorities anymore. It's cold. If it weren't for the parents checking in with him as often as they do, I don't think he would even have time to look at it again."

"Well, I don't want to know the details. I'm an officer of the court, and I have a duty to report criminal behavior if I know about it."

"I just need to see if Trini shows up at his house. From there, maybe I can figure something out."

"You're not planning on breaking in, are you? No, wait, don't tell me." Lisa held up her hands. "I don't want to know."

"Just make sure your phone is charged and on," Jen joked. "In case, you know, you need to bail us out of jail or something."

"This is crazy. I mean, how do you know he has anything to do with Trini?"

"Because she was trying to tell me he does." Charlie pulled the picture of Trini sitting on her bike at the end of her driveway from her purse and handed it to Lisa.

"Is that blood?" Lisa's voice rose a half-octave. She brushed her thumb across the dark brown smudge.

"Yeah. It appeared as soon as I picked up the picture. Only it was fresh then."

Lisa blew out a heavy sigh. "I don't like this."

"Fine, you don't like it. Is that going to keep you from bailing us out if we get into trouble?" Jen asked.

Charlie reached into her purse and pulled out missing flyers for four other girls and laid them on the breakfast bar. "All these girls went missing over the last twenty-five years, and that doesn't even count Trini and Macey or the ones who never made it to the Internet."

Lisa picked up a flier.

Her face softened as she stared down at the picture of the smiling girl—Melissa Benton. "Did they all go missing from the same area?"

"Close enough," Jen said. "Show her."

Charlie pulled the map from her purse and laid it out on the counter. Jen had marked the areas where the six girls had gone missing.

"I couldn't find anything in any of the newspaper articles I read online that tied them together," Jen said.

"Well, other than that they were all in my dream," Charlie said.

"That won't exactly hold up in court though. You need physical evidence for this to work."

"I know," Charlie said, "which is why I want to get in that shed."

"I just really don't like this at all," Lisa said, folding her arms and blowing out a deep breath. "It is not just the legal implications I'm talking about. This is seriously dangerous. Do you know how many people own guns in this state?"

"I know," Jen and Charlie said simultaneously. They glanced at each other.

"But if we don't do this, Lisa, he could do it again, and if he does, that blood will be on our hands too," Charlie said.

Lisa's mouth flattened into a straight line. "Fine. But you better call me immediately when you're finished. Jail or no jail."

Charlie grinned. "We wouldn't have it any other way."

***

"I'm only gonna ask this one more time and then I'm not gonna ask again," Jen said.

"You promise?" Charlie gave her cousin a side-eyed grin.

Jen ignored her. "Are you sure you don't want to call Jason just to let him know what you're doing?"

"I'm positive." She cocked her head. "I'd rather ask for forgiveness, not permission, in this case."

Charlie turned into the subdivision and headed toward Kern Street.

"Okay." Jen shifted her gaze to the side window and stared into the bright sunny neighborhood. Her hands held tight to the plain brown box on her lap. The scent of fried chicken permeated the car interior. "I won't ask again."

"Good." Charlie stopped at the stop sign and looked in the rearview mirror. All clear. She pivoted to face her cousin. "Let's go through this one more time."

"Okay."

"We will knock on the door. Tell him we're delivering food. And get ourselves invited in, no matter what it takes."

"Are you sure this man is a senior?"

"Pretty sure. I did some online searching for the address and the last name Hatch and found Henry

James Hatch Jr. Sixty-three years old. I could've paid fifty dollars and gotten his Social Security number if I'd wanted it."

"Ugh," Jen said. "That reminds me. I need to change all my passwords."

"Don't we all."

"I wonder if people call him Henry James?"

"Why does it matter?" Jen asked.

"I don't know, it just seems like seriously deranged killers all have three names."

"First, we don't know that he's a deranged killer. For all we know, he's just some little old man who hates dogs taking a dump in his yard."

"So, he poisoned it?" Jen shook her head, her voice incredulous "Sure, and there's nothing deranged about that."

A horn beeped behind Charlie's car, startling them both.

"All right, all right," Charlie said, putting the car in gear and turning right on to Kern Street. They wound their way down the street, passing little brick ranch houses.

"You know, it really worried me when you first started working with Jason."

"You were?" Charlie smiled. "Why?"

"Don't get me wrong, I like Jason, but he was kind of a jerk at first."

"Yeah, but he's turned out to be a good guy."

"Yeah. He has." Jen's pensive gaze settled on Charlie as she spoke. "I was afraid this work might harden you too much. Make you hate humanity."

"Yeah, well, what's your assessment so far?" Charlie asked.

"So far, so good. Same old Charlie." Jen smiled. "Except for the whole breaking into people's houses thing that is."

Charlie laughed and pulled into the driveway. She put the car in park and took a deep breath. "You ready?"

"As I'll ever be," Jen said. Her hands gripped the box lunch sitting on her lap. She'd scrawled the address across the top. "What happens if he won't take the food?"

"We'll jump off that bridge when we get to it. Come on," Charlie said.

The two women exited the car and headed toward the front porch. Charlie's heart thudded in her throat so hard she was afraid her voice would shake when he finally came to the door. She pressed the button next to the door. They waited for several minutes before ringing it again. Charlie pressed her ear to the door.

"I can hear the TV. He's gotta be in there."

"Should we be worried? I mean, if he really is an old man, what if he's hurt or worse?" Jen asked.

Charlie rapped her knuckles hard on the front

door. A moment later, it swung open. A sour-faced man wearing an oxygen cannula strung over his ears appeared. His thin white hair receded halfway on top of his head, revealing dark brown liver spots. His wild bushy eyebrows reminded Charlie of silver caterpillars she'd seen in one of Evan's science books. Fluffy, but deadly.

"Whatever you're selling, I ain't buying it." He leaned on a walker with four feet that disappeared into cut tennis balls. The cannula just below his nose was attached to a long piece of tubing that disappeared deep into the house. "Now, get out of here before I call the police," he grumbled. He started to slam the door and Charlie stuck her foot into the opening.

"Wait," Charlie said. "We're not selling anything. We're just here to deliver your lunch."

Cautiously he opened the door a little wider, his eyes scanning each of their faces. "I didn't order no food. Now, get out of here."

Charlie refused to move her foot. "Isn't this 1232 Kern Street?"

"Yeah, so?" he challenged.

"That's the address we have." Charlie glanced at Jen. "Isn't that right?"

"Yes." Jen held up the box. She tipped it a little so he could see the top. "We're supposed to deliver this to 1232 Kern Street."

"Why?"

"As part of our senior outreach program at Palmetto Point Methodist Church," Jen said. It amazed Charlie at how smoothly she lied. There wasn't even a tremor in her voice.

"I don't go to the Methodist Church. I don't go to church at all."

"Huh." Jen puckered her mouth. "Well, that's really strange, because this is the address they gave us. They even wrote it on top of the box."

He eyed the box and then glanced up at each of them again. There was a grayness to his skin and lips, and his dark eyes were sunken into thick folds of skin.

"Gimme just a second and I'll call them and see what's going on. Maybe they got the address wrong." Jen handed Charlie the box. She pulled the phone from her pocket and walked away.

"We'll get this all straightened out, sir." Charlie pasted a smile across her face. "I appreciate your patience." He continued to look at the box. Charlie threw a quick glance over her shoulder at her cousin at the bottom of the steps. Jen walked in a circle talking on the phone. Charlie wondered if she was speaking to someone or if was it all just for show. Maybe she had called Lisa.

A few seconds later, she pressed a red circle on

her screen and tucked her phone back into the pocket of her jeans.

"Well," Jen said looking serious, "I'm not sure exactly what happened. They said this is the address, but I told them you didn't want the food. They told me just to throw it away. Which is a real shame because it really smells delicious."

His gaze never left the box and his tongue darted from his mouth, licking his lips. "What is it?"

"Fried chicken, mashed potatoes with gravy, green beans, cornbread and honey butter and for dessert some apple cobbler. Can you tell me where your trashcan is? Do you mind if I just toss it in there?" Jen took the box from Charlie and looked around as if she was looking for the large green bins the county provided.

The man's nose flared a little and Charlie thought he might lose his cannula. She suppressed a smile. Her cousin was good at manipulation. Maybe a little too good.

"Well, let's not go crazy now," he said. "I mean, it has my address on it."

"Oh, I thought you didn't want it," Jen said.

"I never said I didn't want it. I just said I didn't order it," he protested. He took one hand off his cane and held it out. "I'll take it. I don't like to see food wasted like that. Shameful."

"Yes, sir, it is. I will definitely have to let them

know how you feel about that," Jen said. He struggled with the box and his cane, almost spilling it.

"Here." Charlie grabbed him by the elbow, helping him keep his balance, and Jen took the box. "Let us help you. I mean it's what we do."

He eyed them both again, but finally nodded. Charlie walked beside him, and Jen followed closing the door behind them.

The small foyer opened to a small living room. The scent of old age and solitude permeated the air—a mix of decay and mustiness, menthol, and rotting newsprint. The cold stagnant air tasted as if no one had opened a window in years.

Charlie looked over the house trying to remain objective. The grubby, green and brown shag carpeting was threadbare in some places, showing the promise of oak flooring beneath it. Stacks of magazines and newspapers lined the walls and covered every available surface. A new flat-screen television sat in the corner almost directly in front of a dingy, brown recliner. The faux leather had cracked and peeled in places, and someone had made repairs with gray duct tape. The long tubing of his cannula attached to a bottle of oxygen sitting at the base of the chair. A metal tray table held an array of medications within reach.

"Is there another tray table, sir?" Jen looked around.

He grunted and sat down in his chair, wheezing a bit as he pointed to the stand with the three remaining tray tables folded up next to the television.

Jen took one from the rack holding them in place and unfolded it, placing it in front of him. Charlie watched Jen place the box on the tray table, her mind racing. How could they stay long enough for her to get a look around? She eyed the refrigerator through a small hallway.

"Let me get you something to drink." She pointed to the closed door next to the pass through. "Is the kitchen through here?"

He coughed and nodded at the same time. His face turned red, and his wrinkles deepened as he hacked and wheezed. Jen patted him on the back and looked up to Charlie. Jen's blue eyes widened and her usually sunny expression morphed into a be-careful look.

Charlie nodded. She headed into the small kitchen, listening as Jen tried to soothe him. Was this old man—broken and dying now—the monster? Charlie's heart settled at the base of her throat, beating in a hard, steady rhythm—a ticking clock reminding her to work fast.

The almond-colored laminate counters of the kitchen were dingy and stained. The distinct odor of mold and curdled milk permeated the air. Dirty dishes and empty food cans and containers covered most of the countertops. A fly crawled out of an old empty milk container and Charlie's stomach turned. A small dining table covered in more newspapers and used paper plates backed up to the far wall. Next to it another door led to a darkened hallway.

She scanned the dingy, pine cabinets and started with the farthest ones out of sight of the pass through. He couldn't see her with his chair turned toward the television, but she didn't want to take the chance. Adrenaline pumped through her, and she opened and closed the doors quickly, pretending to look for a glass.

There were plenty of dishes and plastic containers stuffed inside. She found coffee cups, mugs, and jelly jar glasses with cartoon characters on them in the cabinet closest to the sink. She glanced through the door at her cousin, who fawned over the old man sitting in his chair. At the back of the kitchen was a door with a paned window. She could see the shed in the backyard. What was in there that Trini wanted her to see so badly?

A blast of cold blew down her back, and she shivered as she looked for the source. Her gaze went to a vent in the ceiling. She held her hand up to it, but only a trickle of cold air filtered across her fingers. The hair on her arms and neck stood up, and she suddenly sensed someone watching her. Slowly Charlie looked over her shoulder, halfway expecting the old man to be standing in the door staring at her. Instead, a girl with familiar red hair and faded blue eyes peeked at her from the hallway. Charlie's breath caught in her throat.

"Trini?" Charlie whispered. The girl didn't say a word but pointed toward a yellowed plastic key-holder in the shape of a house hanging next to the door. The hooks were empty. Where were the keys?

Jen cleared her throat, making Charlie look her way. Jen's eyebrows rose, and she nodded toward the old man. *Hurry-up*, her blue eyes said.

Charlie grabbed one of the jelly jar glasses and headed to the old avocado green fridge. She opened the freezer and pulled out an ice tray. The ice cracked and popped as she twisted the plastic. She dropped a couple cubes into the glass. As she went to put the tray back, something silver caught her eye. Inside the freezer door's shelf sat a jar with no top. She lifted the jar to get a better look at its contents— silver and brass keys. Her chest filled with icy dread. She glanced at the doorway where Trini had stood. The girl was no longer there. Charlie took a deep breath and reached inside. The frozen metal burned her fingertips, but she pulled out the ring with a dozen or more keys dangling from it. Most were too big to be padlock keys, but there were several that could have matched the size. Charlie slipped the keys into her pocket. Quickly, she finished filling the glass with water and headed back into the living room.

"Here you go." Charlie handed him the glass, her voice steady, almost cheerful.

"You gonna be all right here by yourself?" Jen asked. The concern in her voice was real, and Charlie hoped her cousin's empathy wouldn't be wasted if this man turned out to be the monster.

"I'm fine," he said. He didn't look up, instead he speared the green beans with a plastic fork and shoved them in his mouth.

"Is there anything else we can do for you while we're here?" Charlie asked.

He grunted and stopped eating. He looked up at Charlie's face with narrowed eyes full of suspicion. "No. Y'all can see yourselves out now."

Charlie forced a close-lipped smile. "Well, enjoy your lunch."

He grunted again, picked up the fried chicken thigh and dug his yellow-stained teeth into it.

"You have a blessed day, sir," Jen said. "Come on, Charlie. We have other deliveries to make."

Jen inched up to her and looped her arm through Charlie's, giving her a gentle pull toward the door.

Charlie threw one last glance over her shoulder before they left the house. If it had been another person or a different day, maybe she would've felt sorry for him for having to spend every day alone in a house that smelled like rot and mold, surrounded by nothing but junk and newspapers.

It was then she realized Jen was wrong. This work had changed her. Had made her harder. It had just lifted the rosy glasses she used to see people through and exposed the darkness inside. Now, she knew that evil didn't always look the way it did on television or in movies with some maniacal villain. Sometimes it just looked like a sad old man, rotting away in his loneliness.

Once they were out the door and down the steps, Charlie stopped and gulped in deep breaths of clean fall air. "I swear to god, the air in there smelled like death."

"I know. I thought the same thing. I bet he's got mold and dry rot going on. Poor old man. He's got lung cancer."

"Yeah?" Charlie said.

"Yeah. Did you get anything?" Jen asked.

Charlie glanced back at the front window. The old man stood there watching them. A chill skittered across her back, and she headed to the car. "Come on, let's get out of here."

CHAPTER 20

"What happened?" Jen asked for the fourth time. Charlie didn't answer, instead she just kept driving, ignoring the icy keys digging into her hip. "Charlie! Answer me! You're freaking me out."

Charlie slammed on the brakes, jerking them both forward. Jen heaved in air and pressed her hands against her chest. "I'm sorry," Charlie finally said. "Are you all right?"

"I'm fine," Jen said, but her voice sounded strained with fear. "Are you all right?"

"Yeah. I didn't mean to scare you." Her voice shook a little when she spoke. "I took some keys."

"What?" Jen glared at her, incredulous.

"When I was in the kitchen, I found some keys in his freezer." She swallowed hard. "And I stole them."

"Oh, my god," Jen said. "What if he goes looking for them? He's gonna know it was you."

"I know," she whispered.

"Charlie, we should take them back."

"And tell him what? 'Sorry, but are these yours? They seemed to have jumped into my front pocket'? I think he would have me arrested."

"Do you think they're keys to the shed?"

"I don't know." Charlie shook her head. "I'm going to go back tonight and find out."

"Charlie. I don't think I can go with you," Jen said, sounding horrified.

"I'm not asking you to."

"I don't think you should go either. I mean, he's a dying old man."

"I know," Charlie said. "But he killed those girls. I know he did."

"You could be wrong. You've been wrong before."

Charlie pulled the car over onto the side of the road and put it in park before turning to look her cousin in the eye. "I saw Trini. Inside the house."

"Did she tell you definitively this is the man who killed me?" Jen's cheeks reddened.

"No. But she pointed me to the keys. He killed her. I can feel it."

"Maybe it's not him, maybe he has a son or—"

"It's him, Jen. I love your big heart and I know you want to feel sorry for him because he's a broken old man who's dying from cancer and needs oxygen to live, but trust me when I tell you, it's him."

"What are you gonna do?" Jen asked.

"I'm gonna find some evidence. Prove he took Trini and Macey and all those other girls I saw in my dream. I will make sure he pays for it."

"So, you're God now?" Jen said.

"No, I'm not God. But I'm not afraid to make someone pay for their crimes. I'm also not about to let my sympathy for a sick old man stand in the way, especially if he's a murderer. What if it was Ruby? Would you feel differently then?"

Jens eyes widened with shock, as if Charlie had slapped her. She grew quiet for a moment. When she spoke, her voice was flat. "He kills little girls."

"Maybe not now. But, yeah, I believe he has."

"Oh, my god," Jen muttered and covered her mouth with her hand. "I felt sorry for him." Suddenly, she opened her car door and leaned out just in time to be sick.

Charlie rubbed a circle between Jens shoulder blades, offering comfort. Jen wiped her mouth with the back of her hand and sat up. "I'll go with you if you want."

"No. It could be dangerous."

"Are you going to take Jason?"

"No." Charlie met her cousin's steady gaze and did not flinch.

"Then I'm going. End of discussion," Jen said.

"Yes, ma'am," Charlie relented.

"I'll call Lisa, Daphne, and Evangeline and make sure we have a protection spell in place. For us both."

* * *

EVANGELINE TOOK TWO PLAIN COTTON SACHETS FROM the pocket of her sweater. She'd sewn them shut and strung them onto a black silk chord. She slipped a sachet around Charlie's neck first, smiling and meeting her niece's eyes as she did it. Then she did the same for Jen.

Charlie clasped hands with her cousins, Lisa on one side and Daphne on the other. The five women formed a circle in Charlie's small living room. Charlie had left Evan in the care of her uncle and had avoided his questions when Evangeline's little truck pulled in behind Charlie's at the cottage.

"Salt and herbs, nine times nine," Evangeline began, "Guard well these women I love from harm." She closed her eyes, and Charlie watched curiously as Jen, Lisa, and Daphne followed suit.

"Light flows through you. Light reinforces the talismans hanging around your necks. The pentacle of protection. The black tourmaline. The protection herbs."

Charlie felt a warmth begin in her belly. It

stretched in opposite directions, toward her head and feet, until it encompassed her entire body in heat and light.

"Keep them safe as they face the darkness ahead and protect them from those who would inflict harm, both mental and physical," Evangeline said. "So mote it be."

"So, mote it be," Jen, Lisa and Daphne echoed her words in unison.

"So, mote it be," Charlie chimed in last. Not that she didn't believe in the ritual and its power or the talismans hanging around her neck. Even after all these years of taking part in her aunt and cousin's pagan ways, she felt like a fraud. "You're both wearing tourmaline, right?" Evangeline asked.

Charlie nodded and pulled out the necklace with the pentacle pendant and the two black beads strung on either side of it. Jen held up her wrist, showing a leather band with a large black tourmaline wrapped in silver wire fastened to it.

"I still think this is a bad idea." Lisa chewed on her thumbnail.

"Are you sure there's no way we can involve Jason?" Daphne asked.

"No," Charlie said. "My plan is to break into the shed, take some photos and get out. I'm not taking any physical evidence with me."

"You both have some latex gloves, right?" Lisa

asked. "Just in case you have to touch anything?" Jen nodded and pulled two pairs of gloves from her pocket.

"If there's a window," Lisa lowered her voice. "Make any evidence you find visible. It'll be much easier for Jason to get a warrant."

"I'll keep that in mind," Charlie said. "Thanks, Lisa."

"And make sure y'all text us as soon as you're safe," Evangeline said.

"Or as soon as you're arrested," Lisa chimed in, but there was no joking in her voice.

Charlie opened the bag slung across her body holding her wallet and DSLR camera. She checked the battery one last time to make sure it had plenty of juice and double checked that she had inserted a memory card before she flipped the power button off and tucked the camera back into the padded insert.

"You ready?" Jen asked.

Charlie slipped on a black knit hat to cover up her pale blonde hair. "As ready as I'll ever be, I guess."

"Let's do this." Jen said.

* * *

CHARLIE PARKED HER CAR BEHIND A DUMPSTER FILLED with construction waste on a street where there was new construction going on. Then, camouflaged in black clothes, she and Jen walked into the woods that backed up to the row of houses along the cul-de-sac where the old man lived.

They came out of the woods near the center of his next-door neighbor's yard. The moon glowed in the sky, lighting their way, and Charlie had no need for the flashlight yet. They slunk through the darkness together in absolute silence, focused on the goal of getting into the shed, getting their evidence, and getting out as quickly as possible.

Charlie made her way around to the door of the shed. The middle and bottom padlocks were easy to break into and popped right open, but the one at the top was harder to reach. Charlie had to stand on her tiptoes to jiggle the key in the rusty lock.

"Dammit," she muttered. "I should've thought to bring some WD-40. This thing doesn't want to budge."

"Let me see if I've got some," Jen whispered.

"You keep WD-40 in your purse?"

"Yeah." Jen rifled through the bag. "Shoot. I think I lent it to Daphne last time she was having problems with squeaky hinges at the salon."

"Hello?" The small desperate voice of a child called. "Hello? Please help us."

Charlie dropped to flat feet. "Did you hear that?"

Jen stopped digging and looked around. "Hear what?"

Charlie pressed her ear against the door. "Hello?"

"Help! Please help us!"

Adrenaline flooded through her. "Hang in there! We're coming."

"Charlie, shhh." Jen looked around.

Charlie stood up on her tiptoes again, jiggling the key in the lock again, harder this time.

"Careful," Jen scolded in a harsh whisper. "You're gonna break the key off. Just hang on." She went back to digging through her bag. "Here it is." She pulled a small spray can with a straw taped to the side from her bag and handed it to Charlie.

Charlie slipped the straw into the sprayer and directed it into the bottom of the padlock. The acrid chemical smell filled the air and the slick liquid dripped down her fingers. She put the key back in and twisted it a few times. Finally, it moved and popped open. She removed it and pulled the door out just enough for them to slip inside the darkness.

Charlie twisted the flashlight until the beam flashed around the shed. She looked for the child belonging to the voice she'd heard.

Dust and mold stung her nostrils, and the smell of rotting grass and motor oil coated the back of her throat. Charlie sprayed light around the edges of the walls.

"Hello?" she said. The shadows of garden paraphernalia hanging from the walls distorted in the light. She made out a weed whacker, a leaf vacuum and blower, various sized rakes and shovels, a spade, and a post-hole digger. A couple of rusty lawn mower blades hung on a nail by the door. On the floor, there was a large lawn mower with a bag attachment. But there was no sign of a child.

"Does it seem small to you in here?" Jen peered around the room with her own penlight.

Charlie swung her light to each of the four interior walls. "Compared to the outside, yeah, it does." Charlie walked over to a wall holding different types of rakes and shovels. She knocked on the wooden wall. It sounded hollow.

"Help," a small child's voice said. "Please, help me. Please."

Charlie's heart jumped into overdrive, hammering hard against her rib cage and she searched for a way in.

"Hang on, we're coming," Charlie said. "What's your name?"

"Please help me," the child's voice cried again.

"Jen, help me."

"What's going on?"

"Please help me," the voice sounded smaller and more distant.

"Don't you hear that child? Is that an ax over there?" Charlie pointed her flashlight beam at a tool leaning against the wall on the opposite side of the door.

Jen reached down and grabbed the ax by the handle and handed it to Charlie. "Charlie, what is it?"

"I hear a child crying for help."

"Charlie, I don't hear anything," Jen hissed.

"Please don't leave me here, please." The child's words wrenched Charlie's heart.

"Step back from the wall, okay?" Charlie swung the ax before Jen could stop her.

It only took two good swings to rip through the thin plywood. With the third swing the ax got stuck and when she yanked, the tools came crashing to the floor.

"Well, if nobody knew we were here before, they do now," Jen muttered. The wall hung askew just enough to see behind it. The stench of rot hit them both hard, and Charlie dropped the ax and covered her nose with the crook of her elbow.

"Oh god, I'm gonna be sick," Jen said.

Charlie pulled her cell phone out of her back pocket and quickly called Jason. He picked up on the first ring.

"Jason, I need you to come. It's important."

"What's happened? Did you have another encounter with Brianna?"

"No, nothing like that." Charlie closed off the

back of her nose and her voice became nasally. "But I think I found our missing girls."

"What? Where the hell are you?"

"I'll explain everything once you get here, but you need to call your forensic friends. I'm pretty sure there are bodies here."

"You see bodies?"

"Not exactly. But I see blood."

"Real blood or ghost blood?"

"Real blood," Charlie said with irritation. "Jen sees it too."

"Oh, god," Jen moaned nearby. Charlie found her cousin standing over a large cooler on the floor, with her hand over her mouth. All the color had drained from Jen's face.

"Oh, shit," Charlie muttered. "Jason, there's a body in a cooler." She flitted the beam across a row of nearly identical coolers. Her heart dropped into her belly, and she fought the urge to be sick. A flash of metallic blue caught her eye, and she shined the beam toward its source. A dusty girl's bicycle leaned against the back wall in the corner. Charlie recognized the blue, white, and silver plastic streamers hanging from the handles. "Trini Dolan's bike is here too. I also see a couple of scooters and a skateboard."

"Gimme the address, I'm on my way," Jason said.

"What are you doing in my shed?" a harsh voice called. Charlie turned to find the old man holding a pistol in one hand and propping himself up with his cane with the other.

Charlie raised her hands in the air, still holding onto her phone. "Mr. Hatch, we came back to check on you, sir," Charlie lied. "And I heard a child crying. It was coming from this shed."

The man gritted his teeth. "I don't know anything about that. Get out of my shed. Before I call the police."

"You don't have to worry about that." Charlie inched forward. "I've already called them."

"What?" He stepped backward and glanced at the door.

"Yes. I couldn't leave a trapped child here. So, I had to break in and call the police."

"I don't know what you're talking about."

"I think you know exactly what I'm talking about, Henry. I think it's weighing on you. Maybe even killing you. Why don't you put the gun down and we'll talk? Figure this out."

"Not a chance in hell," he said.

* * *

Ten minutes later, Jason arrived with Marshall Beck in tow and enough backup to take out a small army. The police cars lined up all along the cul-de-sac, their lights flashing. The old man was not in view, but Jason knew they were still alive. He'd listened to Charlie and Jen talk to the man in quiet, soothing tones, trying to keep him calm on his phone, trying to keep him from shooting them.

"All right, how do you want to handle this?" Beck fastened his bulletproof vest in place. Jason surveyed the scene.

"We should go up the neighbor's driveway and come around the backside of the shed, see if we can get a look in. Charlie said there's a window."

"Why on earth was she here?" Beck asked.

"From what I overheard, she said she was there to check on him. I guess they had delivered food to him through some sort of outreach. And she heard a child crying. Said it was coming from the shed, so she went to check it out."

"And you buy that?" Beck said.

"Yeah," Jason said flatly. "I do."

Beck narrowed his eyes. "All right," he said. "I'll go instruct these guys. And then we'll head around back to see what we're dealing with."

"Good," Jason said.

They got out of the car, and Jason removed his weapon from its holster and grabbed his flashlight from the center console. A few minutes later, he and Beck quietly made their way alongside the house next door and cut across the side yard around to the shed. He slunk along the outer wall and peeked inside through the window.

Jen's flashlight pointed to the ceiling because she'd raised her hands—giving Jason just enough light to see the scene. The old man propped himself up with a cane and held a gun in the other. Charlie was closer to him than Jen, and she was still talking. Beck signaled for them to keep moving around the perimeter of the shed toward the door.

Jason tilted his head to the opposite direction, where he moved so they could each cover one side of the door.

Jason overheard Charlie say, "Look, the police are here. See the lights? I think you should put the gun down and we should just all go talk to them about this."

"There's nothing to talk about. You're the ones trespassing."

"Why don't we just go out and talk to the police, then?"

The man fell silent, "No. I don't want to go talk to the police. They're gonna want to start poking around, and I don't want them in here."

"Well, it's a little late for that, Henry," Charlie said. "I can tell you from experience that you holding that gun is not a good scenario with a bunch of cops around. The best thing you can do right now is to put that gun down and give yourself up."

Beck signaled that he would go in. Jason shook his head. But Beck ignored him.

"Police!" Beck charged into the shed with his weapon drawn. "Put your gun down and your hands in the air."

The old man turned slowly, pointing the gun at Beck.

"I can't do that. I can't let you take them. They belong to me."

"Sir, put the gun down now." Beck didn't take his eyes from his target.

"Please, Henry, put the gun down," Charlie said, sounding panicked. "They will kill you."

"This is all your fault, you little bitch," Henry snarled. He pivoted quicker than anyone could have anticipated, and aimed for Charlie's head. Two shots rang out, and a scream pierced the night.

CHAPTER 21

Henry fell to the ground. It took Charlie a second to realize she felt no pain, had not been shot. Quickly, she stepped forward and kicked the gun away from Henry's hand. Marshall and Jason rushed inside, but Charlie ignored them and knelt next to Henry's prone body.

"Henry," she said softly. "Tell us what you've done. You can't go until you tell the truth. Did you kill those girls?"

Blood wetted his lips, spraying a fine mist across his chin as he spoke. His blue eyes fogged with pain. "Mine."

Charlie felt them before she saw them. They shimmered in the shadows, casting back the darkness. Charlie looked up as they surrounded her and Henry.

Any fear they may have had didn't mar their beautiful faces, some of which she recognized immediately. Trini, Macey, Givens, and the young girl who had ridden past her on her bike. The other girls were faces from missing person fliers, but some she had not seen before. How many girls had he killed? Their tormentor was dying. Finally, they would be free.

One of the older girls bent over him and spit on him before casting her eyes skyward and disappearing. A soft rustling sound came from the other girls, and Charlie's heart quickened. Were they going to pick up one of the garden tools and stab into him? She would not blame them if they did.

"I know," Charlie whispered to them. "I know what he did to you. I'll make sure the world knows too. You can go now."

"Charlie?" Jason knelt next to her. He placed his hand on her shoulder and looked around the room.

The old man let out one last wheezing breath and his eyelids fluttered. A moment later Henry Hatch stood staring down at his body. Confusion and fear deepened the lines and folds of his old face. The girls who had not departed huddled together, their fearlessness melting away. His eyes widened when he saw them.

"Don't be scared. He can't hurt you anymore," Charlie said. "Go on now."

One by one, the girls cast their eyes toward the ceiling and disappeared.

Trini stood frozen, staring into the dark shadows of the corner. His glowing amber eyes appeared first, then he emerged from the darkness as if it had borne him. Trini's face twisted with fear and she shook her head, running to the back of the building. Her body disappeared before it connected with the exterior wall.

"Trini, wait," Macey Givens called after her, following her friend.

Charlie watched in horror as the reaper took his scythe and struck it through the center of Henry's heart. The old man's spirit screamed in agony. Charlie squeezed her eyes shut and tears of sorrow traced over her cheeks, falling onto the dusty floor. When she opened them again, Henry and the reaper had disappeared.

"Charlie?" Jason asked. "You okay?"

Charlie nodded and looked at her friend.

"Yes," she said. "I think I know why the reaper was following me now."

"What?" Jason asked. She knew he was trying not to look at her like she was crazy, but it still came through his hazel eyes.

"Nothing," she said. "I'll tell you about it some other time."

"Okay. I need to take you down to the station to give a statement."

"All right," she said. "Then I just want to go home and hug my kid."

CHAPTER 22

On Friday afternoon, Charlie walked into the café and took a seat at the lunch counter. She leaned forward on her elbows, fighting the tired seeping into her muscles. It had been the longest couple of days, and she was grateful to have gotten to the end of the week without being arrested for breaking into Henry James Hatch's shed. Somehow, the sheriff's deputies bought her story and didn't push too hard on how she got the keys to it or why no crying child had been found. She knew she probably had Jason to thank for that. When it was all said and done, they were more concerned about what they found in the shed. They were still sorting out the bodies, but the count was up to nine. Charlie worried about Trini and Macey—had they finally moved on? It was impossible for her to say. Once the dust settled a little, she would go back to the Givens woods and see what she could find.

Evangeline came over and put her hands on Charlie's arms, giving her a half hug. "Hey there, sunshine." Evangeline took the empty seat next to Charlie. "How are you feeling?"

"Good—exhausted but good."

"Well, I'm glad to hear it. I really appreciate you picking me up. Brett Henderson swore he'd have my car back to me by this afternoon, but you know how that goes."

"It's no problem, Evangeline. I'm happy to do it." Charlie peered up at the chalkboard menu on the wall behind the counter. Her stomach growled.

"We just have to wait until Dottie comes in at five, then we can leave." Evangeline said. "Is there anything I can get you in the meantime? Iced tea?"

"Tea sounds good." Charlie leaned forward.

"Lots of ice no lemon," Charlie and Evangeline said simultaneously.

Evangeline laughed and shook her head. "Child, you think I don't know you by now?" She picked up a clean glass sitting on a rubber mat that ran half the length of the service cabinet behind the lunch counter. She scooped it full of ice, took one of the tea pitchers and filled the glass.

She placed the glass down in front of Charlie.

"How about a piece of pie while you wait?"

"Thank you, but no, ma'am. I don't want to spoil my appetite."

Evangeline winked at her. "Smart girl. Jen's making fried chicken."

"There ya go." Charlie smiled and picked up her glass and sipped the sweet tea. Just the way she liked it. The bell above the door rang and a tingle of recognition spread through Charlie's senses. She resisted the urge to turn and look as Tom Sharon sat down at the counter next to her.

"Well, if it isn't Charlie Payne. It's been quite a long time since I've seen you, my friend," he said a little too loudly.

Charlie glanced around at the nearly empty café.

"I don't think Miss Cookie heard you." She jerked her thumb toward the older woman with perfectly coiffed silver hair, wearing a bright aqua colored suit and every piece of jewelry she owned. Miss Cookie didn't look up from the farthest booth on the far wall but licked her thumb and turned the page of the worn paperback romance in her hands.

"Yes, but I think she's a little deaf, isn't she?" Tom quipped.

Charlie laughed and finally let herself look at him. His stark good looks still didn't fail to overwhelm. His golden-brown eyes glittered with humor. Tom leaned in and lowered his voice. "I just don't want anyone to get the wrong idea. I don't want to make trouble for you, Charlie."

"I appreciate that." Charlie's cheeks slackened and her smile faded.

Evangeline returned from the kitchen and stopped in front of Tom. "Good afternoon, Mr. Sharon. How are things going over at the new mortuary? Have y'all opened up yet?"

"Yes, we've opened the doors. We had our first funeral this week. Myra Burns."

"Oh, my gosh, that's right. I forgot about Myra. I was so sorry to hear that she had passed," Evangeline said.

"She was the last of the Burns', wasn't she?" Charlie asked.

"She was. I wonder what they'll do with that property now? She probably hasn't lived there in thirty years, and it's dilapidated. I don't think she has any heirs."

"Maybe the county will tear it down." Charlie took another sip of tea.

"They should," Evangeline absently poured Tom a glass of tea and set it down in front of him. "At least that would keep the kids from vandalizing it."

"Why hasn't she lived there?" Tom took the lemon wedge perched on the edge of the glass and squeezed it into the tea before tasting it. Charlie wrinkled her nose.

"Well, the poor thing went into a home after she had a nasty fall and broke her hip. Never came out. I used to go by and see her every once in a while. After her hip healed, she enjoyed living in the home, so she moved from convalescence to assisted living. I think she was just lonely. And she was rich enough that she didn't need to sell the house, so unfortunately it just sat there and rotted."

"That's a real shame," Charlie said.

"It won't be sad for the developers that get their hands on it, I'll tell you that," Evangeline said. "That property is probably worth a fair penny these days. It's got a marsh view and could easily be subdivided."

"I guess that's what they call progress." Charlie shrugged.

"Tom, are you here for some supper or are you just here to visit with our fair Charlie?" Evangeline asked.

"Maybe both if I can talk Charlie into joining me," Tom said, raising his eyebrows, his face hopeful.

"Oh I'm sorry. It's Friday night. I always try to have dinner with my family."

Tom's face deflated. "It's silly of me to think you wouldn't have plans."

"I really am sorry. But it's probably not a good idea, anyway, at least until I have this custody thing sorted."

"Of course," Tom said.

"So." Evangeline leaned over the counter in front of Tom and smiled widely. "What are you doing for dinner, Tom? I would be overjoyed to have you as my guest for dinner." Charlie gave her aunt a pointed look. Evangeline's eyebrows raised, and she brushed off her niece's questioning glance. "What? I can't have friends to dinner?"

Charlie sighed. "Well, of course, you can."

"Listen, I really don't want to make trouble for Charlie." Tom held his hands up in surrender.

"Nonsense. And don't you worry about Scott." Evangeline narrowed her blue eyes. "I can handle him if it comes to it."

"Evangeline," Charlie warned.

Evangeline picked up her order pad, ripped out a check, and turned it over. She quickly scribbled the time and address. "We eat dinner promptly at seven. Dress is casual so you don't have to wear your suit."

"Yeah, and you can bring Uncle Jack some whiskey if you really want to kiss some ass," Charlie said.

"What kind of whiskey?" Tom asked.

"Don't you listen to her," Evangeline said. She tucked the piece of paper into the front pocket of Tom's dark gray suit. "Don't be late."

Tom glanced at Charlie, his expression full of uncertainty. "I won't come if you don't want me to."

Charlie sighed and looked at her aunt.

"You know you want him to," Evangeline goaded.

Her cheeks filled with heat, and she glanced at Tom. "Just make sure you park behind my uncle's house. Okay?"

"Great." Tom beamed. "Now, seriously, what kind of whiskey should I bring?"

* * *

"I LIKE HIM," EVANGELINE SAID WHEN THEY WERE halfway to her uncle Jack's house.

"Evangeline. I like him, too, but that's not the point. Scott will use every means available to him to keep me from getting custody. Especially since I outright challenged him. If that means not having a relationship with Tom, then that's what I'm gonna do."

"You know I've been wondering," Evangeline said. "Why haven't you asked us for help on that matter?"

"Because there's nothing you can do."

"My love, there is plenty we could do to help you, but you would have to let us."

"Evangeline, please don't do anything crazy. I don't need Scott ending up dead somewhere."

"Nobody's gonna kill Scott. He still Evan's father.

We respect that. And I'm not talking about dark magic. But we can appeal to the forces of good and light to help with your custody case. It might help keep Scott straight. Instead of dirty tricks, like threatening you for having a relationship with another man."

"I hadn't really thought of it like that."

"Well, if you would just accept who you are—"

"I am not a witch," Charlie protested.

"Sweetie, you have just as much witch blood flowing through your veins as the rest of us Payne women. We all have unique talents and we have all learned how to exploit them. And there's nothing wrong with that. Yes, Lisa, Jen, and Daphne are all better at traditional magic. But that little talent of yours of communing with the dead and seeing the future? That's as witchy as it gets, honey."

"Maybe it is," Charlie snapped. "But I'm not ready to deal with that now. About all I can handle right now is fighting for Evan and doing my job."

Evangeline placed her hand on top of Charlie's arm. "I'll leave you alone about it for now. But denying who we are catches up with us in the end. We're here for you, that's all you need to know."

A bittersweet pang spread throughout Charlie's chest and her throat tickled with emotion. "Thank you."

"That reminds me. I want to give you something."

Excitement lit up Evangeline's face, and she reached for her bag. She rifled through the oversized denim tote before finally pulling out a small velvet pouch. She opened the drawstring and emptied it into her palm. A large polished black stone covered the center of her hand.

"I want you to take this and keep it with you at all times. Put it in your pocket, put it in your purse, just make sure you keep it with you."

"Black tourmaline?" Charlie took the stone in her hand and wrapped her fingers around the cool, smooth stone. A sense of calm immediately swept up her arm, dispersing its energy through her.

"I already have a couple of beads on my necklace."

"I know. But this one is supercharged, and I've already blessed it, so it will give you more protection. Jen told me about your concerns about the reaper and that worrisome spirit you've been dealing with."

"She shouldn't have told you that. I didn't want to worry you."

"I s'wannee girl, you make me crazy. What's family for if not to help you with your troubles? You really need to work on asking for help."

"Yes. ma'am," Charlie glanced at her aunt and smiled. It warmed her heart to be so loved. She shoved the stone into the pocket of her jeans. "I'll keep it with me."

"Good." Evangeline gave her a smug grin. "I've been keeping a secret of my own."

"I know. It's been driving Jen crazy."

Evangeline chuckled. "She and Daphne are the nosiest girls I've ever met."

"Well, are you gonna tell me or are you gonna make me wait, too?" Charlie asked.

"I plan on telling everybody at dinner tonight. Well, except for Jack, because you know."

Charlie nodded. Her uncle Jack would absolutely lay down his life for anyone of the women in his life —and he recognized that all of them were talented and special—but it was better not to flaunt the cause in his face. As a doctor, he always looked for the rational reason behind things. There was nothing rational about her ability to hear snippets of his thoughts or see the dead the way she did. Or to know that company was about to arrive or have her food work like a magical balm for any situation like Jen. Or Lisa's ability to find any lost object. Or Daphne's talent for making any woman, or man, for that matter, feel like the most beautiful version of themselves and then project that to the rest of the world. Or Evangeline's ability to heal not just the broken or wounded body, but the soul. Ignorance was bliss when it came to Jack, and happily, he seemed to like dwelling there. So many times he overlooked things, chocked them up to coincidence or ignored them all together.

"I'm excited to hear about it, whatever it is," Charlie said.

"Well, just between you and me, they chose me to be a leader of the SCoW." Evangeline beamed and folded her hands onto her lap.

"What is that again?" Charlie asked.

"The Southern Coalition of Witches," Evangeline said proudly.

"Oh, Evangeline, that's fantastic. Why haven't you told us before?"

"Well, that's part of it. I couldn't. But I'm done training now, so I can share the news."

"I am so proud of you."

"Thank you, Sweetie. That means the world to me." Evangeline flipped on the radio before landing on a station playing classical music, letting them each get lost in their own thoughts.

* * *

"It's about dang time y'all got here," Jen scolded as Charlie and Evangeline walked through the back door.

"Sorry." Evangeline reached for her purple apron hanging on the hook beside the door. "We had to wait for Dottie. I didn't want to just leave the restaurant without somebody there to manage it."

"No, I suppose that would be bad." Jen flipped the chicken frying in the heavy Dutch oven.

"What's wrong?" Charlie asked. "Why are you so contrary?"

"Nothing's wrong. I just—Ruby's been underfoot and so has daddy."

"Well, I'm here now. You need me to help cook?" Evangeline sidled up next to Jen and surveyed the situation.

"Could you bread the squash for me, please?" Jen pointed to the sheet pan full of thin slices of yellow and zucchini squash. "I salted them, and they've been sitting there for twenty minutes sweating."

"I'll get right on that." Evangeline quickly tied her apron strings around her trim waist and got to work.

"I'll set the table," Charlie said

"Don't forget," Evangeline said. "We need an extra place setting."

"Why?" Jen asked, wiping her hands on her apple green apron.

"Evangeline invited Tom for dinner."

"Really?" A smile stretched across Jen's lips.

Charlie rolled her eyes at her cousin's excitement and sighed. It would be hard to fight them off if they all ganged up on her.

She opened the cabinet and counted out enough

plates and napkins and set off for the dining room. A few minutes later Lisa and Daphne wandered in. Daphne pulled out the chair at the end of the table where Uncle Jack usually sat.

"So," Daphne started, "it must be serious if we get to meet the boyfriend."

"He is not my boyfriend, Daphne." Charlie folded a blue and white napkin and placed it across the plate in front of her.

"But he is sweet on you, right?" Lisa asked.

Charlie fiddled with the silverware, making sure the placement of the forks, spoons, and knives was perfect. "Well, that does not a boyfriend make."

"No, if it did, then Charlie would have definite problems because she has so many boys sweet on her," Daphne chided.

"Oh, my god," Charlie said. "Did you two come in here just to give me a hard time or do you plan on being useful?"

Daphne gave her a sly smile.

"Then get out. Go do something else." Charlie waved her hand at them, shooing them.

"Charlie has a boyfriend. Charlie has a boyfriend," Daphne sang in a childlike voice.

"Daphne," Lisa scolded. "What are you, nine?"

"You're just jealous," Daphne snapped.

Lisa threw up her hands. "What the hell do I have to be jealous about? I have a boyfriend."

"I know, and that's all he will ever be."

"You realize that we're not defined by our relationship status, right?" Lisa put her hands on her hips and cocked her head. She frowned.

"All right, that's enough," Charlie said, using the same tone that she used with Evan when he talked back. "God, I can't take your bickering tonight. I like Tom, and yes, he likes me, but we cannot date now. But I'm not gonna rule anything out for the future, okay? For now, just back the hell—"

The sound of someone clearing their throat stopped Charlie mid-rant. She straightened up and closed her eyes, taking a deep breath. Dammit. She turned toward the source of the sound.

Tom stood in the doorway. He raised his hand and wore a sheepish smile on his lips. "Please, don't let me interrupt."

Charlie's face burst into flames, and she offered a weak smile.

"You must be Tom." Daphne rose to her feet, smiled exaggeratedly and stretched out her hand. "We haven't met formally. Although I believe you've come into my shop. Who does your hair?"

"Daphne, Jesus, back off. Let the man breathe. He doesn't need the kind of work you offer at your salon," Lisa chided.

"What? Everybody needs a good stylist." Daphne sniffed.

"Yes, they do." Tom smiled and flashed his gaze toward Charlie. "I'd be happy to give you my business."

Daphne gave Lisa an up-yours look and let go of Tom's hand. "Well, stop by the shop anytime. I'll make sure you get in no matter how busy I am."

"Thank you." Tom nodded. "Evangeline said that you were in here. Anything I can do to help?"

"I'm almost done." Charlie pointed to the table. All the plates and silver were in place.

"What should I do with this?" He held up a bottle of dark amber liquid in an elegant curved bottle.

Charlie chuckled. "You should give that to Uncle Jack."

"Rye whiskey?" Lisa took the bottle and inspected it. "Russell's Reserve. Daddy may just fall in love with you." She handed the bottle back to him.

"A little bird told me that was his favorite."

"Yes, it is." Lisa nodded. "Well played. You're definitely hitting all the right marks."

"I'll be the judge of that," a voice said as it entered from the other door leading to the living room. "How do you do there, young man?"

"Good evening, sir," Tom said. "I take it you're Uncle Jack."

"I am," Jack said. "I don't think we've been formally introduced. "

"No, sir, we haven't. I'm Tom Sharon, and this is

for you." Tom offered him the bottle of whiskey.

Jack whistled and then smiled. "You sure know the way to a man's heart. You sure you don't want this one as your boyfriend? I'll take care of the first one."

Charlie laughed nervously. "Nobody needs to take care of Scott. Okay?"

"You sure?" Jack said. "I always thought he'd make great crab bait."

"That's really unnecessary." Charlie shook her head.

"Remind me never to get on your bad side, then," Tom said.

"It's not daddy that you need to worry about." Lisa's tone was light but there was a darker warning beneath.

Tom's gaze leveled on Lisa, and the smile he wore disappeared from his face. He tipped his head a little. "Of that, I have no doubt."

Lisa nodded.

"Come on, Tom. I'm done here. Why don't we go out back? I'll show you the river," Charlie grabbed Tom by the elbow and ushered him through the house before he could respond. He followed her down the back steps, and they walked side by side across the wide expanse of lush green grass. They passed the little shed that housed her uncle's lawn tractor and other gardening tools. He walked close enough that the back of his hand brushed against hers every once in a while. The touch of his skin sent a thrill through her, and even though she knew better, she didn't put a stop to it.

"So, how has your week been?" They moved onto the short path through the pine trees lining the shore.

"It was…" Charlie hesitated. "Busy."

Charlie stepped onto the wooden deck built on the edge of the embankment and headed down a steep set of steps leading to a T-shaped dock.

A small Jon boat rested on the very end of the left side of the T. A larger boat hung in the air attached to the boat lift running parallel to the dock.

Charlie walked all the way to the end and stopped. She folded her arms across her chest and breathed in the briny marsh air. The setting sun glinted across the water, winding through tall golden marsh grass like a smooth gray-skinned snake.

"It's incredibly beautiful here," Tom said, edging next to her.

"This is my favorite place in the world."

"I can see why." Tom shoved his hands into his pockets. "I like your family."

"It seems they like you too. Maybe you should date them," she teased.

Tom laughed. "Maybe I should." His arm brushed against hers and he rocked on his feet. "Can ask you a strange question?"

Charlie chuckled. "Can I stop you?"

His eyes narrowed, but a grin played at the corners of his mouth. "No."

She shrugged. "Go ahead, then."

"Evangeline is not married to Jack, is that correct?"

Charlie laughed out loud. "No, they are definitely not married. Although, they sometimes spar like married people. Jack was married to my Aunt Ellen. Evangeline is Ellen's sister."

"Is she your mother's sister too?"

"No—my father's."

"Well, you're all very close. It's nice to see and be around."

"They are definitely a lot of fun."

"I find one thing curious though."

"What's that?"

"Why you call Jack uncle and his wife aunt, but you don't call Evangeline the same?"

Charlie toed a screw that had worked itself out of the wood about an inch. "She just always wanted us to call her Evangeline. Payne women are quirky that way, I guess. We called our grandmother Bunny because everybody else did. Her real name was Florence, and she always said she was too young to be somebody's grandmother." Charlie laughed at the memory.

"I see."

"Do you have any other questions about my family?"

"Just one. Your son isn't with you tonight?"

"No, he's spending the night at his grandmother's."

"I see. I'm sorry I won't get to meet him."

"Now, it's my turn ask you a question."

He laughed and gave her a sly grin. "You may ask."

"Exactly why did you show up at the café today?"

"I came in to get some dinner. You being there was just a bonus."

Charlie's stomach flip-flopped and heat flooded her cheeks. She quickly glanced away. "I see."

"I know we can't date right now. But I like you, and if we could at least be friends…"

"Friends are good. I can always use another friend." She leaned slightly into him.

"That settles it."

Charlie let her gaze drift back to the marsh grass. It had been so long since she'd felt so comfortable with a man. She swallowed back the bitterness coating the back of her throat. It was so unfair that Scott could date whoever he wanted, but she couldn't. Even though she was glad of it, friendship seemed a hollow consolation prize.

CHAPTER 23

Charlie flipped open the folder on her lap and thumbed through some still photographs that Jason had dropped off this morning for her to look at. He'd spent hours going through the video from Haley's security system. He had mentioned seeing some interesting things, but it wasn't until he had slowed the footage down frame by frame he captured images of something. He'd given her the photos because what he captured made no sense to him.

With a quick glance to her right and then her left, she made sure no one was watching her. She shifted in the chair right outside Scott's hospital room, waiting while Evan visited with his dad. Scott had asked her to stay, but she thought it more important Evan have some time alone with his dad since he hadn't seen him in almost a week. There were a couple of nurses at the station, but they appeared to be too engrossed in their work to notice her.

Her nostrils flared as she took a deep breath and closed her eyes. She laid her hand on top of one photo and let her mind drift. Images flooded her head.

Scott's door opened, and Charlie opened her eyes. Evan appeared, his slim tanned face more solemn than usual.

"Dad wants to talk to you."

Charlie snapped the folder closed and shoved it back into the tote at her feet. She stood and gave Evan's shoulder a gentle squeeze. "You wait here, okay, Bud?"

Evan nodded and took a seat. Charlie took a deep breath and forced a smile before entering the room.

"Hi." She cringed at the perkiness in her voice and knew Scott wouldn't buy it. Her lips stretched across her face, making the muscles taut. "You look so much better."

"I feel better. I'm hoping they'll let me out of here in a few days."

A pang of disappointment spread through her chest. She wanted Scott to get better, she really did, but she wanted more time with Evan.

"That's great." The muscles in her face ached.

"Will you please wipe that smile off your face? You're not fooling anyone." He scowled.

Charlie dropped the fake smile. "Oh, thank god."

He held out his hand and softened his tone. "Will you come sit by me?"

Charlie took a seat in the chair next to the bed. She didn't take his hand. His lips curved downward, and he dropped his hand back to the bed. His fingers bunched up the light cotton blanket covering his legs in a fist.

"What's going on?"

"They told me I died. Did you know that?"

"No one told me." Charlie met his intense gaze. "Do you remember what it was like?"

His eyes became glassy and distant. "Yes. I saw… you."

Charlie called up a smile. Only this time it was real. "Where was I?"

"I think you were at work." He peered into her face. "You had on one of those headset things."

"Okay," she mumbled. "Do you remember what you saw? What you… felt?"

"Not really. Just you. You saw me, didn't you?" he whispered, as if saying the words aloud would give them too much credence.

"Yes." There was no more reason to deny it.

"All these years I've known you were intuitive. Shrugged it off when you would say or do things outside the confines of logic. I know I made you feel —" He paused and blinked away shiny wetness glazing his eyes. "Crazy."

"Yes," she mouthed the word.

"And Evan he's…so much like you. Do you know what it's like to love someone so much who reminds you of someone—"

"You hate?" Charlie asked.

"No. Someone who broke your heart."

Charlie could taste salty tears in the back of her throat. Her voice cracked, and she sniffled. "Just for the record. I know exactly what that feels like."

"How do we get it back?"

"Get what back?"

"Us." Pain twisted his expression. Had she ever seen him so vulnerable before? Not that she could remember. "I miss you so much, Charlie."

"Oh, Scott." Charlie sat back in her chair, mulling over her words, choosing them carefully. What would happen if she said the wrong thing? Would he banish her from Evan's life forever? She took a deep breath. "Do you know why I left you?"

"Because you didn't love me anymore." His fingers tightened around the blanket and his sharp chin jutted out a little.

"No," Charlie said. "Because you never believed in me. Because I felt less than."

"Less than," he parroted.

Charlie shrugged. "It doesn't matter now. It's all water under the bridge."

Scott opened his hand, turning it palm up. "I believe in you now."

Charlie stared at his hand, watched as his fingers twitched, beckoning her to take it.

"Come home. I can be different. I *am* different."

Charlie took his hand in hers and rose to her feet. She leaned over him, looking him straight in the eye. It would so easy to move back home and start over. All her worries would be over and there would be no chance of losing Evan. Tears leaked from her eyes. "You will always be my first love, but you are not the only one who's changed. I'm sorry, but I can't." Quickly, she pressed her lips against his forehead. "If you really want to believe in somebody unconditionally, believe in Evan. He's the one who needs you to."

Scott closed his eyes and his shoulders sagged. "He told me this would happen. I guess I should have listened."

"What? That I would reject you?" She sighed. "I guess it's so clear that even an eleven-year-old could see it."

"No, he told me, he told me I should get my lungs checked after my bike accident. I told him I was the doctor and to stick to being a kid." Painful silence reared up between them, broken only by the beep of the machines monitoring his heart. "I don't know how to fix this, Charlie. How do I fix this?"

Charlie sat on the edge of his bed and took his hand in both of hers and steadied her gaze on his. "The first thing you can do is take him off that medication you have him on. I know you thought it would help him focus. But all it does is make him feel nothing. And for somebody like Evan or me—not feeling is akin to death."

"But he feels so much. Too much for someone his age." Scott's lip quivered, his jaw tightened. The heart monitor beeped faster as his blood pressure went up.

"Listen to me," she said. "The only way for Evan to learn how to deal with his feelings is to *feel them*. All we need to do is love him and support him. But most of all, we need to believe in him. Do you understand?"

Scott lay back against his pillow and closed his eyes. "I'm very tired all of a sudden."

"Okay." Charlie slipped her hand out of his and stood up. She brushed the back of her hand across his cheek. "I'll let you get some rest. Please think about what I said."

Scott put his hand over hers, holding it to his cheek. He nodded and let it go. Charlie rose from the bed and slung her messenger bag strap over her shoulder. Halfway out to the door he said, "Charlie. I love you."

Tears stung the back of Charlie's throat. "I know."

"I really am different, you know."

Charlie smiled through unshed tears. "I know."

CHAPTER 24

It was only ten o'clock, but Emma Winston could barely keep her eyes open. She couldn't remember the last time she'd gotten a good night's sleep. Bad dreams had plagued her since that night ten years ago, but she'd always got enough rest to be functional. Since Haley's death, sleep had become almost impossible. She climbed into bed and stacked the pillows behind her so she could sit up. She pulled her Bible from her nightstand and placed it on her lap. Then she reached inside the drawer and pulled out her thirty-eight special. It was stupid to think the gun would do any good against a ghost, but it made her feel better to have it close. She checked the safety and then set it down on the bed next to her. Her white Persian cat jumped up on the bed and meowed at her before settling in next to her feet.

Emma opened the Bible and brushed her fingers over the words of Psalm twenty-three.

"Yea though I walk through the valley of death, I will fear no evil. Do you hear that, Brianna? I will fear no evil!" she said to the empty room. Part of her waited for some sort of response, but most of her was grateful that it didn't come. She laid one hand on the Bible spread across her lap and the other hand on her gun, ready for anything.

* * *

THE SOUND OF GROWLING AND SPITTING ROUSED HER from sleep. Her eyes fluttered open and as soon as her brain and body caught up with what she saw, her heart sped into overdrive, slamming against her rib cage, beating its way to the back of her throat. Her fingers tightened around the handle of her weapon, and she raised it up, pointing it directly at the diaphanous glowing Brianna Fiorello.

The spirit's eyes were darker than she remembered the girl's ever being. An unreadable expression on her pale face. Her cat stood guard at the end of the bed, goofed up like a big white cotton ball, her back arched. Her cat growled louder.

"Get out of here, Brianna," she said, her voice shaking almost as much as her hand.

"Do you think that will work? Do you really think

you can kill me again?" Brianna spoke in a voice that sounded like knives scraping cold porcelain.

"I will do whatever it takes to get you out of my life, Brianna, once and for all."

The spirit threw back her head and laughed. "You think this is funny? You think it was funny to kill Haley?"

"No funnier than when you killed me."

"It was an accident. We did not kill you."

"You just keep telling yourself that. Whatever helps you sleep." Brianna chuckled and faded into nothing. Emma blinked hard and looked around, expecting her to pop back up again. Her cat growled and hissed one more time before finally meowing. She headed back toward Emma's lap, displacing the Bible. Emma dropped her hand holding the gun and let the weapon lay on the bed. Then she scooped up her cat in her arms and scratched the ball of fluff behind the ears.

"She's not gonna kill me too," Emma said to the cat. The cat replied by purring loudly. Suddenly, she gave the cat a quick kiss on the nose and laid her on the bed. She hurried downstairs and dug through her purse until she found what she was looking for. She pulled the simple cream-colored card and turned it over before picking up her cell phone and dialing the number printed on it. It rang twice before a sleepy voice finally answered.

"Hello, is this Charlie Payne?"

"Yes, it is."

"I'm sorry to bother you, so late but this is Emma Winston. And I really need to see you tonight if possible."

* * *

All the marble and mirrors in the Marquis Hotel gleamed in the yellow light of old-fashioned light bulbs. The key to a place like the Marquis was to walk in like you owned the place. Charlie held her head high with one hand wrapped around the leather strap of her messenger bag. The bar was across the lobby directly in front of the receptionist desk, just as Emma said it would be.

Charlie walked through the brass double doors and walked along the rows of tables and booths until she came to the last one where Emma Winston sat nursing a large glass of wine. Charlie slid into the booth across from her. A nearly empty bottle of Chardonnay sat in the center of the table. Charlie wrapped her hand around its neck and read the gold label.

"Would you like a glass?" Emma asked. There was a fresh bruise high on her left cheek and the circles beneath her eyes reminded Charlie of the blackout that football players used to reduce glare.

"Well, it's good to see you've been sleeping," Charlie said wryly. "What is she doing to you?"

Emma gulped the last bit of wine in her glass and slipped the bottle out of Charlie's hand. She tipped it and the golden liquid filled the glass almost to the top, emptying the bottle.

Emma shook her head and smiled sadly. "Boy, you don't waste any time, do you? No small talk, huh? No 'how's your family' or 'what's the weather like in Topeka'?"

"Have you ever been to Topeka?"

"Nope. Not once." Emma took a sip of her wine.

"Well, honestly, it's after midnight, and I've never been one for small talk." Charlie laced her fingers together and placed her hands on the table.

"You know you'd never make it in a sorority then. We are the queens of small talk."

Charlie forced a smile. "You know I came from one of the outer islands, right? What exactly would you like to talk about, Dr. Winston?"

"So formal. I mean, you've already been the harbinger of death. You should at least call me by my given name."

"Fine. Emma. Why did you need me to come all the way downtown?"

Emma wrapped both her hands around the bowl of her wine glass. Her eyes became unfocused as she spoke. "I thought if I left my house. That I would somehow be safe. That if I wasn't in the house, she couldn't get to me."

"Who couldn't get to you?"

Emma let out a high-pitched nervous laugh, but still she didn't look at Charlie when she spoke. "You know who."

Charlie let her hand slip down to the pendant hanging around her neck, and she brushed her thumb and forefinger across it. "I brought you something."

"You did?" Emma sat back, her face wary.

"Yes, I did." Charlie opened the flap of her messenger bag and dug around for the little velvet box her cousin had given her. She pulled it out and placed it on the table in front of Emma, pushing it toward her. Emma's blue eyes widened.

"Ooh jewelry? On a first date?" Emma said teasing. She reached for the blue velvet box and flipped open the top. "You certainly know the way to a girl's heart."

"I'm glad that you're joking about it," Charlie said. "It means she hasn't broken you yet."

Emma took the silver pendant from the box and brought it closer to her face so she could make out the symbol. "Is that what I think it is?"

"It's a pentacle."

"Doesn't that—?" She paused and looked around,

then finished in a whisper. "Isn't that a satanic symbol?"

"No. Although the Satanists have taken it and flipped it. The symbol itself is for protection against evil."

"Evil," Emma echoed. "Is that what she is? Evil?"

"I don't think she's inherently evil. But I think she's angry, and a lot of times when spirits are angry, it's because they die angry. The emotion just consumes them after death. Poisons them. I think she's spent the last ten years growing stronger and angrier."

"I just don't understand. Why she's so angry with me?"

Charlie sat back against the condition of the booth. "Isn't it obvious?"

"Isn't what obvious?" Emma laid the pendant down on the table.

"She's angry because you killed her."

"I don't know what you're talking about." Emma's gaze leveled on Charlie.

"Part of what I do, how this whole thing works for me is, I have dreams. I had a dream about you and Haley dropping Brianna off at some abandoned old house in the middle of nowhere, wearing only her pajamas, in the middle of the night. When I see Brianna's ghost, she's wearing those pajamas."

"Haley and I did not kill Emma, if that's what you're insinuating."

"Maybe. Maybe not. But she believes you did. She's not gonna let it go until you're dead too."

"We did not kill her. I swear to God."

"You can swear to whoever you want, won't change anything."

"You have to help me." Emma reached across the table and her hand clamped onto Charlie's wrist. "You said you could help me."

"Fine." Charlie glanced down at Emma's hand. "First, take your hand off me. Second, tell me what you and Haley did to Brianna."

Emma's hand released Charlie's wrist, and she pulled it to her quickly, cradling it against her body as if Charlie's tone had somehow stung her.

"We didn't do anything," Brianna insisted. "We even filled out a missing person's report. Now, would we have done that if we had killed her?"

"I don't know. Maybe." Charlie sat back and took a long look at her. Emma was scared, but she wasn't telling the truth. "Maybe you did it to cover your tracks."

"If we wanted to cover our tracks, we would never have drawn any sort of attention to ourselves," Emma said.

"Either way, it doesn't really bode well for you."

"Why?" Emma asked.

"Because obviously Brianna believes you're responsible. Otherwise, why would she haunt you?"

Emma picked up her glass and took a long, slow sip from her wine.

"The alcohol's really not going to help you," Charlie said. "It actually makes it easier for her to access your dreams."

"I don't know what you're talking about. I haven't been dreaming about her."

"You can lie to yourself all day long, but Brianna is the one in charge. Why do you think you're so bruised?"

"Will you help me?" Emma asked. "Please?"

"Why should I? I mean, honestly? The police will probably rule Haley's death a suicide, and if they don't, then it will be ruled an accident. You can't be implicated at all. And Brianna can't either because nobody's gonna bring up the fact that Haley died at the hands of a ghost. Maybe letting you die the same way is the only way that Brianna gets any justice."

"Oh, god," Emma croaked. "I did not kill her." Emma put her face in her hands and cried. Charlie wanted to feel sorry for, but something inside her just wouldn't allow it.

"Even if—and that's a big if, you didn't kill her directly, you need to own up to your responsibility. She's not gonna stop until you're dead."

"Well, I can't let that happen." Emma sniffed and

wiped the tears off her cheeks. "I am a Mu Theta and we do not give up. If I do die, my blood will be on your hands because you didn't help me. And you can bet your bottom dollar that I'll come back and haunt you.

Charlie cocked her head and narrowed her eyes. It was on the tip of her tongue to tell her to get in line, but instead she just laughed. "You're good. I'll give you that."

"So you'll help me?"

"Well, the last damn thing I need is somebody haunting me on purpose."

A smile stretched across Emma's lips. "Thank you. I promise you won't regret it. What do we need to do?"

"Well, the first thing we need to do is go to the store. I have some supplies that we need."

"There's a Harris Teeter right down the street."

"Do you have your car? Mine's parked all the way up on Broad Street."

"Yes. Of course, I do."

Charlie held her hand out. "Keys please. You're certainly not driving."

* * *

CHARLIE AND EMMA PAUSED IN FRONT OF ROOM 308. Emma held her key card in her hand but didn't move to insert it. After another minute, Charlie took the key card from Emma and slid it into the lock until the little green light appeared. The lock clicked and Charlie pushed open the door. The two women quickly went inside.

The room was nicer than any Charlie had stayed in, at least since she divorced Scott. There was fine mahogany furniture—a carved headboard and matching nightstands and dresser. There was a television hanging on the wall where a mirror normally would be—which Charlie thought to be a good thing. The fewer mirrors they had to deal with, the better.

In the middle of the bed was a white long-haired cat with large blue eyes and a flat face. Its tail swished back and forth. Its gaze followed them into the room.

"You brought your cat?" Charlie said.

"Of course. You didn't think I would leave her at home, did you?"

"No—actually it's good that you have a cat. Some believe they're guardians of the underworld and can ward off the dead."

"Did you hear that, Blizzard?" Emma sat down on the bed next to the cat and scratched it behind the ears. "You're mama's little guardian."

Charlie rubbed the back of her neck, losing her patience. "Have you actually seen her here yet?"

"No, not yet. Hopefully never. I was kinda hoping

you could help keep her away from me." Emma stared at her expectantly, her eyes punctuated by the dark circles beneath them.

"When was the last time you slept, Emma?"

Emma shook her head and tightened her arms around herself. "It's been a while. Since before Haley even died."

"Are you sure you don't want to tell me what happened with Brianna?"

"There's nothing to tell," Emma said. "Now, are you gonna help me or not?"

"Yes," Charlie said, fighting the urge to just leave Emma to Brianna's mercy, or lack thereof. "I will help you. Which door is the bathroom?"

Emma pointed to the left door on the wall of the tiny foyer leading into the room. The door was shut.

"All right," Charlie started. "I'm going to go in there by myself first and check it out."

"Is that a good idea? What if she tries to kill you too?"

"I'll be fine."

"You sure?"

"Oh, yeah, her beef isn't with me, it's with you and Haley."

"All right. If you think that's best."

Charlie handed Emma her cell phone. "Do not come inside, even if I'm screaming. Do you understand me?"

Emma nodded quickly.

"But if I tell you to help me then I need you to call the first name on my favorites list. Do you understand me?"

Emma looked down at the phone in her hands. "Jen," she said softly. "If you call out help me, you want me to call Jen."

"Yes. Tell her I'm in trouble. Tell her the address and then go downstairs and wait for her."

"You want me to call your cop friend?"

"No. He can't help me with this kind of trouble, but she can."

"Okay," Emma croaked.

Charlie opened the door and flipped on the light to the bathroom. She stepped up to the edge of the granite counter. In the mirror, she could see Emma watching from the bedroom. Her large blue eyes stared intently at Charlie's reflection and she smiled, trying to reassure her.

Charlie closed her eyes and drew in a deep breath, focusing on the rise and fall of her chest. Her mind cleared and her eyes opened and closed again. Long, slow blinks. The mirror fogged and the scene shifted. The light in the bedroom behind her changed. The bright bluish fluorescent light was gone replaced by the hazy gloom of night. Thunder boomed overhead, making Charlie jump and glance at the ceiling. When she brought her attention back to the mirror, she was no longer alone in the bathroom. Brianna stood right behind her. The temperature in the small space plummeted and out of instinct Charlie glanced over her shoulder. Her breath stuttered in her chest. There was nothing there except Emma, standing in the same place watching her.

"You okay?" Emma said.

"I'm fine." Charlie called up a smile and pushed the door closed. She pressed her palm flat against the wood door. Dread coiled around her heart and squeezed, making the deep breath she attempted harder. Finally, she turned around to face the mirror.

Brianna stood just on the other side of the sink staring out at her, as if she was looking through a window.

Not a window. A portal.

Charlie's gaze shifted from her translucent face to the blood-soaked T-shirt she wore.

"Do you remember how that happened?" Charlie pointed to the girl's chest. Brianna blinked and tilted her head as if she were unsure whether or not what she was seeing was real. The hair on the back of Charlie's neck prickled. "If you tell me where you are, I can help you, Brianna."

Brianna's eyebrows raised and her mouth opened, forming a perfect 'O.' "How do you know my name?"

"I know a lot about you, actually. I know you

went missing ten years ago. I know that Haley and Emma are responsible. Looks like you took care of Haley yourself, but if you'll let me, I'll make sure you get justice. I can help you pass on to where you're supposed to be."

A thundercloud shrouded Brianna's face and her eyes darkened to where Charlie could only see black hatred. Her lips twisted into a snarl and the anger rolled off her, pouring into Charlie. She swallowed back the bitter taste of bile, threatening to make her vomit.

Brianna raised one hand, her forefinger pointing. Her words sounded venomous in Charlie's ears. "You tell Emma she's next."

"Brianna, don't—" Brianna crossed the barrier of the mirror so fast Charlie had no time to react. The spirit wrapped its fingers around her throat and slammed her up against the door hard enough that Charlie saw stars. Charlie clawed at her throat only to find nothing there. Still she couldn't breathe. She gasped and fought against the apparition's grip.

"Charlie?" The doorknob rattled. Emma sounded like she was crying. "Charlie? Are you okay?"

Brianna's attention shifted to the voice coming from behind the door, and her grip loosened enough for Charlie to breathe. Charlie dug into her pocket for the piece of polished black tourmaline Evangeline had given her. She touched the stone to her throat.

Brianna screamed and pulled her hand to her chest, cradling it, as if she'd been burned. "You bitch!"

"Fine. If that's how you want to play it, then that's exactly what you're gonna get." Charlie pulled a fistful of salt from her other pocket and tossed it into Brianna's diaphanous body. The hard-white crystals dusted the floor. Brianna screeched, her face twisting into a mask of pain and fury. Charlie pulled out another handful of salt and showed it to the spirit.

Brianna spit in Charlie's direction. The room temperature plunged, and Charlie's breath puffed in enormous clouds.

"Stay out of this, bitch, or I swear I will come after you too." Brianna hissed then turned and scrambled back through the mirror. Charlie fell forward onto her knees, gasping and coughing. Her hand went to her throat. She crawled toward the door and turned the lock on the knob and pulled it open.

"Oh, my god! What happened?" Emma whined.

"Emma don't come in here," Charlie said, her throat feeling like she had swallowed a handful of rocks. "I saw Brianna." She coughed again and rubbed the skin of her neck where Brianna's icy fingers had squeezed. Would there be bruises? It wouldn't be the first time a spirit had left its mark on her.

"Did she hurt you?"

Charlie cleared her throat. "I'm okay. But I need you to be honest with me now. Where did you and Haley take Brianna that night? The night you say she disappeared."

"I don't know what you're talking about," Emma said.

Charlie gritted her teeth and pushed herself to her feet. "Fine. Don't tell me. Keep your little secret until your dying day. Which I presume will be a lot sooner than you think. I'm done here." Charlie slipped the tourmaline back into her pocket and got to her feet. She grabbed her bag off the bed and slung it over her shoulder.

Emma let her get as far as the door before crying out, "Wait! She'll kill me!"

Charlie wrapped her hand around the doorknob and turned it. Light from the hallway spilled into the room through the crack as she opened the door. Emma pushed the door shut, putting herself between the exit and Charlie.

"You cannot leave me here unprotected. You promised!"

"I did. It's disappointing when someone breaks a promise, isn't it? I bet that's exactly how Brianna felt when you and Haley broke your promise to her. Now, move or I will move you."

Charlie yanked on the door again, forcing Emma forward. From the bathroom, they both heard someone whisper Emma's name over and over again.

Charlie stepped out into the hallway, and Emma grabbed hold of her arm, giving it a tug. Tears streaked the young woman's face, and her eyes pleaded with Charlie. She twisted her wrist out of Emma's hands.

"Stop!" Emma said. "Fine! You win. I'll tell you what you want to know. But you have to help me."

CHAPTER 25

Once Charlie got Emma calmed down and poured a ring of salt around the bed so the woman could get some sleep, she slunk out of the hotel and made her way toward East Bay Street. Even at nearly one-thirty in the morning there were crowds of people milling around, and she mixed in with them, glad for the anonymity. Even though she hated crowds they were often a good shield, especially when the emotions were positive. For someone as sensitive as she was, the mood of the crowd could sway her more easily than she liked to admit. The streets of downtown Charleston in early September were almost always filled with vacationers and tourists. Never once had she walked away from downtown feeling anything but happy. She welcomed the influx of emotion floating around her, letting it lift her out of the fear and anxiety that made her body shake.

"Charlie?" a voice came from behind her. "Charlie Payne?"

Charlie stopped in her tracks and turned around to find Tom Sharon's beautiful brown eyes fixed on her. A smile stretched across his lips, revealing his perfect white teeth. Her heart fluttered in her chest. How did he do that?

"If it isn't my own personal stalker," Charlie teased and couldn't stop herself from smiling.

His expression shifted from one of joy to concern as he drew closer. "Oh, my god, what happened? Did someone hit you?"

Charlie's hands instinctively went to her cheek where Brianna had struck her head against the door.

"Nothing really. It was stupid. I fell," she lied.

"Tom?" the man standing beside him said. At nearly six three, Tom was tall, but this man loomed over him by at least four inches. He looked like an older version of Tom, with a little gray at his temples and a few wrinkles. But his eyes were a fiery coppery gold. He smiled, but nothing about him made her heart flutter. Instead, a cold warning spread through her chest. She took a step backward.

"Forgive me." Tom glanced at the man. "Charlie, this is my older brother, William. William, this is the young woman I was telling you about."

"I see." William smiled, but it never reached his eyes. "It's nice to meet you. I've heard a lot about you." William offered his hand and Charlie's breath caught in her throat. She didn't want to touch him. Didn't want to see whatever images might float through his head or spirits that might have attached themselves to him. She called up a weak smile and looked to Tom for help.

Tom touched his brother's elbow and shook his head slightly. "Charlie's very sensitive to touching people."

William's fingers twitched, and he closed them, letting his hand fall to his side. His smile morphed into a scornful leer. "Yes, I've been known to be sensitive myself from time to time."

"Sorry," Charlie muttered. "It's really not personal."

"Of course, it's not," Tom interjected. "William and I were just having a late supper and time just got away from us. He runs the branch over off Calhoun."

"Right. It's the original, isn't it?"

"Yes, our great-great-grandfather opened it in 1802."

"Really? I had no idea that it'd been around so long."

"Oh, yes." William nodded. "After all, death is always with us, and someone must attend to its needs."

A chill skittered down Charlie's spine even though it was still almost eighty degrees. She folded her arms across her chest and hugged them tightly to her.

"Indeed." Tom gave his brother an embarrassed side-eyed glance. "Charlie, can I walk you to your car?"

Charlie shook her head. "That's really not necessary."

"Oh, let him walk you to your car, dear." William's tone oozed with condescension. "It isn't often that my brother takes such a shine to someone."

Charlie shifted her feet and fought the urge to turn and just run. Her cheeks tightened with the force of her smile. "All right."

"I'll see you on the weekend, William?"

"Yes, of course. We must get that taken care of before someone else—" William fixed his gaze on Charlie. "Gets hurt."

Charlie's gaze went from Tom to William and back to Tom again.

"We have a piece of property that has an old house on it that's not very secure." Tom explained. "There have evidently been signs of squatters, and we don't want anyone to get hurt."

"No of course not. What are you going to do?"

"We're looking at having the building razed."

"Oh."

"Yes, it's been in the family forever. The county zoned it commercial several years back, and we thought of opening another branch there, but really, it's so far out it doesn't make much sense." The gray suit William wore draped his tall, lean form perfectly. Charlie folded her fingers against her palm to keep herself from reaching out and touching the fabric to see if it was made of wool. It was such a warm, muggy night. She couldn't imagine wearing such heavy material. Even Tom, who wore a suit to work, was dressed in a pair of black twill shorts and a pale gray and white polo shirt.

"What will you do with it, then?"

"Sell it," William said. "You wouldn't be interested in forty acres of land with an old house on it, would you, Miss Payne?"

"Me? No." She laughed nervously.

"That's too bad," William said. "Well, I must be off now. I have an early day tomorrow. It was very nice to meet you."

"Nice to meet you too."

The two brothers gave each other a curt nod. William spun and headed in the opposite direction, back into the bustle of East Bay Street. Charlie watched him for a moment, in his dark gray suit disappearing into the crowd despite his size.

"Well, that was interesting," Charlie mumbled.

"I'm sorry if he made you uncomfortable. He can be intense."

"Yeah, I got that." She tilted her head and gave him a half smile. "Regardless of your brother, it's kinda nice to see a friendly face."

Concern etched lines in his forehead, and he stepped closer to her. "Why are you downtown this late?"

"Meeting with a client." She shrugged and muttered, "Sort of a client."

"A sort of a client? Not sure I like the sound of that."

"She's just someone who did a bad thing a long time ago, and now it's come back to haunt her. Literally."

His eyes darkened and his brows grew together. "You're taking precautions, right? When it comes to these… sorts of things."

"As best I can."

The toes of his gray hiking shoes touched the toes of her black ballet flats. "It's getting late. Would you think it weird if I asked to follow you home?"

Charlie chuckled. "I guess that all depends on what your intentions are, Mr. Sharon."

Tom raised his hands in surrender. "I just want to see you home safely, that's all."

"Who says chivalry's dead?" She smiled. "All right."

"Great. Where are you parked?"

"Up on Broad."

"That's a bit of a walk in the dark, isn't it?"

"Don't worry, I won't let the boogey man get you," she teased.

He made a chuffing sound in the back of his throat, but his lips curved up. She grabbed him by the wrist and turned him around, heading toward Broad Street. Tom pulled her hand into the crook of his elbow and Charlie's fingers tightened around his arm. It felt so good to be with him. She almost never wanted it to end, which was a funny thought. It had been such a long time since she'd felt attractive to someone. Mostly when she thought of herself, the words weird or strange were the first to pop into her head, which were definitely not attractive qualities in her mind.

Other than being part owner of a funeral home and having a penchant for black clothing, Tom was anything but weird or strange. Charlie sighed and leaned her head against Tom's upper arm. She was so tired.

"Listen I appreciate the offer but there's something else I need to do. I'm not gonna go straight home."

"All right." He eyed her. "It's not dangerous what you're thinking of doing, is it?"

"No, course not," she lied.

"Then let me go with you."

"Why would you want to go with me?"

"Because I like being with you. Don't you like being with me?"

"More than I'd like to admit," she said. "Let me ask a question. How do you feel about ghosts?"

"Why?" His mouth spread into a wide grin. "Are we going ghost hunting?"

"Yes," she said. "I just need to make one phone call."

"You're calling your deputy friend?"

Charlie frowned. "Okay, I need to make two phone calls."

* * *

"What is this place?" Tom put his black sedan into park.

"Mu Theta Chi sorority uses it for hazing," Charlie said. She stared into the dark windows of the old house, searching for any sign of movement. Her breath caught in her throat when the face of the young woman appeared in the upper left window.

"I thought hazing was illegal in this state," Tom said.

"Yep, it is," Charlie said. "My client called it a test of worthiness. Whatever that means." Charlie glanced at the red digital numbers on the clock on the radio.

"What are we waiting for?"

"My cousins," she said.

"Why?"

"They will help me trap her."

"The spirit that's been plaguing your client?" Tom asked.

"Yes."

"What will you do with her once you have her?"

"Banish her. I hope," she said. *And if that fails,* she thought, *there is always the reaper.*

"And you and your cousins can do this?" His voice was full of curiosity, not fear or disbelief. Her heart swelled.

"Yes," she said.

"How?"

The lights from Lisa's white BMW shined into Charlie's rearview mirror, and some of Charlie's anxiety eased. She looked at Tom, giving him a mischievous grin. "Magic," she said. "Come on."

She was out of the car before he could respond, waving her hands. Lisa pulled up next to Charlie and parked. Her three cousins piled out. Jen and Lisa wore somber expressions, but Daphne's was more excited. More curious.

"I can't wait to add this to our videos," Daphne

almost sang the words. She gave Charlie a quick hug. "Oh, hi, Tom, the not boyfriend."

Charlie pinched Daphne's side.

"Ow!" Daphne whined. Charlie raised her eyebrows and gave her cousin a stern warning look. Daphne's lips twisted into a frown momentarily. "Fine, have it your way."

"Are we all ready for this?" Jen asked. She dug through her messenger bag and pulled out a small paper sack. "Tom, I have a few things for you."

"For me?" He glanced at Charlie, uncertainty filling his eyes.

"It's okay," Charlie reassured. "Just a couple things to help protect you."

"From the spirit?"

"Yes." Jen opened the sack and began rummaging through it. "Now, I didn't have time to put together a full protection kit so these are just a few things that will help keep you safe. You'll need to stick with one of us." She held up a silver pendant hanging from a black silk cord.

"Just exactly how are you going to trap these spirits?" He bent forward to allow Jen to slip the talisman over his head.

Jen pulled three Rowan's crosses from her messenger bag. "With these."

Two of them were simple — twigs crossed and wrapped with red thread joining them together. The third one was more complicated — the twigs crossed in such a way that when wrapped with red thread it formed a hexagon. The center was wrapped in yellow and white threads, and it looked like an eye staring out at them. A God's eye cross.

"And exactly how do those work?"

Jen gave him a smile but didn't answer his question. "Okay, so the pentacle will help to protect you. Here is a small bag of salt and a black tourmaline." She pressed the small stone bead into his palm. "It was the best I could do on short notice."

"It'll be fine," Lisa glanced at the expensive gold watch wrapped around her wrist. "Can we get this show on the road? It's almost three, and I've got an early meeting tomorrow."

"Of course," Charlie said.

"Is Jason coming?" Jen asked. "I have a sack for him too. You know, just in case he forgot to bring some of his things."

"I called him and left a message, but he hasn't called me back. I gave him the address, though, so that if he checks his messages at least he'll know where I am."

"And that you're not alone," Lisa said.

"Yes," Charlie said. "And that."

CHAPTER 26

The front door was locked, which Charlie found to be odd. Most of the windows had been broken out. What was the point in locking the front door?

"Hang on just a minute." Lisa went back to her car, opened the trunk and returned carrying a small pry bar. She stuffed the flat end between the doorjamb. With one hard yank, the ancient door splintered and opened wide.

"Well, that's one way to do it." Jen pushed past her sister, holding one of the red threaded Rowan's crosses in her hand. She stopped in the foyer and looked around. There were two sizable rooms on either side of the wide foyer and a staircase that led up to a second floor. The foyer led to a hallway running along the staircase toward the back of the house. Charlie moved in close to her cousin and turned in a circle, surveying the room. The house was old, not as old as some she had been in, and it reminded her of the large foursquare styled house she had grown up in with her grandmother Bunny. On one side was a dining room. Dark rose-colored walls, dingy cracked plaster and exposed wooden lath that looked like dingy gray bones that made her skin tingle with heightened awareness. Something dead lived here.

An old buffet with a cracked glass front and one door missing was the only stick of furniture left. A living room or a parlor sat directly across from the dining room, uninviting, whatever it was. Water wept down the plaster, leaving floor-to-ceiling stains. Built-in shelves flanked a brick fireplace centered between two enormous windows on the far wall. A ratty nest made of pine straw and paper filled up one corner of the bottom shelf. The stench of mold and rat feces hung in the air.

"Do you see anything?" Jen asked softly.

"No." Charlie shook her head.

Daphne came in holding her phone up. A red circle on the screen blinked. Lisa and Tom entered, both wearing cautious expressions on their faces.

"What's the plan, Charlie?" Lisa asked, glancing around, rubbing her arms.

"We should split up," Charlie said. "Each take a Rowan's cross."

"I don't think we should go by ourselves," Daphne said.

"No, Daphne's right," Jen said. "We should go in pairs at least."

"I want to be paired with Tom," Daphne said.

Jen, Lisa, and Charlie all shot their younger cousin a what-the-hell look at the same time. Tom chuckled but turned it into a cough.

"What?" Daphne shrugged and looked as if she'd been caught doing something wrong. "He's tall and a man."

"So?" Lisa asked.

"You can't blame a girl for trying. I mean, Charlie's not interested in him so—"

"Daphne!" Jen said.

"What? She's not."

Lisa just rolled her eyes. "You're coming with me."

"Jen?" Daphne said, her voice full of pleading.

Jen held up her hands in surrender. "Sorry, you kinda set yourself up for that one."

Charlie snickered. "Tom, why don't you come with me?"

"Yes," he said, sounding relieved. "Good idea. You, too, Jen."

"Why does Jen get to go with them?" Daphne whined.

"Come on. You know perfectly well why." Lisa held out her hand. "Can I have one of those?"

Jen handed her one of the Rowan crosses.

"Here, Charlie, you take this one." She handed Charlie the God's Eye cross.

"Daphne and I'll do a sweep upstairs," Lisa said.

"That sounds good," Charlie said. "We'll take the downstairs." She reached out, holding her hand palm down. Her cousins circled around, each placing their hand on top of hers. Charlie glanced up at Tom and he stepped into the circle, placing his hand on the very top.

"Guardians of the East and West be with us now. Powers of the North and South fill our souls with light and protect us," Lisa said.

"So mote it be," Jen said.

Lisa, Daphne, and even Tom echoed the words. As usual, Charlie chimed in last. She glanced up at Tom, unsure what to think of his joining so easily in the quick prayer and ritual. She would ask him about it later. Right now, they had a spirit to catch.

They dropped hands, and Lisa and Daphne headed up the steps.

"Be careful," Jen said. "Some of that wood looks rotted."

Lisa raised her hand and gave her sister an

acknowledging wave. Daphne followed close behind her, never pausing her video.

From the corner of her eye, Charlie saw one of the windows raise in the dining room. "Jen, Tom," Charlie whispered and motioned for them to follow her. As she approached the window it slammed shut, shattering what little glazing was left. Charlie jumped when Jen placed a gentle hand between her shoulder blades and crept up next to her.

"Do you see anything?" Jen asked.

"Just what you see," Charlie replied.

Tom stared through a second door leading to a small serving space. "I saw some movement through there."

Charlie nodded and headed through the door. It appeared to be a butler's pantry. Glass-fronted cabinets floating above a marble counter and more cabinets below. Inside one cabinet were crystal glasses coated with a thick layer of dust. Something crunched beneath her feet and she looked down to find shattered remnants of a bottle ground to almost fine powder.

A door on the opposite side of the one they came through swung open of its own accord. Jen wrapped her hand around Charlie's arm and gave it yank.

"Brianna?" Charlie called. "I know you're here."

They found themselves in what was once a kitchen. There were no appliances left, only rust stains on the floor where the refrigerator must've sat and scorch marks on the wall where the stove must have been. The grimy cabinets might have been white or cream at one time, but now they were just a dingy gray. Rat droppings dotted the top of the faded butcher block counters, and the stench of something dead permeated the air. Charlie fought the urge to vomit, bringing her arm across her face, so she could bury her nose in the crook of her arm. Jen covered her nose and mouth with her hand and a soft moan escaped her lips.

Tom did not seem to be affected by the smell. His eyes narrowed, scanning every corner of the room. His expression was alert. Cautious, but not fearful.

"I can't—" Charlie finally said. She turned around and headed back toward the butler's pantry. The swinging door moved back and forth rapidly, as if two children were batting it in the game. It didn't open far enough or slow enough for them to move through it. Charlie tried to grab it, but it slammed her fingers in between the door and the jamb, and she cried out, jerking her hand back.

"Are you all right?" Tom cradled her hand. "Can you move your fingers?"

Charlie tried to wiggle her fingers and pain exploded from her pinky and middle finger. She cried again.

"Looks like they may be broken," he said. "We need to stabilize them."

"I can't breathe in here," Charlie said.

Tom wrapped his arm around her shoulders and led her and Jen through the kitchen. The cabinets in the kitchen opened and closed, slamming over and over as they passed across the dingy linoleum floor. Tom got them out of the kitchen into a hallway adjoining a small room with windows overlooking the backyard.

"Do you have a flashlight?" Tom asked.

Jen dug through the bag slung across her body. She pulled out a silver flashlight about the size of an ink pen, with an adjustable beam. She turned it on and shined the bright light on Charlie's hand.

"I need to stabilize her fingers with something. You wouldn't have a pen or something hard and long and thin in that bag of yours, would you?"

"Oh, yeah, of course. Hold on." She handed him the light and continued to dig.

"Any chance you have any tape?"

Jen pulled out two small rolls of washi tape and handed them to Charlie, who took them in her good hand, weaving her thumb through the wide holes of the rolls.

"Wait, a minute. It looks like I have a couple popsicle sticks."

"Ruby's?" Charlie said.

"Yes, but they were for projects, not popsicles." She handed them to Tom. "They're clean, I promise."

"Perfect," he said. "I'll trade you." He swapped the popsicle sticks in Jen's hand for the light. Gently, he stretched out Charlie's middle finger.

She gritted her teeth and sucked in her breath, counting through the pain. He pressed one of the popsicle sticks on the underside of her finger and wrapped tape around the finger and popsicle stick just tight enough to cause fresh pain to shoot through her hand.

"Sorry," he said.

Charlie gave him a weak smile. "It's okay."

He went to work on the second finger.

"You're handy to have around. Where did you learn this?" Charlie asked.

"Well, as a mortician, I had to study anatomy, but I'm also certified in first aid with the Red Cross." He smiled.

"And here I thought you were just another pretty face," Jen quipped.

He ripped the last piece of tape off and wrapped it around the top of her pinky, covering her fingernail. "That should do it."

Charlie pulled her hand to her chest, cradling it. "Thank you."

A scream pierced the air, making all three of them jump.

"Daphne," Jen muttered and headed out toward the hallway. Another scream followed closely, sounding like Lisa. Jen hurried down the hallway.

"Jen," Charlie said. "Wait." Charlie and Tom made it through the door just in time to see Jen turn a corner. Another scream echoed through the house, making every hair on Charlie's body stand up.

"Jen, wait!" She and Tom broke into a run, trying to catch up with Jen. When they turned the corner where she had gone, there was no sign of her. They had wandered into what looked like a den. There was another fireplace, and hanging over it was what looked like an ancient deer head.

"Where did she go?" Tom asked.

"I don't know," Charlie said, glancing around. Her eyes settling on an old stuffed buck's head hanging over the fireplace. The fur had loosened and fluffed with age and from bugs burrowing into the wood form. The glassy eyes stared at them, unblinking. "I don't like it in here. We need to get out," Charlie said.

"Agreed," Tom said.

When they turned to leave, the door slammed shut and the lock clicked. Charlie wrapped her hand around the brass door handle giving it a good twist, but it wouldn't budge.

"Dammit, Brianna! Stop it! Come out and talk to

me!" Charlie screamed at the ceiling. "I can help you. Let me help you."

An old picture frame holding a pastoral painting fell from the wall. The corner of the frame hit the ground, breaking it into two pieces. One piece of the sharp wooden frame punctured the canvas.

Charlie and Tom both jumped and faced the now broken painting heaped on the floor against the wall.

"Brianna, tell me where your body is. I will help you cross over. I promise Emma will pay for what she's done to you. Please," Charlie said.

"No!" the voice screamed down the chimney. "I will make sure Emma pays."

"I can't let you do that." Charlie pulled the God's Eye from the back pocket of her jeans and held it out in front of her. The incantation that Jen had taught her was short so that she would easily remember it but standing in front of the fireplace Charlie's mind drew a blank. Dammit. What were the words?

She closed her eyes and tried to recall. Something about the elements, but she couldn't remember the order. Why hadn't she practiced it more?

"Brianna," Tom's tone calmed Charlie immediately. She shifted her gaze from the fireplace to his steady presence. "If you act on your anger, and you hurt Emma, you only hurt yourself more, and you will pay a far worse price than Emma ever will."

"Can you hear her?" Charlie whispered.

Tom nodded, not taking his eyes off the fireplace. "Brianna? I know you believe in hell."

"Of course, I do." Brianna hissed, her voice echoing down the chimney and spreading through the room. "I'm already there."

"You think this is hell now?" Something beneath his soft, deadly tone made Charlie want to recoil. She'd had no idea he believed in such things. There was still so much she didn't know about him. "You have not even begun to experience real hell."

Ash, old wood, and long dead coals exploded out of the fireplace. The thick black and gray cloud threatened to choke Charlie. She coughed and gagged. She turned away, squeezing her eyes shut. She searched for the door handle, giving the door a good shake once she found it again.

It took several moments, but the dust finally began to settle, and when it did, Brianna stood in front of the fireplace—her form almost as black as the chimney soot that covered them. Charlie had seen her like this before, in the memory of Haley's neighbor, Mr. Baker.

Brianna's chest heaved, as if she was breathing heavily and her eyes burned red. She had her gaze locked on Tom, who had not moved from his spot in the middle of the room.

Charlie quickly moved from the door, stepping in front of Tom, holding up the God's Eye cross out for protection. The twigs and threads quivered beneath her fingers like they might fall apart in her hand.

Brianna laughed and sauntered over to Charlie, as if she had no cares in the world. She held up her hand in front of the spirit trap.

"Did you really think this stupid craft project could hold me?" She swiped her hand to the right, and the cross flew out of Charlie's hand and bounced off the wall, landing not too far from Charlie's feet. "You have to believe in the magic for it to work, Charlie."

The old buck's head on the wall shook and shivered, and for a moment Charlie thought she saw it bow its head as if it were about to charge at her. She blinked hard, trying to clear her head. Something in that smoke had really gotten to her.

"Did Emma tell you what really happened?" Brianna hissed.

"She told me they left you here alone overnight. She told me that they found you dead the next morning and were afraid, so they covered it up."

The deer head shook more violently. Its antlers pointed straight at Charlie. If the long dead creature still had a body, she felt for sure it would have come for her already.

"Lies!" Brianna screeched.

"Then tell me the truth!" Charlie screamed.

Brianna opened her mouth, emitting such a high-pitched scream that what little glass was left in the windows shattered. Charlie's hands flew to cover her ears and dizziness swirled through her head. She felt a warm hand wrap around her wrist, pull her close. Tom tucked her in between his arms, and they spun around until they were facing the wall opposite the fireplace. The shrill scream stopped and something sharp poked her in the back. Charlie winced, pulling her body away from Tom's chest. The weight of him grabbing onto her shoulders almost brought her to her knees. She lunged forward, glancing back over her shoulder. Tom stumbled around, trying to keep his balance before his legs gave out and he sunk down to his knees. Brianna's dark form loomed behind Tom, staring at him.

It took a moment for Charlie to understand what she was seeing. Dark bloody flowers bloomed on his gray and white cotton shirt where the tips of antler protruded through his chest and abdomen.

"Oh, god, Tom," Charlie muttered, moving toward him as quickly as she could. She grabbed his arms, trying to keep him from falling backwards, from landing on the deer head and driving the antlers deeper through his body. Blood trickled from his lips and his hips gave way. He teetered backward.

"No," Charlie said, giving his arms a yank. "Please, Tom, you have to try. I can't hold you up." His amber eyes looked glassy and unfocused. All the color had drained from his face. He loosened one of his hands and touched her cheek with it.

"Behind you." Tiny droplets of blood splattered across his chin and lips as he spoke. His gaze flitted over her shoulder and his eyes fixed and wide.

Charlie glanced toward his gaze. Brianna hovered behind her. In one swift motion, the spirit raised her hand across her body and backhanded Charlie, knocking her across the room. Tom crumpled to the floor onto his side.

Charlie lay there for a moment, facing Tom. The light in his amber-colored eyes was fading fast. They'd had no time to get to know each other beyond their few meetings, and now they never would. His eyes opened and closed slowly.

"Please don't leave, Tom," she whispered.

One side of his lips curved up a little.

"I'll be okay," he said. "Take her." His eyes flitted to the God's Eye lying on the floor near her head. Charlie gave him a nod and wrapped her hand around the exposed twigs. She groaned as she pushed herself to her feet. She was going to hurt tomorrow.

Charlie stepped around Tom's body and held up the twig cross.

"Goddess of the moon and sun, I call upon your aid. Put the spirit where she belongs, with others like her, let her fade.

Earth, wind, fire and air, return this spirit to whence she came and soothe her anger and her fear. So, mote it be."

Brianna screeched in horror and pain. Her once beautiful face, metamorphosing into a shrieking leer as she charged at Charlie.

Charlie held her ground, repeating her verse again. Brianna's shriek faded the closer she came, and her apparition seemed to be caught in the trap's web. Charlie's arm shook as the trap's magic pulled Brianna inward by pale ephemeral tendrils. Brianna tried to change course but couldn't, as if she were caught in a tractor beam. Unable to stop herself or her fate. The spirit faded, and the shriek became nothing but an echo.

The door flew open and her cousins and Jason rushed into the room. The twig cross thrummed in her hands.

"She's gone," Charlie said. "The trap worked."

Jen rushed forward and took the cross.

Charlie knelt next to Tom's motionless body. His skin was still warm, but there was no pulse in his neck. Sorrow swirled through her chest, black and overwhelming, threatening to pull her in. "Tom?"

Jen's hand, warm and small, touched her shoulder. "Charlie, honey."

"Tom!" Charlie shook his shoulders. No response.

"Come on, sweetie, Jason's here. We need to go talk to him, tell him what happened."

Tears and grief shook her body with such violence she couldn't move. Jen knelt next to her and wrapped her arm around Charlie's shoulders. Beneath her hand, Tom's arm twitched. Charlie hiccupped and sniffed back her tears.

"Oh, god, Tom?" A spark lit the darkness in her heart. "Tom?" His arm flailed without purpose. "Daphne! Call 911!" She shouted at her cousin, pointing to the phone in her hand. Daphne stared at her dumbly, her wide blue eyes blinking fast.

"Why do we need 911?" Jason stepped into the room. One look at the scene, and his cautious expression morphed into understanding. He took the cell phone hanging from his belt and made a call.

Tom's body began to convulse, his arms and legs flailing uncontrollably. Jen pulled Charlie backward, getting her out of the way. Her heart hammered in her throat as she watched, unable to understand, or stop what was happening to him. Maybe she had not captured the ghost at all. Maybe Brianna had figured out that she could jump into the body of the newly dead. Charlie had seen that happen before.

She held her breath when he stopped moving. Waited for him to rise. She started toward his body, but Jen yanked her back, clutching her hard by the waist. "No, Charlie, no."

The two women stared, unable to look away as the body transformed. The beautiful face she had come to the admire so much retreated into a black cloak and his dark wavy hair dissolved into a hood. Only his amber eyes remained. The reaper rose and his gaze fell on Charlie. *I can explain*, his silky voice floated through her consciousness.

Charlie stood up and faced him.

"Charlie, don't," Jen and Lisa pleaded behind.

The spark of hope she felt a moment ago, transformed into a wildfire, spreading hot and fast through her body. A dull roar filled her ears.

"You? This whole time? It's been you."

"I—" he began.

Her arm reared back almost as of its own accord, and struck out, connecting with something solid. The sound of her cousins and even Jason gasping as she slapped the reaper registered deep in her brain. This was dangerous. What if he turned on her? Killed her? There was nothing to stop him.

His bony pale hand floated to the side of his hood, where her hand had marked him.

"How dare you?" she demanded. "I trusted you. Cared for you!"

"I'm sorry," he whispered. The fire in his brown eyes faded to nothing, and only a black void stared back at her. He turned, and in a blur of shadows, fled through the window. A piece of glass hanging on by a thread of glazing compound fell to the ground and shattered.

Jen was by her side first, then Lisa and Daphne together. A torrent of tears, both angry and sorrowful, brought her to her knees. The only thing that kept her from completely falling apart was the feel of her three cousins' arms enveloping her, lifting her up with their light and love.

* * *

CHARLIE STOOD NEXT TO JASON'S DODGE CHARGER, facing him.

"What's gonna happen to Emma?" she asked.

"Well, thanks to Lisa's location thingy—"

"Spell," Charlie corrected. Jason paused. His lips twisted into a scowl and the line between his brows grew deep. Maybe it was too soon.

"Yeah, well," he said flatly. "Now that we have a body, I expect things will go differently from the first couple of times we talked to her. I just hope forensics will turn up something proving she was involved."

"She told me she and Haley didn't kill her."

"Maybe." His eyes looked warily at the old house behind them. "We'll see what the evidence says."

"For what it's worth," Charlie added, "I don't think the noose we found around her neck was as an accident."

"Nope, things like that rarely are."

Charlie glanced at Jen, who had carefully put the trap holding Brianna's spirit into a specially blessed black velvet bag.

"What are y'all gonna do with her spirit?"

"I'm hoping that once her parents bury her body and everything comes out, that we can take her to a sacred place and help her move on for good."

"And that'll work?"

Charlie called up a half-smile. "Yeah, I'm pretty sure it will."

CHAPTER 27

Charlie pulled into Scott's driveway and put her Honda into park. She took the large casserole Jen had made and carried it with the two potholders from her kitchen. She pressed the doorbell with her elbow and a moment later Scott answered the door, smiling.

"Charlie!" Scott said, sounding entirely too chipper.

"Who are you and what have you done with my ex-husband?" Charlie joked.

"I told you, I'm a changed man." He smiled and shook his head. He stepped to one side. "Come on in."

"Aren't you supposed to be in bed resting?" Charlie walked into the foyer.

"I am resting. What've you got there?" He gestured to the dish in her hand. "It smells great."

"It's a veggie lasagna. Jen made it, I didn't, so it's definitely tasty. We figured meatless would be healthier."

"Wow, thank you." He lifted the corner of the aluminum foil covering it and sniffed again. "Can't wait to dig in. Please tell Jen thank you for me."

"I will."

"Do you have a few minutes? I need to talk to you about something."

"Sure, let me just put this in the kitchen."

Something about him was different. There was a lightness to him she had never seen before. Gone was his stern tone. Maybe almost dying had really changed him. Only time would tell though. She followed the hallway next to the staircase toward the back of the house and to the large beautiful kitchen. Everything was spotless, as if no one ever cooked, thanks to Cora. Charlie put the lasagna into the refrigerator and left the instructions for warming it on top of the foil.

She fought the cloud of dread filling her chest as she made her way to Scott's study. The last time she had been here they had fought. Maybe this new and improved Scott would somehow keep that ugliness from happening again.

Her heartbeat quickened as she approached the

open door, but her anxiety faded almost immediately once she entered.

He had changed the study around. The desk no longer loomed before two chairs. Instead, a leather couch dominated the wall, and Scott had moved the desk in front of the window so that when seated, he could look out. It was much more open and inviting now, and it felt less like she was visiting the principal's office.

"I like the new layout." She smiled widely.

"Yeah? Thanks." He glanced around. A peaceful smile curved his lips and he took a seat on the couch, patting the space next to him. "I thought it needed a change."

"Well, it feels better in here."

"I totally agree." He nodded.

Charlie sat on the opposite end of the couch and pivoted toward him. She took one of the red plaid pillows and placed it on her lap, hugging it against her body. Scott eyed her and frowned. She braced herself for a scolding.

"You look like you're preparing to be taken to the woodshed." Scott sighed and shook his head. "I'm sorry."

"For what?" she asked.

"For making you feel that way."

Charlie squeezed the pillow tighter. "It's okay."

"No, it's not. You deserve better."

Charlie opened her mouth to protest but stopped herself. She called up a smile. "Thank you." She put the pillow aside and rested her hands on her lap. "Wall down. Better?"

Scott smiled and nodded. "Better."

"All right," she said. "What did you want to talk about?"

"Custody of Evan."

Charlie shifted in her seat and folded her arms. Wall up. "Okay."

"I fired my lawyer this week after I had him draw this up." He hopped up from the couch and grabbed a legal sized manila folder from his desk. He handed it to her.

"What is this?" She flipped it open and read the first few lines. "Scott?"

"It's a new custody agreement."

Heat flooded her cheeks, and she glared at him. "You can't just draw up a new custody agreement without my consent. That's what the lawyers are for."

"Will you please just read it before you get upset?"

"It's like fifteen pages of legalese. You want me to just sit here and read it?"

"Why don't I condense it for you? Then take it to your lawyer and have him look it over before you sign it."

"What does it say?"

"Basically, that you and I agree to share custody of Evan. That you will have him every other week. That we will share holidays. I will have him for Thanksgiving, Christmas, and Easter on even years and you will have him on odd years."

"What about Paramore's?"

"There are no restrictions on Paramore's, other than Evan's approval. If he feels uncomfortable, then it's his right to speak up about it and you and I both have to abide by his wishes."

"And you feel comfortable giving that sort of power away to an eleven-year-old?"

"Honestly, our eleven-year-old is much wiser than most forty-year-olds. What about you? Do you trust him?"

"I do. Evan's a very good judge of character. He always has been."

"He gets that from his mother."

Charlie dropped her hands to her lap, and she stared at him in awe. "You really have changed, haven't you?"

Scott beamed. "I really have."

"Wow." Charlie met his gaze. "I'm just sorry you had to die for it to happen."

"Well, I always have had to learn things the hard way," Scott said dryly.

Charlie laughed and shook her head. "That's true, you do."

"Listen, if you want to date that guy again, as long as Ev's okay with it, you'll have no complaints from me."

Charlie gave him a sad smile. "It doesn't really matter now. It wouldn't have worked out."

"Please tell me it wasn't because of me and my jack-assery."

"No. It wasn't. Anyway, I've already forgiven you for being a jack-ass. My uncle Jack hasn't but—"

"It's probably a good thing that I don't have to see him, then."

"Yeah, it probably is." Charlie chuckled.

"You know if you ever change her mind about—"

Charlie winced internally. "Why don't we just concentrate on moving forward, instead of looking back?"

"Sure." Scott nodded. "See? There's that wisdom again."

"Mom!" Evan's voice boomed through the house. "Mom, are you here?"

"I'm in here, babe!" she called. "Should we tell him now?"

"He already knows. My lawyer drafted the whole agreement based on his input."

"Are you serious?" she asked.

"Yep. And just so you know, he's also coming off

the meds. There will be a weaning period, but it shouldn't take but a few weeks."

"Oh, Scott, you have no idea how happy that makes me."

Charlie resisted the urge to throw her arms around Scott's neck and hug him. She didn't want to confuse him. Instead, she stood up and threw her arms around her son as soon he walked through the door.

CHAPTER 28

Three days later, Charlie pulled into the parking lot of Sharon and Sons Funeral Home. The new brick building sat neatly on an acre of land. Trees separated the plot from the hustle and bustle of the main downtown area of Palmetto Point. She gripped the hard rubber of her steering wheel and stared at the front door.

She pulled down the visor and glanced at herself in a small mirror. She pinched her pale cheeks and reached into her purse for the tube of practically nude lipstick. After applying just a touch of the pale beige-pink cream to her lips with her pinky finger, she pushed her hair behind her ears. "You got this," she muttered to her reflection and flipped up the visor, then hopped out of the car.

Her stomach twisted into knots as she walked

through the front door. Cold air slapped her in the face, along with the scent of mums and white lilies—the flowers of death. When she died, she wanted no flowers, unless they were bright and sunny and smelled like life. A stunning woman with dark wavy hair spilling over her shoulders emerged from behind the desk in the nearby office. Her tight navy pencil skirt hugged her slim hips and the deep-v of her silky violet-colored blouse accentuated her long graceful neck.

"Good afternoon. How may I help you?" The young woman wore a somber but friendly expression. Charlie recognized the similarity of the woman's dark gold eyes immediately, and a chill wafted across her spine.

"I'm looking for Tom Sharon." Charlie folded her arms across her chest. "Is he here?"

"Why, yes, he is." The young woman's gaze trailed over Charlie from head to toe. Charlie bit her tongue to keep from making a smart-ass remark she might regret.

"I'm Joy, by the way."

"Uh—nice to meet you, Joy." Charlie shifted her feet, and remembered Tom mentioning his sister Joy. Was she a reaper too?

"I'll just go get him."

"Thank you." Charlie watched Joy disappear down a hallway that ran alongside of her office.

Charlie assumed there were other offices there too. To the left was a set of carved double doors and a podium with an open book perched on it. A pretty but somber poster stood on an easel and in a large simple script it read: Wilson—2 p.m.

Anxiety wound around her heart and squeezed.

"Charlie?" Tom's warm voice was full of surprise. She turned to find him staring at her in awe.

"Hi," she said, trying to keep her voice steady. "Do you have few minutes?"

"Of course. Come with me." Tom gestured for her to follow him. Charlie hesitated a moment, glancing at the young woman who appeared to be watching them with great curiosity. She gave Charlie a closed-lipped smile that made the skin on Charlie's arms crawl. Charlie took a step backward.

"Uh, no." She jerked her thumb toward the exit. "I'd feel more comfortable outside."

The young woman gave Tom a smug look. Tom rolled his eyes and scowled at her. "Charlie, I don't think you've met my sister, Joy."

"It's so nice to finally meet you." Joy extended her hand. "We've heard so much about you."

Charlie's breath stuttered in her throat, and she stared at the young woman's perfectly manicured hand. Tom stepped forward, gently taking his sister's hands into his before lowering it to her side.

"Charlie has a thing about handshakes. I know

you don't want to make her uncomfortable." He gave his sister a pointed look. Her lips twisted and she folded her arms across her ample breast.

"No, of course not." Joy smiled. "It was genuinely nice to meet you, Charlie. I hope we'll be seeing more of you."

"It was nice to meet you too," Charlie said.

Tom stepped forward and took Charlie by the elbow, leading her toward the front door. As soon as they were outside, Charlie shook him off. She turned to face him.

"You look great." A wary smile played at the corners of his lips.

"Thanks," She stiffened her stance and glanced toward her car before steadying her gaze on his. "I need your help with something. Do you have some time this afternoon?"

His face lightened and his lips broke into a wide, hopeful smile. "Let me just go tell Joy where I'm going and I'm all yours."

The knot in Charlie's stomach tightened. "Great."

* * *

CHARLIE OPENED THE PASSENGER DOOR OF HER CAR. "Get in, please."

Tom nodded and did as he was asked. Charlie closed the door behind him and made her way around to the driver's side. She put her hands on the steering wheel and stared straight ahead.

"First you should know. You are not forgiven." She took a deep breath and blew it out. "What you did, pretending to be…to care. It was reprehensible."

He opened his mouth to argue, but she fixed an angry glare on him and his lips closed. He hung his head. "I am so sorry if I've hurt you. It was never my intention."

"What was your intention, exactly? Why toy with me?"

"I wasn't toying. I wasn't. I swear."

Her hands tightened and her knuckle cracked. She took another deep breath. *In through the nose. Out through the mouth.* She loosened her grip. "I have a few questions for you before we go anywhere."

"I figured you would," he said. "You know I'm not going to hurt you, right?"

"What?" She shifted her gaze to him. He gestured toward her hands. She let them fall into her lap.

"Ask me whatever you need to," he said. "And I will answer as best I can."

Charlie twisted her lips, trying to figure out where to start. There were so many questions and so many feelings. It was all jumbled in a ropey, impossible mess inside her heart and mind. She took a deep breath. "How long have you been following me?"

"I haven't—" he started, but the words died on

his lips when Charlie shot him a don't-lie-to-me look. Tom glanced down at the console. "Since the first time you called for me."

"Is that when you took up this pretense?" She gestured toward the building.

He smiled, and a weariness settled into the lines around his eyes. "I told you, death is my business. My family and I have lived in this area for many generations. All this does—" he gestured to the building and then to himself " —is provide a very simple way to collect the souls who are still clinging to this world. Then we ferry them to the other side."

"So, your sister and brother are... they're...?"

"Like me? Yes. They are."

"Why do you look the way you look? Why don't you look like—?"

"A creature?"

Charlie nodded.

"My kind figured out millennia ago that it is much easier to move among the humans if we look human."

"Why do you even need to move among us?"

"Not all souls go willingly. It's our job to find and take the ones that don't."

"How does this... human facade work?"

"It's the same sort of magic your cousin Daphne uses to make her clients love her so much."

"Glamour." Charlie sat back and pressed her head against the headrest.

"Yes," he said. "So, what is this thing you need me to help you with?"

Charlie sighed and straightened her back. Yes, it was good to concentrate on why she'd really come. She turned her body a little so she could face him. "Do you remember the missing child case that I told you about?"

"How can I forget? It's how I met you."

"That was you, wasn't it? That night in the shed? You were the reaper—" Charlie swallowed hard. "Were you following me? Are you always following me?"

"No," he protested. "Believe it or not, it was his time, and he was facing an unfortunate afterlife, so I knew he wouldn't go easily."

"And how do you know that?"

"I can't tell you that." He held up his hands. "Sorry. There are some things that humans are not meant to understand or know."

Charlie narrowed her eyes, scrutinizing him. She didn't sense that he was lying, but maybe her senses were impaired when she was with him. She frowned.

"So, is there a heaven and a hell? Is that why you told Brianna to be careful with her actions, even though she was dead?"

Tom smiled, giving her no answer.

"So humans can't know that?" Charlie's irritation crept into her voice. "We're just left to guess."

He smiled and gazed at her, his face full of peace.

Charlie gritted her teeth and blew her breath out through her nose. "You realize I'm really pissed at you."

"I know." He expression became more solemn. "If you tell me to stay away, I will."

"I haven't decided what I want just yet but I have one more question and a request."

"Okay," he said. "Shoot."

"Did you cause Scott's embolism?"

Tom took a deep breath, and for a moment, Charlie thought he might brush it off as something humans couldn't know. She braced herself for an argument.

"It's my understanding that Scott had an embolism because he fell on his back and it caused a blood clot. Isn't that what you told me?"

"So, you didn't?"

"No, I did not cause his embolism. We don't cause death, no matter what the myths say."

"You appeared though. Was he going to die?"

"Only for a glimpse. Not permanently."

"Was he supposed to die?"

He shook his head, a helpless expression on his face. "I can't tell you that. What I can say is that I've seen other humans change drastically because of a near-death experience. I may have helped him find you. I… I wanted him to know what you are."

"What am I?"

Tom's lips twisted into a smirk. "You know what you are."

Charlie stared at him. "No, I don't, Tom. What are you saying?"

He rolled his eyes. "You and your cousins, your aunt, Bunny, you're all special creatures, just like me."

Charlie's eyes widened. "I am not like you, and neither is my family."

"Charlie." He sighed and she could see him struggling to find the right words. Words like witch and magic. "You already know you are. You feel your power. It's growing inside you, otherwise you would never have been able to capture that spirit the way you did."

Charlie scowled and shifted away from him. She let her eyes settle on the new brick-facade of the building and the two sago palms flanking the door.

"You're never to follow me again," she warned. "It's creepy and disrespectful, and I will not tolerate it. Do you understand me?"

"Of course."

"And I can fight my own battles, especially with my ex-husband. I don't need you to do that."

"I have absolutely no doubt about that. Was that your request?"

She finally looked at him again. "I want you to help Trini Dolan and Macey Givens find their way to wherever it is they need to go. They deserve peace."

He sighed. "I couldn't agree with you more, but they're both very wily, especially Trini, and she protects the other girl."

"I have an idea about how to fix that."

"Okay, I'm listening." The excitement in his eyes gave him away.

"First," she mustered her sternest voice, "wipe that smile off your face. This is nothing but a professional collaboration. Got it?"

He sucked in his smile, but the corners of his mouth didn't comply. "Yes, ma'am."

* * *

"You're sure this is where we'll find them?" Tom looked at the shed, his eyes attentive to any sign of movement. The yellow police tape still hung in place but was coming undone on one side. A good thunderstorm would probably bring it down completely.

"It's as good a place to start as any. Come on." Charlie walked toward the backyard. "They ran off toward the woods, and we're gonna find them, even if it takes all day."

"Well, I'm all for that if it means I get to spend it with you."

"Hey, buddy." She rounded on him, pointing her finger. "What did I say about flirting?"

"Professional. Yes." The smile on his face faded but couldn't quite be quelled. "Right."

"Stop it," she said, fighting her own smile.

Tom breathed in deep and nodded. "Yes, ma'am."

"Now, come on."

They walked side by side into the thick grove of pines behind the house.

"Once we find them, I'll talk to them," she said, keeping her eyes on the ground. The brush and saplings grew too thick to pass in some places. "You need to keep your glamour up until I tell you it's okay."

"Of course."

"And whatever you do, don't show them your scythe. Because you holding it is just downright terrifying."

"No scythe. Got it." The corners of his mouth twitched.

"This is not funny."

"No, of course not. It's not funny at all." He fought against the smile trying to break out across his face.

"I know that you're happy, but you need to tone it down a little. For everybody's sake."

"Yes, ma'am." Tom nodded, and they headed deeper into the woods.

"Trini? Macey?" Charlie called out. "Please come out. I promise it's safe. No one can hurt you anymore."

Charlie felt Tom's hand on her right elbow. He stepped closer and whispered in her ear, "Look to your left near that oak."

The shimmer of the girls' skin danced in the corner of her eye. A relieved smile stretched her lips, and she waved at the two girls standing in the shadows of a tall skinny oak tree. "Stay here for a minute. Let me go talk to them."

Tom gave her elbow a gentle squeeze and nodded. "I'll be watching."

Charlie offered him a weak smile, unsure if that comforted her or creeped her out.

Macey Givens looked almost the same as the photo sitting on the Givens mantle. Her long blonde hair spilled down her back and she wore a red T-shirt and jeans shorts.

"Have you come to play with us?" Macey asked.

Charlie smiled and shook her head. She knelt to their level and peered into the round face of Trini Dolan. Her soft red curls rustled as if there were a breeze blowing.

"Actually, I came to talk to y'all. He's gone, you know." Both girls nodded at the same time. "See that man over there? That's my friend Tom. He has magic powers to help people like you."

"Dead people?" Trini asked.

"People ready to move on. Do you understand what that means?"

"Does it mean go to heaven?" Macey asked.

"For you, it does," Charlie said.

"I don't want to go," Trini said. Her body shimmered and faded to nearly disappearing.

"Trini, wait, don't run. I know you're scared. I promise you there's nothing to be scared of."

Trini disappeared.

"Don't you want to see your mom again? You know she's waiting for you now."

Trini reappeared in front of Charlie, her expression solemn. "My mama."

"Yes. She loves you so much," Charlie picked up a rock and held it in her hand to keep from reaching out to touch the girl.

"I have a baby brother in heaven. Do you think he's waiting for me?" Macey asked.

"I have no doubt he is, sweetie. And I'm sure there are grandparents and aunts and uncles there too. Wouldn't you like to see them?"

Macy's pale pink lips curved up, and she nodded.

"How?" she asked. "How do we get there?"

"Well, for some people, a light appears. Have either of you seen something like that?"

The girls shook their heads simultaneously.

"That's okay. There's another way, but it's really important that you be brave. I promise you, no one will hurt you."

Charlie threw a glance over her shoulder and gestured for Tom to come forward.

Tom smiled as he approached them, his golden-brown eyes glittering.

"Hello, girls." Tom knelt next to Charlie.

"This is Tom. He will take you where you need to go now. Remember what I said?"

"Be brave." Trini stared at Tom, her faded blue eyes wary.

"Be brave," Macey echoed.

"Yes. There's nothing to be afraid of," Tom said.

"You promise?" Trini asked.

"I promise," Charlie said.

Trini glanced at Macey and nodded. Charlie touched Tom's arm, and he stood up. "Don't be scared."

Charlie gave him one quick nod. Tom smiled at her and it sent a fresh pang through her chest. He really was the most beautiful creature she had ever seen.

He dropped his glamour and his black hooded robes appeared. The dark shadow took up the space where his face should've been and the only recognizable thing about him were his golden eyes gazing out at them.

The two apparitions flickered, almost disappearing.

"Be brave." Charlie reminded. "I promise he won't hurt you."

"I just want to help you girls. That's all." His silky voice slid through Charlie's senses. "Truly. Where you're going, there is so much love and light. You'll never be scared and lonely again."

Tom offered his hand. Trini shifted her surprised gaze to Charlie. The girl's chest expanded as if she were taking a deep breath, and she slipped her hand into Tom's. Macey followed her companion's lead, and the three of them headed off into the thicket of trees.

Charlie stood there for a long time, peering into the gloom of the forest even after they had disappeared. When thunder rumbled in the distance, Charlie headed back toward the safety of the yard. She cast a glance at the now empty house. The monster was dead.

The first drops of rain struck hard against her skin as she climbed into her car and sped away beneath the darkened sky.

A NOTE FROM WENDY

Thank you for reading *Wayward Spirits*. I really enjoy coming up with fresh stories (and ghosts) to challenge Charlie's abilities and of course have the cousins tag along.

Charlie's adventures continue in Devil's Snare. Charlie goes on a trip with her cousins to the mountains of North Carolina and her vacation quickly turns into a nightmare when Charlie gets lost in the woods and encounters a not-so friendly spirit, hellbent on making sure Charlie stays with her in the woods forever.

Connect with me

One thing I love most about writing is building a relationship with my readers. We can connect in several ways.

A NOTE FROM WENDY

Join my reader's newsletter.

By signing up for my newsletter, you will get information on pre-orders, new releases, and exclusive content just for my reader's newsletter. You can join by clicking here: https://wendy-wang-books.ck.page/482af1c7a

By signing up you'll be notified about pre-orders, new releases and anything new going on in Palmetto Point.

Connect with me on Facebook

Want to comment on your favorite scene? Or make suggestions for a funny ghostly encounter for Charlie? Or tell me what sort of magic you'd like to see Jen, Daphne and Lisa perform? Like my Facebook page and let me know. I post content there regularly and talk with my readers every day.

Facebook: https://www.facebook.com/wendywangauthor

Let's talk about our favorite books in my readers group on Facebook.

Readers Group: https://www.facebook.com/groups/1287348628022940/ ;

You can always drop me an email. I love to hear from my readers.

A NOTE FROM WENDY

Email: wendy@wendywangbooks.com

Thank you again for reading!